The
Beginning of the End

The
Beginning of the End

Mira Yeoh

This book was written and illustrated by Mira Yeoh.

Copyright © 2020 Mira Yeoh.

All rights reserved.

ISBN-13: 9781736701904

Dedication

To Mom, Dad, Nina & Jeremy-
Thanks for all your support!

Contents

Arguing

Chapter 1

June 4, 2473

"Rizo!" Rizo's nine-year-old sister, Anala, called. "Riiizzzzooo!"

"Calm down, Anala! What's the fuss?" He asked. Personally, Rizo thought his younger sister had a habit of overreacting. However, no one ever said that to her face, unless they wanted her to over-overreact. And nobody wanted that to happen. At least, anybody who knew Anala.

"Don't say CALM DOWN!" Anala said. "I NEED to be this way!"

"And why is that?" Rizo asked with a sigh.

"Because! WE have to SAVE the WORLD!" She said, as if it were obvious.

"Anala. You are making my beak hurt with all of this shouting," Krackers interjected, with as much dignity as a genetically modified, super smart parrot can muster.

"And all of you are making my head hurt!" Edward Duarte was the head scientist and leader of the Gryffin movement. The Gryffin was a group of scientists, ex-generals and lieutenants trying to throw off the Netrhaphalin.

The Netrhaphalin were robots that were meant to help in war, with AI that scientists perfected- until the robots became too smart and took over the whole earth. With their laser shooting eyes, their capability to shrink and expand, and their intelligence that surpassed the ancient scientist Albert Einstein, Earth was now at the Netrhaphalin's mercy, and their leader, Kano.

Rizo and his sister, along with another girl named Mikaela, had been taken from an orphanage under the cover of night to the underground base of the Gryffins. The Gryffins' plan was that they would raise as many kids underground as they could, away from the manipulative Netrhaphalin so they could eventually overthrow the robots. "Influence a whole generation to do the right thing" was their plan. However, after Rizo, Anala, and

Mikaela were taken from the orphanage, the Netrhaphalin had cracked down on the whole world, making it almost impossible to go above ground. They had lessened their restrictions lately, but orphanages were still heavily guarded.

The Gryffins now had to work with the three kids they had, along with Krackers, a genetically modified parrot, and Hope, an early Netrhaphalin created when the artificial intelligence had not been "perfected." Edward Duarte had re-programmed her himself, putting limits on her AI and giving her an extremely optimistic personality. Rizo thought he regretted not giving her at least a sense of how dire things were.

Dr. Duarte covered all of his shortcomings with criticism. He frequently remarked how useless Hope, Rizo, Anala, Mikaela, and Krackers were, possibly because he thought that three kids couldn't change anything. However, Rizo suspected that Dr. Duarte was really just angry at himself for only taking three kids at a time and failing to carry out the rest of his plan.

"All of you need to tone it down. You're supposed to be reading, for Gryffin's sake!" If Rizo was to rate Dr.

Duarte's aggravation level on a scale of one to ten, it was definitely a seven going on eight.

"Yes, Dr. Duarte! We were just having fun! Everyone was just joking, right?" Hope looked around, smiling cheerfully.

"Uh, sure, Hope," Rizo mumbled. The way Hope expected everything to be perfect was a little annoying sometimes. Even Dr. Duarte looked around, as if to say, "We all know Hope is like that- what's the truth?"

"Hope's right, Dr. Duarte," Mikaela said quietly, but not entirely truthfully, with just a hint of fury in her voice.

"Hope is AVSALUTELY right!" Anala agreed, in her usual loud manner.

"It's *absolutely*, Anala," Krackers said haughtily.

"Krackers," Rizo said sternly. Rizo hated when Krackers acted all high-and-mighty- especially with Anala. She couldn't help it if she was dyslexic. There were treatments that could help her, but Dr. Duarte couldn't risk taking her up to the surface to be helped by a specialist.

"Okay, but when I come back, I expect to see you reading, not squabbling like a bunch of parrots!" Dr.

Duarte stormed out of the room, muttering something about all of them being useless.

"What's WRONG with parrots?" Krackers called to the departing back of Dr. Duarte. Dr. Duarte ignored him, continuing down the hall.

"Nothing," Anala told him soothingly. "Parrots are PERFECT!" Rizo was pretty sure that this opinion of Anala's would quickly change. She was less about being consistent and more about being whatever felt right for the moment.

"Oh yes!" Hope agreed, flipping her half- sphere head in the air while her body remained floating. "Parrots are perfect! Everything is!"

"Not the Netrhaphalin," Rizo reminded her.

"Well, what about me?" Hope asked. "I'm a Netrhaphalin, and I'm fine, aren't I?"

"Well..." Krackers started.

"Don't be MEAN, Krackers!" Anala scolded. "Hope, you are AWESOME!"

Rizo grimaced. Anala was passionate about being compassionate, which was great, but she laid it on a little thick sometimes.

"Oh, awesome!" Hope said. "Mikaela! Did you hear that? I'm awesome! I mean, you're awesome, too, but nobody's called *me* awesome, you know, because I'm a Netrhaphalin and all, but-"

"I get it," Mikaela told Hope dryly.

"Awesome!" Hope did another flip, missing the curt tone in Mikaela's voice completely. "I wonder if they have a song about how everything is awesome. It would go 'Everything is awesome! Everything is cool! Everything is amazing!' and then 'Everything is awesome!'"

"Yep, that would be AWESOME!" Anala agreed.

"Okay, can we please stop saying the word 'awesome'?" Krackers asked. "It's starting to not sound like a word anymore. Also, what you're referencing was a very old song that was featured in a movie."

"I TOTALLY understand!" Anala promised, ignoring Krackers' lecture. "I won't use the word 'awesome' for the REST of the DAY!"

"Wish that were true," Krackers muttered.

"Well, Anala," Rizo asked her slyly, trying to trick her into saying 'awesome', "How is your history project going?"

"Yeah," Mikaela said, catching on to what Rizo was doing and joining in, "I heard it's amazing! Amazingly horrible. Dr. Duarte's always going on about how bad your spelling is."

Rizo glared at her.

"Oh, that?" Anala shrugged. "It's okay. I'm JUST getting to the COVID-19 pandemic in 2020. I mean, it's ancient history. How fun can ANCIENT HISTORY be? ANCIENT HISTORY! I mean, yeah everybody FREAKED out and it was a HUGE blow to the ENONOMY or something and then they had to POSTPONE the OLYMPICS but HONESTLY, how is that INTERESTING? I can't WAIT until I get to the Uprising of the Netrhaphalin. THAT will be TOTALLY EPIC and AWES-"

"Wait for it..." Krackers whispered.

"-AMAZING!" Anala finished, glaring at Krackers.

"Well," Krackers muttered, "it was worth a try. Besides, it's Economy, not Enonomy."

"I HEARD THAT!" Anala yelled. "And I don't care!"

Rizo rolled his eyes. Anala almost never had mild feelings. Most of her sentences ended with exclamation marks.

"Anala..." Rizo tried.

"DON'T 'Anala' ME!" Anala said. "YOU are NOT the BOSS of ME!"

"Okay! Okay! I was just trying to keep the peace," Rizo backed off, raising his hands to look harmless and sitting down on a hover chair. He floated it to the far side of the room, away from his sister and the racket she was making.

"It is COMPLETELY PEA-" Anala started.

"Anala, if I have to tell you one more time to stop yelling, you are going to regret it," Mikaela told her in a low, ominous voice. Rizo had heard this voice once before, when Mikaela was fed up with his sister. Anala had ignored her and had promptly got knocked unconscious. Dr. Duarte had been livid, and Rizo had almost lost his temper at Mikaela, who still thought that Anala deserved to get clobbered.

Mikaela's personality was heavily influenced by her past, which Rizo didn't know much about. All he knew was that she had been trained to fight from the day she learned to walk because her family knew they would be targeted by the Netrhaphalin. Rizo didn't know why, and he didn't know how she ended up in the orphanage, as Mikaela never said anything about her family or past, but he knew she was not to be messed with, no matter how quiet she usually was.

Rizo knew for certain that she hated the Netrhaphalin and usually acted irritated around Hope. She really only trusted Krackers, who rode on her shoulder most of the time. Mikaela acted quiet but annoyed around everyone else, especially Anala. Now Rizo's sister backed down under her glare, looking wary.

"Rizo, you wouldn't let her do that to me, would you?" Anala asked hopefully. Mikaela just glared at her.

"Um, I'm really for keeping the peace around here," He said.

"Well, your sister is *disturbing* the peace," Mikaela practically growled. "so get her to stop carrying on and yelling *right now.*"

"Oh...okay," Rizo stammered. "Um, Anala, try to be a little less loud."

"All right," Anala agreed. "but MIKAELA doesn't have to THREATEN me!"

"She was...threatening you?" Hope asked, bewildered. "Nobody would do that! Why would they do that?"

"Don't worry, Hope," Mikaela told her with a half sigh, half growl. "Everyone is fine."

"Everything is *completely* fine," Krackers added from his perch on Mikaela's shoulder. "Except for the fact that Mikaela and Anala just had a fight, and the fact that the world is being controlled by robots, and, oh, the fact that we're hiding from them and that they can find us at any moment, and the fact that-"

"No way!" Hope exclaimed. "No one would do those things! No one!"

"Yes, dear, you're very right," Mikaela told her crossly, with just a hint of sarcasm. "Everything is one hundred percent perfect."

"ANY-" Anala started loudly, before she caught the glare Mikaela was shooting her way. "Anyway, Krackers, are all of the things you just said true? They can't be true, right?"

"Oh no, another Hope," Krackers muttered before saying, "In the medium to worst possible scenarios, yes."

"Really?" Anala squeaked before turning to Mikaela and Rizo. "Both of you are thirteen, right? YOU know better than a talking PARROT! He's lying, isn't he?"

"Not really-" Rizo started before Krackers interrupted him.

"I BEG YOUR PARDON!!" Krackers squawked indignantly. "Parrots are perfect. You said so yourself!"

"YOU AREN'T!" Anala told him. "YOU have NEON feathers underneath your wings! NORMAL parrots don't have those! NORMAL parrots are PERFECT! YOU are NOT NORMAL! THEREFORE, YOU ARE NOT PERFECT!"

Rizo glanced at Mikaela. She had that I'm-so-bored-and-annoyed-right-now-I-can-hardly-stand-it face on again, so he decided not to bother her.

"You did not just say that," Krackers glowered.

"YES I DID! AND I'LL SAY IT AGAIN!" Anala was yelling by now. "PARROT, YOU ARE SERIOUSLY DELUSIONAL AND FLAWED! YOU ARE-"

"WHAT DID I SAY ABOUT KEEPING QUIET!" Dr. Duarte roared. "All of you are BEHAVING DISGRACEFULLY. You are being COMPLETELY useless! The only thing you *are* useful for is getting us killed!"

"But-" Anala started. Dr. Duarte looked at her severely, then sighed. He growled something unpleasant. "Come here, all of you. You impudent brats make it *very* clear that I have to tell you why you just put our lives in jeopardy."

KANO

Chances

Chapter 2

June 3, 2473

"Sit down," Dr. Duarte barked. "I'm going to go straight to the point. When you yell, scream, and be generally aggravating and useless, you can alert the Netrhaphalin that we're here."

"How?" Anala asked, her eyes wide. Krackers sighed heavily. Rizo shot him a glare. Krackers was very smart and helpful most of the time, but he had little patience for those who didn't know as much as he did.

"The Netrhaphalin keep a very close eye on the world nowadays," Dr. Duarte explained. "If they sense disturbances, they will without question go and check it out. All of you yelling is enough to cause a disturbance. If you must argue, keep your discord refined and quiet."

"But what if-" Anala protested.

"That is an order, not a suggestion, Anala," Dr. Duarte told her firmly. Addressing everyone, he said, "Now, everyone in this organization has a lot of work to do every day, and it would be very helpful if certain children did not go around yelling and putting our lives and hideout at stake, not to mention being generally useless. Understood?"

"Yes, Dr. Duarte," Rizo, Anala, and Hope said together.

"Krackers? Mikaela?" Dr. Duarte asked.

"Fine," Both of them agreed.

"But Dr. Duarte," Anala started. "We're bored, and that's why we're fighting and being 'useless'. Why can't we help you do whatever you're doing all day?"

"Well..." Dr. Duarte hesitated. "There are a lot of dangerous, not to mention expensive equipment in the lab room. I don't think I can or should trust you with all of it. Maybe..." He trailed off.

"Yes?" Mikaela prompted.

"Can any of you hack a computer?" Dr. Duarte asked.

"Um, of course!" Mikaela and Krackers' reply was instant.

"I think so, I mean, I like to work with technology," Rizo said uncertainly. "I could probably figure it out."

"Uh, not really?" Anala answered, looking downcast.

"Okay," Dr. Duarte sighed. "Mikaela, Krackers and Rizo, I want to test your skills. Anala and Hope, hang out here and play a game."

"Sure!" Hope exclaimed. "Come on, Anala!"

"Okay," Anala told her, slightly disappointed. "Does this mean I'm really useless?"

"Of course not!" Rizo exclaimed. His sister was certainly not useless, no matter what anybody said.

"Anaaaaala!" Hope called from the game room, where she was setting up holographic *Crush that Robot.*

"Coming!" Anala called back. Even though she was sad now, Rizo knew she would be herself soon. She and Hope were best friends, though Rizo thought Anala mostly liked how Hope never criticized her.

"This way," Dr. Duarte pointed to a door marked LAB. Beside Rizo, Mikaela was practically bouncing up and down in excitement. Rizo was excited as well. They had never gone in the lab and were strictly forbidden from even looking inside of it.

Dr. Duarte unlocked the door with his fingerprint, led them inside, then locked the door behind him. He led them past other scientists looking at holograms and mixing different vials of colored liquid together. He brought them down a long corridor to a room marked TECHNOLOGY. He motioned them inside, then shut the door.

"Wow," Rizo breathed. The room was full of BETALINKS and other gadgets. He had heard of the time when humans had access to even better technology than this, before the Netrhaphalin had taken it all away from them. There had only been one BETALINK in the orphanage, and only the staff were allowed to use it. It only had 2 holographic screens. In a corner, Rizo could even see a DELTALINK and an EPSILIONLINK which had 4 and 5 holographic screens, respectively. Rizo couldn't resist being excited about all of these LINKS and gadgets. *I shouldn't, though,* he thought. *LINKS are pretty ancient.*

24

We only made them because that was the only technology we were permitted to have.

It was very rare to have an EPSILONLINK, which had 5 holographic screens. It was the best LINK a human could have. A DELTALINK was pretty rare as well.

"Do not touch anything other than this BETALINK," Dr. Duarte told them sternly while pointing to a huge LINK on a desk riddled with circuits and resistors. Mikaela, Krackers and Rizo just nodded. Rizo assumed they were all as overwhelmed as he was by the explosion of BETALINKS and laptops and the fact that the Gryffins had this much advanced technology.

Dr. Duarte turned on another LINK across the room.

"This is our testing machine," He explained. "This is the LINK we hack into to test barriers and techniques. It currently has the security of one of the Netrhaphalin's database NETLINKS."

"Cool," Rizo said. NETLINKS were like high- speed, holographic, super-smart, pocket-sized discs that the Netrhaphalin used to store data in, scan surrounding areas for suspicious activity, and were also used as weapons, as they could double as tasers if a

Netrhaphalin's eyes were being used to shoot lasers somewhere else. They had been taken away from all humans in the Uprising of the Netrhaphalin, along with other even cooler technology.

"If you can hack it, without any trace of you being in the computer, you can help," Dr. Duarte told them. "If you can't, well... let's just say this is a *very* rare chance to prove your worth. Meaning it is one of your *only* chances."

"If you don't give us many chances, then how can we prove ourselves?" Rizo asked. He started to think that Dr. Duarte was not being entirely fair with them. *You shouldn't be surprised*, a voice said in his head, *when has Dr. Duarte ever been fair?*

"Don't worry, we got this," Mikaela looked ready to burst with excitement. "We can be very useful, you'll see."

Rizo was astonished to see Mikaela so animated. Mikaela's natural resting state was quiet, bored, and a little vengeful.

"We *will* see," Dr. Duarte grumbled, as if he was already regretting his decision to let them help. Mikaela ignored this comment and sat down in front of the hologram. Her fingers flew across the keys of the LINK.

"You can go," She told Rizo. "This will take a while, so you don't have to wait here until it's your turn."

"Okay," Rizo said, exiting the room.

"Wait!" Dr. Duarte called. "You'll need my help to exit the lab."

"Oh, yeah," Rizo said. He followed Dr. Duarte as he walked briskly down the hall, into the lab, then out again.

In the game room, Anala and Hope were focusing on the game of Crush that Robot.

"DO you REALLY want to do THAT?" He heard Anala ask Hope.

"Why not?" Hope asked her, confused. Anala shook her head and immediately captured one of Hope's robots. Rizo didn't want to interrupt them, so he went to the library instead. He loved the library. He loved all the books and the peaceful feeling that came with them. Usually, he loved fictions. Even old fictions like *Justice Boys* were interesting, as fascinating as new fictions like *The Star Riders.*

Before Dr. Duarte had realized that Anala was dyslexic, Rizo had tried to get Anala to read some of the other girly-girl books like *Poems, Lathania*, but she had refused. She almost never went into the library because she hated reading.

Today, however, he looked for a book on hacking. He really needed to brush up his skills on how to hack a NETLINK if he was going to be of any use to the Gryffins. He found a book called *Beginning Hacking,* sat down, pulled out the disk inside the book, and pressed play. A hologram popped up and began rapidly scrolling through the words as a voice dictated them through a surround sound speaker. *"The first thing you have to do before you hack is...."*

> > >

Three hours later...

"Rizo, it's your turn," Mikaela pushed a button on the disk, and the holograms faded away. The excitement and confidence had faded from her voice, making it sound...disappointed? That was unusual. Mikaela was a lot of things, but she was rarely *disappointed.*

"How did you do?" He asked before he noticed the downcast expression on her face.

"I left a trail behind that led straight back to the LINK I used," She explained glumly.

"Oh, sorry," Rizo told her, his confidence wavering. If Mikaela couldn't hack the LINK posing as a NETLINK successfully, what were that odds that he could? Mikaela looked at him with a quick glare, as if to say, *"I don't need your sympathy."*

"Go on," Krackers told him. "Dr. Duarte is waiting."

Rizo nodded and went back to the lab and down the hall to the technology room. The table looked a bit worse for wear, as if Mikaela had taken her frustration out on it a few times.

"Good luck," Dr. Duarte told him. "Get comfortable. I'll see you in a few hours."

"Uh, okay," Rizo answered, before he realized that Dr. Duarte had left.

Rizo sat down.

He took a deep breath.

Let's do this, he thought.

Time to prove he was useful after all.

Working Hard

Chapter 3

June 4, 2473

Rizo hunched his shoulders. He had been working for hours now, and he was sure he'd missed dinner. After every barrier he cracked as stealthily as he could, there seemed to be an even trickier blockade waiting for him. Sometimes he thought he was going in circles. *I've seen that block of commands before*, he thought. *Am I losing it?* He shook his head to clear it. He couldn't fail. Not if he wanted to be useful. If he could prove himself, then maybe he could prove that his friends were useful, too. Then they would be busy all the time. Then there would be no more fighting. There would be peace, for once.

Okay, he thought. *Focus. You're doing this for your friends.*

It was harder to focus as the barriers became more cryptic.

Traps that made you leave obvious trails behind were scattered throughout the code.

Confusing mazes to crack.

Rizo could just see himself failing miserably.

No! He told himself. *You absolutely cannot fail. That is not an option!* Rizo took a deep breath. *You can do this,* he assured himself. *You have to do this.* Another voice rang in his head: *It's impossible. You will fail. You were always useless. Absolutely useless.* Rizo closed his eyes, trying to shut down the warring thoughts in his head. He had to do this. He *had* to. Maybe other thirteen-year-olds would just give up- well, maybe not Mikaela, but he wouldn't. He couldn't. This might be the only chance he had to earn Dr. Duarte's respect, or, at least, show him that he wasn't *completely* useless after all.

He used the last of his mental energy to squeeze through (hopefully) the last barrier. *Please let me be in,* he thought. *Please, please, please.* He closed his eyes as the computer processed his code. *I hope I did it* went through his mind as he opened his eyes. And he was in. He had done it! Now his mind was racing. *I've done it, but what if I left a trail? If so, I've failed. Really truly failed. Just like Mikaela.* However, he was also thinking, *I got in! I did it!* And then back to: *But what if I messed something up?*

He felt distinctly nervous as Dr. Duarte checked his work.

"Rizo..." Dr. Duarte looked at him sternly. *Oh no,* Rizo thought. *I messed up. I failed.*

"Rizo, you hacked this laptop perfectly," Dr. Duarte told him. A thousand thoughts were whirling around Rizo's mind. *What? I did it?* and *No way! This is a trick!* and *I DID IT! I am awesome!* and *He has to be lying.* and even, *I beat Mikaela? She is going to be SO MAD!*

"But?" Rizo asked, somewhat afraid of the answer to that Dr. Duarte would give to him.

"No buts," Dr. Duarte cracked a rare smile. "Consider yourself useful after all."

"Really?" Rizo couldn't help but smile back. "So what can I do?"

"You can start scanning the area for NETLINKS," Dr. Duarte told him. "When you get a signal, try hacking the NETLINK. Remember, be *very* careful. If you mess up, we're in big trouble."

"I know," Rizo assured him. Dr. Duarte gave him a skeptical look that probably had something to do with the huge smile on Rizo's face.

"I know! I know, my face looks weird," Rizo protested. "But I understand one hundred percent." Dr. Duarte still looked doubtful.

"How about you have Mikaela check my work as I go?" Rizo asked. He hoped that suggestion would clear the unconvinced look on Dr. Duarte's face *and* give Mikaela a job.

"I guess," Dr. Duarte said, rubbing his forehead. "I hope I won't regret this."

"Don't worry, you won't," Rizo promised.

"Arhgggg," Dr. Duarte growled, looking indecisive. "I *really* hope I'm not making a terrible decision here."

"You aren't!" Rizo told him. "You will be *very* glad you let us help."

"This seems like a bad idea."

"It was *your* idea!" Rizo was getting a little agitated now. He had passed the test. If he could hack the equivalent of a NETLINK then, he could do it again, surely. Why couldn't Dr. Duarte trust him?

"I'm going to get Mikaela's input," Dr. Duarte finally decided. "Don't you dare do anything while I'm gone."

"Fine," Rizo told him, annoyed. How could Dr. Duarte tell him that he'd performed perfectly, then not trust him to do just as well the next time? Dr. Duarte nodded, then turned and left. Rizo just sat at the desk, fuming. He'd proven himself, and yet Dr. Duarte *still* had doubts about him. *Calm down*, he thought. *Don't get all mad. I bet Dr. Duarte has a good reason for his skepticism.*

Nevertheless, it was still INFURIATING. *Calm down*, he reminded himself. *You don't have to be like Anala when you get mad.*

Rizo closed his eyes and tried to shut down this train of thought. It was not only unproductive, but also decidedly hostile and not very nice. Rizo hated thinking mean thoughts. It was one thing to observe the disagreeable traits of others, it was another thing to get angry over them. Plus, he always felt guilty after being horrible to someone. Well, horrible by his standards. Anala obviously had no problem with yelling, while Mikaela apparently had no issues with knocking someone out for being noisy.

Just then, Dr. Duarte reappeared with Mikaela at his side, who looked slightly annoyed that Rizo had managed to do what she hadn't.

"So, you did it," Mikaela deadpanned.

"You don't sound that excited," Rizo observed. He frowned. Why didn't Mikaela sound as enthusiastic as he thought she would?

"Well, I-" Mikaela sputtered.

"All right, you two," Dr. Duarte interrupted Mikaela's stammering. "Do you want to do this or not?"

"Yes!" Rizo absolutely wanted to do this. He wanted to be useful. He looked at Mikaela expectantly.

"I guess," she mumbled.

"You guess?" Rizo looked at Mikaela, dumbfounded. He inspected her more closely, not that he expected to deduce what she was feeling. He was terrible at figuring out human emotions. "I thought you wanted to do this."

"I did," she said, looking down.

"What?" He asked. Now he was *really* confused. Mikaela had always acted like she had a purpose, and he thought she had been dying to prove that, even in little ways.

She shook her head. "You don't understand."

"Um," he said uncertainly. "Sorry?"

"*Well*," Dr. Duarte looked impatient. "Let's assume everyone gave an enthusiastic yes. Supposing this happened, emphasize on *supposing*, I would need to walk you through some more safety precautions."

"Safety precautions?" Rizo groaned. "Can't you trust us? I mean, I did fine, right? What else do I need to know?"

"Stuck up- slime weasel," Rizo thought he heard Mikaela grumble under her breath.

"Excuse me?" He asked politely, although he was rather offended.

"You think you're so smart," Mikaela fumed.

"Okay, what? I really have *no idea* why you're acting *so weird*," Rizo was getting more bewildered by the minute.

Mikaela just growled. Rizo was now pretty sure Mikaela was mad. That was the one human emotion he could usually identify. Also, it was the one emotion he usually wanted to quell. He had thought he was good at calming people down, but he had no idea how to pacify

36

Mikaela when he didn't know what was making her mad in the first place.

"I see that letting you guys help was clearly a stupid decision," Dr. Duarte muttered under his breath. "You haven't even started yet, and it's a disaster."

"Mikaela's the one making this difficult!" Rizo burst out. "I really don't understand what's happening!"

"Rizo," Dr. Duarte sighed. "Come over here. Mikaela, you can go for now."

"No way!" She exclaimed.

"Mikaela, this is important," Dr. Duarte told her.

"I know what it is. You're going to tell him why I don't want to help like this! It doesn't matter. I'll tell him myself. I don't want to help as a backup person. I want to be in the front line. By myself. So now you know. So now you know why I don't want to do *this.*" Mikaela looked around defiantly.

"I'm sorry," was all that came out of Rizo's mouth. He was surprised that his mouth worked at all, he was so shocked by Mikaela's outburst. "I- I didn't know."

"Of course you didn't," she said bitterly. "You don't understand. You never have, and you never will. Your parents just died of a car crash, right? The autonomous driving programming was flawed or something. It was just a freak accident. It wasn't your fault. You couldn't have saved them. That's why you will *never* understand me or anyone else who's ever been hurt by the Netrhaphalin." With that, Mikaela stormed out of the technology room.

"Okkkaaayyyy," Rizo said, looking at Dr. Duarte. "I did not understand *that* at all."

"That's sort of her point," Dr. Duarte sighed. "as even *I* don't know much about her past. All I know is that her family was targeted, then taken away by the Netrhaphalin, never to be seen again. She somehow survived and got taken to the orphanage we took you from."

"That's... scary," Rizo commented.

"Exactly," Dr. Duarte said. "I think she believes it was her fault her family got caught, because they depended on her or something. Therefore, she doesn't want to depend on anyone and also wants to prove that she can do what she couldn't all those years ago." He paused, listening. "What was that?"

"Me, and you're wrong," Mikaela stepped into the room. "I heard all that. I have already proved myself, many times. And I don't depend on anybody because I don't trust anyone."

"Even me?" Rizo asked, hurt.

"You're a gray area," she replied.

"Better question," Dr. Duarte cut in before Rizo could protest about his trustworthiness. "How did you hear all that?"

"I just made a scene to see how you'd react," Mikaela shrugged. "I doubled back and listened through the door."

"Well, now, I don't trust *you*!" Rizo burst out. "That was sneaky and devious, not to mention mean."

"Well, you were being mean, too," Mikaela pointed out. "So I thought I should return the favor."

"I was being mean?" Rizo asked. He instantly felt a wave of guilt crash over him. "I'm sorry."

"I know you didn't *mean* it," Mikaela rolled her eyes. "You're a peace-loving sloth who is always nice and tedious."

"Okay, now you're just being horrible for no reason," Rizo pouted.

"Enough!" Dr. Duarte looked impatient *and* furious, not a good combination. "These theatrics have gone on too long. Both of you are wasting my time. Are you going to help, or not?"

"I'm in," Rizo said.

"Fine, but only because I enjoy annoying Rizo." Mikaela smirked.

Rizo had a sudden feeling that this was when everything would go wrong.

Confusion

Chapter 4

June 5, 2473

"Let's DO this!" Mikaela had an extremely gleeful smile. It was the day after she had agreed to help hack NETLINKS with Rizo, and he could already see the million ways this whole 'working together' plan could go south.

Mikaela's frizzy, dark brown hair flew out behind her as she skipped down the hall to the technology room. That was odd. Mikaela always had her hair up in bun or ponytail of some sort, never loose. Also, Mikaela *never* skipped. *Oh well,* Rizo thought. *It's probably nothing. Besides, when did I ever think about a girl's hair? Or her behavior?* He followed her down the hall, a little less enthusiastically. Dr. Duarte trailed both of them, looking concerned.

"I don't think this is a good idea," he said for the thousandth time. "I really don't."

"We KNOW!" Mikaela called from behind the main hacking computer. "But we're doing it ANYWAY, regardless of what YOU think!" Her voice was unusually high and gleeful.

"What's wrong with her?" Dr. Duarte whispered to Rizo, looking confused. "She sounds like Anala today."

Rizo shrugged. "I don't know," he replied. *It's nice to know that Dr. Duarte also thinks that Mikaela is acting weird, though. I'm not just imagining it.*

Mikaela was rummaging through a bin of circuits when both Dr. Duarte and Rizo came in. She quickly got up, looking startled.

"Uh, hi! YOU sure took YOUR time coming here!" She told them brightly.

"Mikaela. Are you okay?" Rizo asked, concerned.

"Of course I am! Why wouldn't I be?" She looked at him curiously, though she sounded worried. Then her eyes went wide in shock and horror at something behind him. He whirled around to see *another* Mikaela walking

42

down the hall, with Krackers on her shoulder. Rizo looked from one Mikaela to the other. His mind was screaming: *What is happening? What is HAPPENING?*

"What are you-" the second Mikaela hissed to the first Mikaela, then cut herself off. "What is the meaning of this!"

"What in the world!" Dr. Duarte exclaimed. "Who are you?"

"Me?" The second Mikaela looked furious. "I'm Mikaela. Who is she? Anala? Hope? Come out here right now, or I will-"

"Calm down, there's no need-" Rizo started.

"Or I will make you regret everything you've done," Mikaela interrupted him, finishing her sentence.

"Okay! Okay!" The first Mikaela took off her wig to expose straight, dark hair in a bun. She glared at the second Mikaela.

"Huh?" Rizo looked at the first Mikaela. She did seem a little small to be Mikaela, come to think of it, but the real Mikaela was so petite, he hadn't noticed.

Meanwhile, the first Mikaela scrubbed off what appeared to be make-up with a towel she produced from her pocket, and Rizo noticed light skin.

43

"Who are you?" He asked. The first Mikaela sighed. Hope flew out of another pocket in her clothes and started expanding. She then scanned the first Mikaela's body, and the rest of the disguise fell away, revealing a frightened girl behind it.

Anala.

"WHAT KIND OF TRICK WAS THIS?" Dr. Duarte seemed ready to explode. "EXPLAIN YOURSELF. NOW."

"I'm- I'm sorry," Anala stammered, flicking her eyes toward the real Mikaela. "I-I j-just thought that it wasn't...fair, yeah, it wasn't FAIR that Mikaela and Rizo got to help and I didn't. I'm so, SO, sorry. I thought that the disguise was pretty cool, though! Hope couldn't get the skin color just right so I had to use LOADS of make-up and Hope put in on me and didn't it look AMAZING? ALSO, oh my GOODNESS it was SO HARD not to yell ALL the TIME but-"

"ENOUGH!" Dr. Duarte glanced up, towards the sky, if they hadn't been underground, muttering unpleasant things. "Anala, you are in *so* much trouble."

"I know," She whispered.

"Anala, come with me," Dr. Duarte told her, rubbing his forehead.

"I have a question," Mikaela tilted her head at Anala. "How did Hope put on the make-up?"

"Oh that?" Anala said. "That was simple. Hope just spray-painted my face with the stuff. It was SUPER easy. The only, uh, problem was that some of it got on the walls. ONLY a LITTLE! We were VERY careful. But, uh, the game room looks a little, um, *browner* than usual. It DOES look VERY nice though. I think it really should-"

"Anala..." Dr. Duarte snarled. "Are you saying that you basically spray-painted the game room brown?"

"Well, we tried REALLY hard to NOT get any make-up on the walls or carpet or anything- at first. But then we sort of disagreed about something and I accidentally, ACCIDENTALLY, sprayed a little on the wall. And then, Hope and I thought it looked nice so we..." Anala trailed off. Rizo could tell she was about to say something she knew no one would appreciate.

"Yes?" Dr. Duarte was frowning heavily now, as if he wasn't sure he wanted an answer to that question.

"We sprayed most of the room," Anala blurted out quickly.

"WHAT?" Dr. Duarte roared. "YOU did WHAT?"
Rizo half expected smoke to come out of Dr. Duarte's
ears, he looked so mad. Rizo had a flash of memory,
back before he was an orphan, when he had drew on the
walls with a permanent marker, not a holographic one.
His mom had looked just like Dr. Duarte in that instant.

"I thought you said we weren't supposed to yell,"
Krackers muttered darkly. "Hypocrite."

"We thought it looked nice!" Anala protested.
"We just went a LITTLE overboard."

"A little?" asked Mikaela, looking incredulous.
"More like a lot."

"Okay, maybe a lot," Anala consented. "But we
had a good reason to!" She clapped her hands over her
mouth, horrified.

"Anala!" Hope cried. "You weren't supposed to
say that!" *Uh oh*, Rizo thought. *When Hope's alarmed,
something is very, very wrong.*

"What was this reason?" Dr. Duarte asked. Rizo
caught sight of Mikaela, who was staring at Anala in
horror. *Or maybe fear,* Rizo observed. *What could
Mikaela be afraid of?*

"I-we-" Anala glanced quickly at Mikaela, who glared at her, then looked away. "Nothing."

"Are you hiding something from-" Rizo started.

"Anala, I know it's something," called Dr. Duarte from the game room. He had gone ahead in a rage, wanting to see the damage for himself. "You wrote this, didn't you? Otherwise, why would the walls have words spray-painted on them saying, 'MIKAELA is dlacknailing- is that blackmailing? Ok, BLACKMAILING us into doing THIS and we think that's NOT alright'?"

KANO

Crisis

Chapter 5

June 5, 2473

"Mikaela?" Rizo turned to his friend. "Care to explain *that?*"

Mikaela blinked. "I don't know anything about that message." She shook her head. "I never asked them to impersonate me. And I would never, ever, blackmail Anala and Hope, no matter how annoying they are sometimes." She sat down on a hover chair and crossed her arms. "That's a nasty trick. I'm not *that* horrible."

"YOU-YOU-YOU, DIRTY LOW DOWN LIAR!" Anala screeched at Mikaela before turning to Dr. Duarte. "SHE IS LYING. *LYING!* Rizo, don't you believe me?"

Rizo hesitated. "Well," he said slowly. "Hope, do you confirm what Anala is saying?"

"I want to say yes, but would Mikaela do- what am I saying? YES! Anala is telling the truth." Hope had an odd look on her face, as if there was a war going on in her computer-mind.

"Mikaela?" Dr. Duarte inspected her face for any hint of emotion.

"I have no idea why they think I told them to do this," Mikaela stated calmly. "I hope we catch the *real* culprit soon."

"But-but-you called us! On the holophone! And told me to act like you and mess Rizo up!" Anala protested.

"Wait, what did you just say?" Dr. Duarte ran his fingers through his hair, worried.

"Mikaela called! She said it was her!" Anala was nearly in hysterics trying to prove herself.

"Anala, what did Mikaela say exactly?" Dr. Duarte asked her.

"I didn't do it," Mikaela grumbled. "Get that through your thick head."

"Quiet," Dr. Duarte instructed her firmly, then crouched to look Rizo's sister in the eye. "Anala?"

"I'm telling the truth!" She wailed. "Mikaela called and said it was her. She said if we didn't pretend to be her and mess Rizo up, she'd kill us. She also said not to tell anyone, but Hope and I reasoned that she didn't tell us to write anything down so we had to-"

"That's crazy. I wouldn't kill Anala and Hope!" Mikaela told Krackers, the only one who was listening to her.

"Oh no," Dr. Duarte snapped upright. "Follow me." Rizo ran along with everyone else to the holophone in the common room. Dr. Duarte checked the numbers of previous callers. After a minute, he muttered something that Rizo would get grounded for saying and tapped a number into the phone.

"Hi, Kyrie," He said to whoever was on the other end of the phone. "We need you to, um, one of the kids is hurt. We need you to come here now... Yes... excellent. See you soon." Dr. Duarte hung up and put the home phone down. He turned to Rizo and Mikaela. "I need you to go-" He started then stopped. Quickly, he picked up the phone, pried it open, then removed a small device that was stashed inside. He flicked a switch, and a blue light emitted from the device, scanning the room. A red flicker caught his eye on the second scan. He zeroed in on it and pulled something off the wall near the clock. He set it on the table, then raised his fist to strike it, then paused. Instead, he spoke into the device. "It was all a mistake, don't worry, Anala. I'm sure Mikaela didn't mean any harm. I'm sure she was joking. Mikaela- NO! Don't throw the-" He slammed his fist into the table, breaking whatever he had found. Rizo guessed it had been a bug, designed to eavesdrop on everyone's conversations.

While Mikaela and Krackers had clearly figured out what was happening, Anala and Hope seemed confused. Rizo motioned for them to stay quiet. Dr. Duarte scanned the room again and again until he was satisfied that there were no more bugs or cameras anywhere. He whirled around to talk to Rizo and Mikaela, but before he could speak, a young woman or an older teenager- Rizo couldn't tell- ran into the room, looking around wildly.

"Da- Dr. Duarte! Who's hurt?" She asked.

"No one," Dr. Duarte replied. "We've been detected, Kyrie."

"Oh, Lord have mercy," Kyrie said. "That's bad. Is it as bad as the Guard-"?

"No. I'm starting the evacuation plan," he told her. "Take care of the kids!" He raced away.

"Oh, bananas," she said. "Kids, and- you two, follow me." She darted to a door marked EMPLOYEES ONLY and punched in an entrance code into an electronic keypad. She let them all through and closed the door behind them. Rizo heard a bang, and the concrete above them trembled.

"Nuts," Kyrie whispered. "All of you, stay close and don't make a sound." She ran down a long hallway, turned left, and then grimaced as she pulled open a drawer marked EMERGENCY ONLY. It appeared empty at first, but then she typed a code on to a hidden keypad. The bottom slid open, revealing a button.

"I really hoped it wouldn't come to this," she sighed, then turned on an ancient radio on her belt. "All clear, Jared?"

"Ready to rock and roll," an unfamiliar male voice answered. "Such a goof," she whispered affectionately as she turned off her radio. Rizo was astounded by the radio in her hand. Radios had been popular centuries and centuries ago. He hadn't known any more existed, though he had loved to study radios when he was younger. He was so focused on the radio that he didn't see Kyrie press the button in the secret compartment. There was a crash, and the walls shook around them.

"Come on," she motioned to a nondescript door on her right. They filed into a dark room. Kyrie locked the door behind her, and they all sat quietly for a moment.

"Kyrie, what's happening?" Anala whimpered, breaking the silence. "Why are we hiding?"

"It's just a precaution, dear," Kyrie reassured her calmly. "No need to worry."

"Okay," Anala appeared to be satisfied, though Rizo, Mikaela and Krackers knew there was something wrong.

"Will Dr. Duarte be alright?" Hope asked.

"Probably-" Kyrie stopped herself. "He will." They sat quietly for a minute, thinking. Rizo was the first to break the silence.

"Um, how old are you?" Rizo couldn't help asking Kyrie. Not only did he want to know, he also didn't want to think about the danger Dr. Duarte was in.

"Seventeen," she laughed at his shocked expression.

"You're in the Gryffins at age seventeen?" Mikaela asked, intrigued.

"I've been in it my whole life," Kyrie responded. "Edward Duarte is my father."

"Really?" Mikaela asked. "You don't look...much alike." That was putting it mildly. Kyrie had light skin, hazel eyes, and long, dark blond hair, while Dr. Duarte had chocolate-brown hair, dark eyes, and a dark complexion that was a little lighter than Mikaela's.

Kyrie laughed. "My father's family is from the Brazil District, and my mother's family is from the Scotland District. They met at school. Many people say that I got my mother's looks, while Jared got his from Dad."

"Who?" Anala asked.

"Jared is my brother. My mother- she died when I was four. She was a scientist, and she got quite a bit of radiation through her work. She had cancer, but we didn't have the medicine to treat it. My father wanted to go to a hospital to get some. My mother told him not to. It would save her life, yes, but then we would be exposed. Dad was heartbroken when she died."

The room fell silent, filled with sympathy.

"I hope Dr. Duarte's okay," Rizo said quietly.

"So do I," Kyrie told him. She looked up. "Hope, what are you doing?" Hope was gliding in circles, shaking her head from side to side.

"Oh, nothing," Hope replied, but continued her strange movements.

"Are you-" Kyrie asked.

"Nice try," Hope sneered, in voice unlike her own. "We'll take it from here."

"What? Who's we?" Kyrie peered into the darkness, confused and panicked.

"You poor creature," Hope sighed. "How wretched it must be to be a human."

"This isn't Hope," Anala said, worried. "She's always nice."

"Hope?" Hope laughed. "An unusual name for a Netrhaphalin."

"Lord have mercy," Kyrie whispered. "Monkeys and bananas." Rizo and Mikaela exchanged horrified glances, accented with fear.

"Run!" Rizo called, already on his feet. He flew down the way they had entered the room.

"No it's a-" Kyrie shouted. Rizo rounded a corner- and hit a dead end. The hall was caved in, completely destroyed.

"Well bless my beak," Krackers muttered. "We're done for."

"Kyrie! How do we get out?" Rizo turned to the oldest person in the room.

"You won't," a voice called, and Rizo saw a hole being blasted into the top of the room. "Don't move."

The Netrhaphalin had found them.

Detected

Chapter 6
June 5, 2473

"Rizo? What's happening?" Anala asked, her eyes wide. She clutched his arm with iron grip.

"We're in big trouble," Rizo responded. It was the easiest answer he could think of, and they were really in huge trouble.

"Round them up!" A voice called. Hope immediately followed the command. Anala squeezed Rizo's arm tighter. His circulation was getting cut off. He freed his arm with a hiss that indicated that Anala should stop hanging on to him.

"Put your hands up," Hope instructed them in the same monotone, creepy voice. Rizo obligingly put his hands up. Mikaela, Anala, and Kyrie did the same. Rizo looked around for Krackers, who was hiding in the shadows. He locked eyes with the parrot, and tilted his head towards the hole in the ceiling. Krackers nodded. He cocked his head towards the Netrhaphalin, then flapped his wings silently and looked at Rizo. *He wants a distraction*, Rizo thought. If capture was inevitable, then he should limit the number of people (or parrots) captured, right? *Well, I'll give him one.* If anything, Krackers could free them later, or tell the Gryffins what had happened.

Rizo glared at the nearest Netrhaphalin, a blue and white robot, and spoke up. "You guys are so lame!" He shouted. Krackers cringed at the flimsy insult. "I mean, if you don't have electricity, you die!"

"Someone can charge us up again," a Netrhaphalin shrugged. "We're not gone for good. Unlike some people in the room. Besides, out batteries last for years before they run out." He laughed, a high pitched, horrible laugh that made Rizo want to fling him across the room.

"Well, well- I-" Rizo stopped. He started waving his hands in the air wildly. "LOOK OVER HERE!" He yelled. "MIKAELA IS TRYING TO ESCAPE!"

"I'm not escaping," Mikaela scoffed. "That's a good way to get yourself killed. Besides, I *like* the Netrhaphalin." Rizo was sure Mikaela was lying about the last part. Mikaela hated the Netrhaphalin with every bone in her body. It was part of who she was.

"SHE'S TRYING TO ESCAPE!" Rizo repeated, louder this time. The Netrhaphalin turned to look at him, and Krackers motioned for him to keep going. Kyrie saw the motion and caught on.

"YOU'RE LYING!" she yelled at Rizo. "I AM NOT ABOUT TO ESCAPE, THOUGH I HATE THE NETRHAPHALIN!"

"You what?" Hope asked. Kyrie had the Netrhaphalin's full attention now. They all turned to her with shallow glares.

"I MEAN WHAT I SAID!" Kyrie yelled. Krackers motioned for more. By now, both Mikaela and Anala had caught on to what Rizo and Kyrie were doing. They started yelling, too.

"I don't WANT to be CAPTURED!" Anala
screeched. "I want to be FREE! I am NOT going with
YOU! NO WAY! NOT EVER!"

"SHUSH! THE NETRHAPHALIN ARE PERFECT!"
Mikaela called. She appeared to be in physical pain by
just saying good things about the Netrhaphalin. Right
then, her face was twisted in a grimace of disgust and
pain.

"STOP IT!" Rizo shrieked, adding to the din. The
Netrhaphalin looked from one person to another,
obviously bewildered by the shouting.

"ROUND THEM UP!" Hope called to them. Rizo
made a fuss, pushing and pulling at his captors. Anala
was kicking and screaming loud enough for everyone to
hear. "YOU ARE HORRIBLE!" She yelled. "I DESPISE THE
NETRHAPHALIN!" Meanwhile, both Kyrie and Mikaela
were putting up a fight, yelling the whole time. In the
chaos, Rizo saw a flash of neon feathers going up the
hole, and then Krackers was gone.

The Netrhaphalin rounded them all up and
brought them to the surface.

"Wow," Anala whispered. "I forgot how bright it is
up here." Rizo couldn't agree more. It hadn't been dark

underground, but he had almost forgotten what the sun felt like. However, the warm feeling the sun gave him vanished quickly as Rizo and the others were transported to a dark building by telecubes.

Telecubes were placed around the cities and connected by thick underground wires. They were heavily guarded by the Netrhaphalin, and were only used with their permission. They worked by breaking you up into little particles and sending them through the wires. At the other end of the wires, it re-formed you. There had been accidents in the beginning, when telecubes were being fine-tuned, but now they worked perfectly.

When Rizo re-formed, he found himself just outside a dark, foreboding building that loomed over them. It looked very out of place next to the bright, floating, egg-shaped buildings surrounding it. In fact, it seemed as if the drab building they were entering had been built hundreds of years ago, like the tunnels they had lived in.

"They're like modern catacombs," Dr. Duarte had said a few years ago when he was describing the tunnels. "Old and crumbling." (Rizo had later searched for what a catacomb was in their library later, and was not pleased.

Were there skeletons around him at that very minute? His nightmares were chased away only when Dr. Duarte had explained that they were in metaphorical catacombs, not real ones.)

Rizo glanced back and saw that Mikaela and Kyrie had already re-formed, and Anala was right behind Rizo.

"It's creepy here," Anala said in a small voice. "I wish Mom and Dad were here. They would make everything better."

Rizo was surprised. Anala almost never mentioned their parents, and had certainly never said that she wished they were still alive, even though Rizo knew she did. He always missed them. It had been awful, the first few days after the accident. Rizo often worried that Anala was stuck in that happy, enthusiastic state because she was afraid of what might happen if she let herself be sad for the parents she had never known.

Rizo put an arm around his sister. "Don't worry," he told her. "We'll find a way out of this."

"I hope so," she said. "I really hope so." So this was Rizo's sister underneath her bubbly (or loud) personality. A frightened, sad girl who desperately wanted to be happy.

What's my real personality? The revelation hit him hard, like his whole life had been in a fog, and now it was clearing up. For so long, he had thought he was a naturally calm person who liked order. He had played calm peacemaker for so long; it was his default personality.

You don't know what to do? Keep the peace. Stay calm. Anala's freaking out because of something? Calm her down, like a good little peacemaker. Not that anything was wrong with wanting peace- Rizo was sure there was always a need for order- but he remembered himself when he was younger, not at all worried about picking fights or restoring peace. He had been so carefree and innovative, something a little different every day, instead of the predictable and boring person he had become in the tunnels.

Well, time to come out of my shell, he thought. *Because if I don't, I may not be able to get us out of here. However, I think I should still hang on to the peacemaking part of me. And the planning part. Those skills might just come in handy.*

"Rizo! Stop daydreaming!" Mikaela waved her hand in front of his face, then smacked his arm.

Apparently Rizo had stopped in his moment of self-reflection.

"OW! Oh, sorry," he mumbled. Rizo tried to keep his mind in the present, but he couldn't help but notice that Mikaela was getting bolder and more ferocious the longer she had to submit to the Netrhaphalin.

Anala stayed close to Rizo as they were herded into the building. Rizo looked around for an escape, but he saw nothing but concrete and gray walls around him. As the Netrhaphalin filed out, he thought he saw- but it couldn't be- a flash of neon feathers as the only way out closed, locking all of them in the semi-darkness.

"How are we going to get out of here?" Mikaela whispered. They all were sitting in the middle of the room. It wasn't comfortable, but it was under a skylight, which made it a tiny bit more bearable than the other dark corners.

"We're getting out?" Anala asked.

"Do you want to die?" Mikaela countered.

"No," Rizo agreed. "They should die, not us."

Mikaela tipped her head at Rizo. "Are you Rizo? Because I thought Rizo was a peace-loving softie."

"I'm different now," Rizo told her, lifting his chin defiantly. "Kyrie? Do you have any plans?"

"Well," Kyrie spoke very calmly and carefully. "I don't think escaping is the best idea." She glared at them, as if to say, *We're being watched, so shut your traps if we want to get out of here.*

"I guess," Mikaela relented, obviously catching the meaning behind Kyrie's look.

"Wait, what?" Anala asked, confused. Rizo rolled his eyes. For a nine-year-old, Anala was not very perceptive.

"Hush up," he told her quietly.

"What? That is ABSURD-" Rizo clapped his hand over her mouth before she spouted any more nonsense. *We need to get out of here fast,* he thought *before Anala ruins everything.*

"What are we going to do?" Mikaela asked, looking up. Rizo glanced up and saw a small skylight. On top of the skylight was Krackers, peering down at them. Rizo gasped, and Kyrie frowned at him. Rizo kept his eyes on the ground, and motioned for Anala to do the same.

"We'll just submit to them," Rizo said. Anala was staring openly up at Krackers, her mouth open.

"Anala," he hissed. She missed his signal and immediately started talking.

"Oh my goodness," Anala said. "I can't believe it's K-" Rizo clamped his hand over her mouth again. She twisted around in protest, trying to get out of his grip. He gave her a very stern look and let go of her.

"Anala," he hissed. "Just be quiet and listen." However, he wondered how Krackers had found them. The only way that was possible was if he had taken the Telecubes.

"I am-" Anala started indignantly.

"Shh," Kyrie interrupted Rizo's sister mid-protest. She looked up, and Krackers waved to them. He made some flapping motions, which Rizo didn't understand, and then flew away.

"I didn't understand," Anala whispered, voicing Rizo's thoughts. "Mikaela?" Mikaela shook her head. Krackers re-appeared a moment later, shaking himself. He beat his wings twice, and Mikaela stretched, throwing her hands out.

"Ahh, I'm tired," she said. "I'm going to lie down for a bit." She lay down, but not before she threw up a hand in an exhausted gesture.

"Me, too," Anala lay down and closed her eyes while Krackers turned around and flew away. Now Kyrie and Rizo were the only ones awake, unless Mikaela was acting. She was probably acting. However, they couldn't wake her, because that would look suspicious to the Netrhaphalin who were watching them through the cameras mounted on the walls of their prison.

"What was that about?" Kyrie asked Rizo in a low voice.

"I don't know," he replied, in the same tone. "Krackers and Mikaela have always been best friends, so they probably devised some sort of communication system that I don't know about."

"And she *had* to go to sleep?" Kyrie asked, exasperated. "We're going to have to wait hours to learn what Krackers told her!"

"Maybe it was part of the signal? Maybe?"

"It's going to be a long day, and possibly a long night, if we don't get out of here. I hope Mikaela wakes up soon, and if she doesn't, I'll wake her. Secret codes are useless if the only people who know them are asleep or not available!" Kyrie said severely.

"You may look like your mom, but you're an awful lot like your dad," Rizo observed.

Kyrie smiled sadly. "That's probably true."

Rizo and Kyrie sat in silence for a while, thinking.

"What are they going to do to us?" Rizo was very concerned about that part, and hoped Kyrie had an answer.

"I don't know, we'll see. It can't be good."

That was...reassuring.

There was another long pause. Again, Rizo broke the silence.

"If you don't mind, I think I'll take a nap, too." Rizo told Kyrie.

"Take a nap. I'll stay up, watching. And thinking."

"Okay."

"Have a nice nap."

Rizo lay down, thinking that this was one of the biggest messes he had ever gotten himself into. If Krackers didn't get them out soon...Rizo didn't want to think about it.

All he knew was that they would be in big trouble.

Communicating

Chapter 7

June 6, 2473

Rizo's dreams were filled with nightmares of his being captured by the Netrhaphalin. They were chasing him and... shaking him? Rizo woke up, shuddering. He looked up. Kyrie had been the one shaking him.

"Wake up, sleepyhead," She whispered.

"How long have I been out for?" Rizo asked.

"Let's see," Kyrie said. "Cover me." Rizo stretched, hiding Kyrie. She bent down and pulled the sole off her tennis shoe. Underneath there was a mini watch!

"It's six o'clock, June fifth." Kyrie reported, then closed her shoe back up. She started a series of jumping jacks and stretches.

"It's an undetectable watch," she explained when she saw Rizo's amazement.

"Cool!" He whispered. "Is that a gorilla?" The face of the watch had a picture on it.

"Yes," Kyrie smiled. "I'm surprised you knew what it was." Rizo shrugged. Gorillas were extinct- for now, anyways- and had been for the last two hundred years. Humans had finally learned how to successfully re-create animals using their DNA when the Netrhaphalin had come and stopped all the research going into saving animals. Some scientists in the Gryffin were hoping to get back to their projects in that field when the reign of the Netrhaphalin had ended. For now, everyone had to live with animatronic animals, which were extremely realistic but still not real. Dr. Duarte was pretty paranoid and had once claimed that he believed that the Netrhaphalin were planning to kill off humans and then replace them with animatronic people. Mikaela had spent a full meal arguing that Dr. Duarte's theory made no sense.

"Should I wake the others?" Rizo asked.

"Sure. I would've waken you all up way earlier, except I fell asleep, too."

"Oh, okay." Rizo roused Anala gently, and was about to shake Mikaela awake when she sat up.

"Finally!" Mikaela said. "Waiting for you guys to wake up took forever!"

"You were up and you didn't tell me?" Kyrie frowned, but continued stretching.

"Why didn't you just wake us up instead of waiting?" Rizo wanted to know. Mikaela shrugged in response to both questions.

"Anyway," Rizo said calmly, before Kyrie completely lost it. "let's settle down." He couldn't help it! Some part of him still wanted to be a peacemaker, and Rizo decided he was okay with that.

"Yes," Kyrie growl-whispered. "We can settle down and Mikaela can give us some answers. What did Krackers tell you?"

"I'm not saying," Mikaela whispered back defiantly.

"Mikaela-" Rizo started.

"I don't want to tell *her,*" Mikaela told Rizo, looking pointedly at Kyrie.

"Why?" Rizo asked.

"A bad feeling."

"Mikaela, seriously," Kyrie said. "What could I do with that information?" She stopped her jumping jacks and sat down, moving to sit-ups.

"A couple thousand bad things," Mikaela replied.

"Mikaela! What is WRONG with you?" Anala whisper-yelled. "JUST TELL us!"

"There's nothing wrong with being careful, calm down," Mikaela rolled her eyes.

"There are some drawbacks that come with being paranoid, though," Kyrie reminded her. "And you are *definitely* being paranoid right now."

"Why should I trust you?" Mikaela asked, crossing her arms.

"I'm Dr. Duarte's daughter. You trust him, right?"

"Not really," Mikaela muttered darkly. "I don't trust Dr. Duarte because I just don't trust him. I don't trust *you* because you led us into an ambush."

"I did *not*!" Kyrie exclaimed. "They must have hacked Hope and found out all they needed to know from her. That's why she was acting weird!"

Mikaela scowled, annoyed that Kyrie had made a valid point.

"Fine," Mikaela said after a minute. "That does make sense. I'll tell you. Krackers just asked how many people I had with me, and I said three."

"And..." Kyrie prompted.

"That's it."

"That's it! That's NOTHING!" Anala exclaimed.

"Why were you so paranoid about sharing that kind of information?" Rizo wanted to know.

"I was just checking," Mikaela told him calmly. "No need to explode."

"I have EVERY right to-" Anala was almost yelling now.

"Anala!" Rizo scolded her. "Quiet!"

"Actually," Mikaela said. "Anala, make a fuss about something."

"Why?" Anala asked.

"Just do it, you'll see later," Mikaela hissed.

"Uh, okay, um, MIKAELA! YOUR SNORING kept ME up ALL NIGHT! I had TERRIBLE SLEEP! IT was HORRIBLE! I...." Anala ranted, pacing around them.

"Okay," Mikaela said under the cover of Anala's shouting. "I didn't tell you this before because I thought someone might hear us, but I think it's safe to say that no one can hear anything but Anala."

"THAT'S RIGHT!" Anala yelled. "I am VERY ANGRY!"

"Anyways," Mikaela continued. "Krackers also told me he wants to get us out through the skylight."

"How?" Kyrie asked, her eyes shining. "When?"

"I don't know!" Mikaela huffed. "I have to wait until he comes back to get more information! Also, he got here by following us to through the Telecubes. There was only one Netrhaphalin guarding the cube, so he just made a distraction and went through."

Kyrie sighed. "That makes sense. All I know is that he'd better rescue us soon, otherwise we'll get carted off somewhere unpleasant."

Anala ran out of breath for the moment, and after minimal attempts at yelling some more, fell silent. They all sat down, thinking and waiting for Krackers to come back.

Rizo guessed they had been sitting in the same place for an hour when Mikaela spoke up.

"Don't look now, but Krackers is back," she whispered.   Immediately, Anala looked up at the skylight while Rizo restrained himself.

"What part of 'don't look now' do you not understand?" Mikaela hissed at her.

"Sorry! I got excited," Anala apologized. Mikaela waved her hand dismissively, but she still looked annoyed.

"Just cover for me," she told them. Rizo snapped to feet and stretched while Mikaela made some frantic gestures in Krackers' direction. Anala yawned, and joined Rizo in the exercises he was doing. Kyrie quickly followed both of them.

Meanwhile, Mikaela and Krackers were having a conversation through panicked flapping and hand waving. After a few minutes, Krackers flew off, and Mikaela joined their workout.

"What's up?" Rizo asked her.

Mikaela just shook her head. "Later," she whispered.

They kept moving for a few more minutes, then sat down. A Netrhaphalin came with water and fruit. Anala wolfed some down, then promptly fell asleep. Rizo,

Mikaela, and Kyrie exchanged worried glances, then left the food untouched, shoving it far away.   Kyrie gave them some water she had smuggled inside, but kept much of it for later. They spent hours staring at each other. Finally, when night was beginning to fall, Mikaela told Kyrie and Rizo her plan in a hushed voice.

"Krackers says that he's found some rocks that he's been lugging up to the skylight. He also found some rope. He's going to smash a hole into the glass, then lower the rope. We're going to have to climb it." Mikaela glanced worriedly at Anala, who was still sleeping. "How strong was that stuff in the food?" She asked.

"I don't know," Kyrie replied. "but she better be up by the time we have to go."

"See, she has to get up now," Mikaela said. "Krackers said he saw a big hover truck pulling into the building that says *TRANSPORTATION*. He thinks they're going to move us soon. I think that makes it pretty clear that we need to get out of here ASAP."

Now everyone looked at Anala. Rizo had to find a way to transport his sleeping sister. He looked around. He saw what looked like a threadbare rug in the far corner of the building.

76

"Can we use that rug over there to carry Anala?" He asked.

"Maybe..." Mikaela cocked her head, thinking. "It would be pretty hard, though."

"I'm not leaving my sister." Rizo told her.

"I know," Mikaela sighed. "Kyrie, do you have any ideas?"

Kyrie shook her head. "I don't see how we could make this work."

"Could we wake her up?" Rizo asked them.

"How?" Mikaela asked.

"Um, shaking her?" Rizo suggested. He went over to her and shook her. Nothing. He slapped her. Nothing.

"Kyrie?" Mikaela turned to the older girl again. "Did you smuggle in anything that we can use?"

Kyrie started to shake her head, but then seemed to remember something.

"I always carry a weak anti-sedative around with me," she said.

"You didn't think that was worth mentioning?" Mikaela cried.

"I forgot I had it until now," Kyrie admitted. "Besides, it might not work." She took a pill out from a hidden pocket in her jeans. "Give her this."

Rizo took the pill. "How?"

Kyrie sighed, and pulled a very small water bottle out of the heel of her shoes.

"Dissolve it in there, then get her to drink it all," she said. "By the way, that's like, the last thing I have with me. No more easy solutions from now on." Rizo nodded. He did as she had told him, then gave it to Anala, drop by drop. When she finally finished, she was still asleep.

"It didn't work," he reported to the others sadly.

"Don't worry," Kyrie told him. "It usually takes a minute."

Rizo waited a few minutes, then sighed. "It didn't work," he repeated.

"Try shaking her now," Mikaela suggested. Rizo got up and shook her lightly. When she stirred, he shook her harder.

"Go awwwwaaaaaayyyyy," she moaned.

"Anala, get up!" Rizo said, shaking her some more.

"I don't waaannnnttt tooooooo," she whined.

"Anala! Wake up!" Rizo told her.

Mikaela sighed. "Here, let me do it." She gave Anala's wrist a good smack. "Wake up, sleepyhead!"

"OW!" Anala sat up quickly. "Hey! That wasn't nice!"

"We are getting out of here, and I thought you wouldn't want to miss the show," Mikaela informed her curtly. "You're welcome."

"We ARE? Really?" Anala asked, her eyes wide.

"Yes, Krackers will be here soon, so get up," Mikaela told her impatiently.

"I can't BELIEVE it!" Anala said. "Let's go!"

"One minute, calm down," Kyrie said. "Mikaela, when is Krackers coming?"

"Any minute now," Mikaela responded. She glanced at the skylight with a worried expression. A few seconds passed, and Krackers appeared at the skylight. He was carrying a large stone. He flew as high as possible, then dropped it. It missed the window entirely. He tried again. This time, cracks appeared in the glass. Krackers dropped the stone one more time, and the glass broke with an alarmingly loud sound.

"What was that?" A Netrhaphalin called from somewhere. One burst into the room.

"The prisoners!"

"Quick!" Mikaela said. They raced over to the rope Krackers was lowering through the hole in the skylight. Mikaela climbed up first with ease. She and Krackers waited as Kyrie hauled herself up. The Netrhaphalin were closing in fast.

"Go, go, go!" Rizo urged his sister. They both got on to the rope with the Netrhaphalin on their heels. Kyrie, Krackers, and Mikaela pulled them up slowly.

"Rizo!" Anala sounded frightened. A Netrhaphalin was trying to pull her down. She kicked off the robot, and Rizo grasped her wrist and pulled her up. This didn't faze the Netrhaphalin. They just flew up and attacked Rizo and Anala again.

"Help!" Rizo called. Krackers flew down and squawked loudly, catching the Netrhaphalin's attention. He clawed one and beat his wings at another. Rizo kicked at his attackers, and some of them retreated out of the building. He was so close now- he grabbed at the glass, ignoring the pain that shot through him as one of the shards cut this hand. He hauled himself up, then turned to help Anala. He took a deep breath. They had made it.

His relief lasted approximately two seconds before everything went wrong. Krackers flew up the skylight, and his eyes widened with terror. Rizo whipped around. He saw at least ten Netrhaphalin behind Kyrie, and another ten behind Mikaela.

Uh oh, he thought.

"Surrender- or die," one of them said.

Adventure

Chapter 8

June 6, 2473

Rizo looked around helplessly. Kyrie and Mikaela had grim expressions on their faces, and Krackers looked livid. Anala, however, looked frightened.

The Netrhaphalin were about to take them off the roof when a hover car pulled up. A familiar Netrhaphalin flew out of it.

"All available Netrhaphalin must report to the nearest Headquarters immediately," it said. This Netrhaphalin was a glossy white and pink- Hope.

"Hope!" Anala gasped. Mikaela shushed her.

"She's not herself right now," Kyrie told Anala. It suddenly occurred to Rizo that they called Hope a 'she' because she had a more feminine name. If Hope had been named something like T27, then they would probably call her 'it.' Because Hope wasn't really herself, Rizo decided to call her and all the Netrhaphalin it for the time being.

"Why didn't you tell us through the NETLINKS?" One Netrhaphalin asked.

"All communications have been destroyed by a resistance group," the first Netrhaphalin reported. Mikaela's eyes widened, and she bent down quickly. The Netrhaphalin ignored her. They were too busy checking their NETLINKS worriedly. When one glanced back at Mikaela, she straightened up at threw a shard of broken glass right at it. It hit it right in the eyes. The Netrhaphalin hovered in midair, trying to fix its face.

"Hey!" It shouted. "What was that for! I can't see!" Mikaela grinned wickedly. She threw two more shards at the Netrhaphalin who turned around to face her. It hit them square in the eyes as well. Rizo had no idea how Mikaela could throw with such accuracy, but he figured it came with the whole knowing-how-to-defend-yourself thing.

The two Netrhaphalin promptly started yelling about killing Mikaela. As the others turned around, Rizo picked up some glass and tossed it at them. He missed. Obviously, he wasn't going to be able to use the glass if he couldn't throw straight. He glanced around and spotted a wrench lying near a fire extinguisher that he thought was installed ages ago. Since the building he was standing on looked old, he was probably right.

He ran over to it. He used the wrench to smash a hole in the case, then grabbed the fire extinguisher. He went back into the fray and handed Kyrie the wrench.

"Use this to fight!" He told her. She nodded and drove back the Netrhaphalin who was trying to grab her and Anala. He inspected the fire extinguisher. The directions on the side of it were worn with age and impossible to read. Rizo twisted random nozzles, aiming the orange can at the Netrhaphalin. He pushed and pulled at the fire extinguisher, but he didn't have any luck. He picked up a piece of glass, and tried to puncture the can. They just needed a distraction....

"Kyrie! Can I borrow that wrench?" Rizo called over the chaos. Kyrie thew it to him in a high arc, then picked up some glass to throw. She dodged the laser beams the Netrhaphalin were shooting at her and threw some glass at them.

Meanwhile, Rizo had caught the wrench, and had started banging the can until he heard a hissing sound. He threw the wrench back to Kyrie, who caught it neatly and promptly slashed it across one of the Netrhaphalin's eyes. This was a smart move, as it blinded them and shut down their laser beams.

"Stand back and get into position!" Rizo yelled. Mikaela retreated, dragging Anala with her. Kyrie and Krackers were close behind. Rizo stabbed the dent he had created in the can with some glass. White foam shot out of the hole as Rizo threw the can into the crowd of Netrhaphalin. The foam flew everywhere. Rizo and his friends remained untouched while the Netrhaphalin got the worst of it.

"Let's go!" Mikaela cried. She grabbed the rope they had used to escape and tied it to a pipe on the roof. She let down the rope and climbed down it quickly. Anala and Kyrie followed her. Rizo went last. He had just touched the floor when more Netrhaphalin burst out of the building. Krackers, who had stayed on the roof, sliced the rope off the pipe and flew down. Mikaela lashed out with the rope, knocking one Netrhaphalin to the ground.

They ran. The gate was open, so they ran right through it. Krackers flew ahead of them, showing them where to go. Rizo had never been so scared. The Netrhaphalin were just behind him, ready to grab him when he ran out of breath. Anala was scared, too. Rizo could tell from the way she was shaking. Krackers flew left, and they all followed.

After a few exhausting minutes, they arrived in a busy marketplace full of other humans. Once they got into the heart of the supermarket, they slowed down and tried to blend in. Krackers landed on Mikaela's shoulder, and Mikaela led the way from there. She led them into a bustling restaurant.

"Do you have any money?" Mikaela asked Kyrie. Kyrie sighed and pulled a one hundred dollar bill out of a pocket. Mikaela looked at the money disdainfully.

"That's it?" She raised an eyebrow dubiously.

"No, but I think I should save some for later," Kyrie said.

"Fine, I'll see what I can do with this," Mikaela grumbled. She ordered some food and asked the robot

waiter for water. It wasn't much, but it tasted good to
Rizo.

"I'm hungry," Anala complained after they had
wolfed down a shared bowl of spaghetti and salad.

"Kyrie only gave me a hundred dollars!" Mikaela
said, glaring at Kyrie. "That was the best I could do!"

Rizo's stomach growled. "I wish we were in the
olden days, when you could get a *whole loaf of bread* for
twenty bucks," he sighed.

"You can't even get a *lollipop* for twenty bucks
now," Anala remarked.

"Anyway, even if Kyrie did have any money to
spare," Mikaela pointed out, bringing them back to the
present. "the cashier would probably get suspicious. No
one uses real money anymore, even when it comes to
small bills. Everyone uses e-cash now."

"How do you even have real money?" Rizo wanted
to know.

"I have my ways," Kyrie responded mysteriously.
"and I'm not telling you any of them."

"Okay," Mikaela said in a low whisper, bringing
them back on track again. "What's our plan? Can we
contact the Gryffins?"

"No," Kyrie shook her head. "They're probably scrambling right now. The Netrhaphalin destroyed one of our main headquarters. I *told* Dad it was a bad idea to bring a Netrhaphalin into our HQ."

"What are we going to do, then?" Anala asked. "I mean, we can't stay here FOREVER."

Kyrie sighed. "Remember what Hope said? There was a resistance group who shut down the communications between them. That wasn't the Gryffins. I think I know who was behind the attack, though I'm surprised they even did such a thing."

"Who?" Mikaela and Rizo asked together. "How can we find them?" What Rizo really wanted to ask was *And why are you surprised that they did that? Aren't they a resistance group?*

However, Kyrie was answering their first question, and Rizo didn't want to interrupt her. "They're called the Rockets, and I've only heard of them, not come in contact with them. However, the rumor is that if you want to talk to them, all you have to do is find an American Museum of Space and tell someone working in the 'Moon Cycles' area, *'We will be at the red planet yet; all we have to do is shoot for the stars.'*"

"What's their response?" Mikaela asked.

"It's '*Yes, I think we can pull it off with lots of hard work. I have heard it's quite nice there. It will take a lot of rockets to get us there, though.*' I know, it's cheesy," Kyrie told them, almost apologetically.

"Will they help us?" Rizo knew this was the important part. If the Rockets couldn't help them, then they were useless to them.

"I think so," Kyrie replied. "I mean, they should. It's not like what they do is legal."

"How do we get to the American Museum of Space?" Mikaela wondered. "Actually, what state are we in right now? I know it can't be far from the orphanage we came from."

"It... is really far, believe it or not. Your orphanage- Dr. Lake Simmons Orphanage- was in Ohio. We're in California now. In the suburbs of Los Angeles, I think," Kyrie cringed at the shocked faces around her. "I... probably should have told you, but that was where our headquarters are so unless..." She trailed off and slapped her forehead. "I'm an idiot," she said. "The telecubes! We could be in a whole other country right now!"

"I don't think so," Rizo said. "I saw a store that said, 'Coco's Bakery, Est. 2353 in Barr City, Nevada'. And I saw a sign that said Welcome to the Super-Super Market of Barr City, Nevada. So we're definitely somewhere else." It made sense. Barr City. It must be pretty important, because Barr was a famous Netrhaphalin who had been one of the leaders of the Uprising.

"That would make sense," Kyrie nodded. "I think the nearest American Museum of Space is in Armi, California. How do we get there?"

"We could rent a hover car," Mikaela suggested.

"We don't have that much money," Kyrie pointed out quietly. "We're already on the run from the law. I think our only option is to *steal* a hover."

"How long will it take?" Anala asked.

"About 2 hours on a hover," Mikaela answered her. "so use the restroom. Kyrie and Rizo can go first, so they can steal a hover. Then I'll take you and we'll join them."

"Got it," Rizo saluted. Anala laughed. He and Kyrie went to the bathroom and came out ready to steal a car. They went outside and looked for some hovers. After a quick search, they found a large hover that was parked close to the ground. Kyrie hopped into it, and she quickly went to work hacking the hover. After a few minutes, she sighed with relief.

"This car's computer has more holes than Swiss cheese," she commented. She punched in some commands. The hover flew over to the restaurant, where Mikaela and Anala were waiting. They got in, and Kyrie entered the coordinates of the American Museum of Space. The hover flew off.

"The American Museum of Space, here we come!" Anala said.

Arial Innovation

Chapter 9

June 7, 2473

Rizo was nudged awake by Kyrie. They had parked near the Museum and gone to sleep in the hover car. Rizo could tell it was early in the morning.

"We have to go," Kyrie said. "It seems like the owner of this hover reported it missing- and the Netrhaphalin tracked it down. Krackers saw them first." Rizo was up in a heartbeat. He looked into the distance and saw three hover cars containing two Netrhaphalin each coming towards them in the distance. He shook Anala and Mikaela awake while Krackers collected some large rocks from somewhere for defense.

"They'll most likely recognize us," Kyrie told them. "We have to go." She entered some coordinates into the car's computer and it shot off. The Netrhaphalin promptly followed them in a high- speed air chase.

"It's them," one of the Netrhaphalin yelled. "They were the ones who escaped!" Anala clung to Rizo as the hovers swooped closer, but he shook her off.

"I have to help Mikaela fend these guys off!" He told her. "You help Kyrie steer." Rizo leaped to the back, where Mikaela and Krackers were standing.

"Help steady me!" Mikaela yelled over the wind. Kyrie had overridden the controls and was now manually controlling the car. She was diving and swooping at hundreds of kilometers per hour while Anala told her what was behind her. Rizo found a crate lying under a seat. He pushed it towards Mikaela. She leaned on it and picked up a good-sized rock. Krackers moved away from her and grabbed a rock, too. When a Netrhaphalin hover car came close, he flew up and dropped the rock on them. It took him a lot of energy to keep up with the cars, so he only did it when he absolutely had to.

Rizo had always wondered why the Netrhaphalin didn't just fly. They had no need for hover cars. He now realized that hover cars could, without a doubt, fly faster than the Netrhaphalin if even Krackers couldn't keep up with them. Krackers was genetically modified to have super speed, so if he couldn't do it, they couldn't either.

"Rizo! Mikaela! Krackers!" Kyrie called from the front of the hover. "Hold on tight!" Rizo, Mikaela, and Krackers got down low and held on for dear life. Two Netrhaphalin shot lasers at them while the hover car flipped upside down as another two Netrhaphalin hovers dive- bombed it. When they were right side up again, Mikaela dragged herself up and threw another rock. It bounced off the Netrhaphalin logo on the side of the car- a world with the letter 'N' on it and Kano's name on the bottom of the world- and fell harmlessly to the ground. More hovers joined the chase- all with the Netrhaphalin logo emblazoned on their sides.

"Mikaela!" Rizo called to her. "Look!" He grabbed a hammer off the floor of the car. "When we flipped, the crate fell over. This is a handyman's car! There are some handymen around after all! This stuff is not all done by robots!"

"It could be a robot's car," Mikaela pointed out.

"True," Rizo said. "but that's not the important part. There's hammers and wrenches and everything! And duct tape! And rope! And instant fusion under UV light wood glue! A ton of wood glue! There's five whole bottles! If we tie Krackers to this car, he could squirt wood glue on all of the Netrhaphalin's windshields without getting blown away! And then the Netrhaphalin won't be able to see!"

"I think that would work," Mikaela said. "it's not like we have any better options. I mean, that I can think of. Krackers! Get over here!" Krackers came over, and Mikaela told him their plan. Krackers agreed to it after minimal grumbling, and Rizo tied him securely to the car. Krackers grabbed the first bottle of wood glue and shot out of the car. Mikaela and Rizo watched as he hovered over the closest hover and squeezed the bottle. A stream of glue fired from the tube. However, instead of the glue hitting the windshield like they had planned, the glue shot out and hit the two Netrhaphalin in the face. They lost control and veered wildly into another hover. Both of them fell out of the sky and onto a grass field. Kyrie expertly flew away from the crash.

Two down, four to go. Krackers flew on and squirted some more glue on a hover that was catching up to them. His stream of glue missed and hit the logo on the car. He signaled that he was out of glue. Rizo pulled him in as Mikaela threw another rock at the same car. It hit the windshield, and cracks appeared in it. Krackers landed on the hover. Rizo gave him another tube of glue, and he flew out again. He fired, and glue sprayed the windshield that was already cracked. The car fell out of the air for a moment, but steadied itself. Krackers shot another stream of glue at the Netrhaphalin inside. He hit his target. They Netrhaphalin lost control and veered straight into the hover Rizo was on. Kyrie cut hard to the left and narrowly avoided the hover. It shot past them and crashed into a skyscraper that read LOS ANGELES NETRHAPHALIN HEADQUARTERS. Immediately five more hovers shot out of the building and saw the wreck lodged in the skyscraper and the chase going on. Two of them went towards the wreck while the rest joined the chase.

So now three down, seven to go. Krackers fired glue into another hover. It slowed down quickly. Another car behind it slammed into it. Both hovers crashed to the ground. Five down, five standing. Kyrie shot away from the Headquarters so that other hovers couldn't join the pursuit as quickly. Krackers came back for another bottle of glue. Rizo handed it to him.

"You know, the tubes you're giving to me are still half full," Rizo remarked.

"They get hard to squeeze so I can't use them," Krackers explained, panting. Rizo nodded and Krackers took off. He fired the glue. The hover he was aiming at fell and crashed. Six down, four to go. Just as they got to two remaining hovers, ten more came soaring in from the Netrhaphalin HQ.

"We're going to have to do something big," he told Mikaela. "We can't keep picking them off. Every time we do, another one comes!" Mikaela nodded. She had been throwing rocks with no avail, and seemed frustrated.

"But how?" She asked. Rizo checked inside the crate. He rooted around for a minute, then pulled out a gleaming sharp kitchen knife out of the crate.

"I wonder why there was a knife in here," he said.

"It doesn't matter!" Mikaela exclaimed. "How can we use it?" Just then, Krackers came back. He handed the last bottle of glue back to Rizo.

"That's it," he said glumly. "We still have ten cars on our tail, and they're gaining on us."

"Don't worry," Rizo said. "Okay, Mikaela, how accurately can you hit a moving target?"

"Down to the center of the bull's eye," she responded confidently.

"Okay," Rizo said. "I'm going to throw one glue tube after another into the air between the Netrhaphalin. You have to hit them on the end and puncture them. Hopefully, the glue will spray everywhere and hit everything. I'm going to tie the rope to the knife so that we don't lose it. Got it?"

"Yes, but you should tell Kyrie what to do. She needs to be able to get out of here if they all crash," Mikaela told him. Rizo ran to the front of the car.

"Kyrie, I'm going to count to five. When I say go, gun the engine. Then land after we lose them and get off quick," Rizo said.

"Got it," Kyrie responded. Rizo ran back to the back of the hover.

"Ready?" He asked Krackers and Mikaela. Krackers was going to pull the knife in once Mikaela threw it. He was holding the rope while Mikaela tied the rope to the knife and secured it with duct tape.

"I don't know if I can throw as well with the rope on the knife," Mikaela said, worried. She tossed the knife at a seat on the hover a few times and took a deep breath.

"I think I'm ready," she said.

"Are you ready?" Rizo called to Kyrie.

"Ready!" Anala called back for Kyrie. Just then, Kyrie cut sharply to the right. They were thrown to the side. Mikaela hit her head hard on the side of the car and passed out.

"Mikaela!" Rizo cried, shaking her. Krackers flew to Kyrie and told her what happened in hopes that she would have something quite literally up her sleeve to help Mikaela. He came back, shaking his head. Kyrie didn't have anything to help them. Rizo shook Mikaela harder. She had to wake up. She was the main part of the plan. Krackers slapped her. He slapped her again.

"Mikaela!" Krackers yelled.

"Give her some time," Rizo suggested. They waited. And waited.

"Rizo! You have to do something!" Kyrie called. "They're catching up!" As if to punctuate her point, a laser beam narrowly missed the hover, forcing Kyrie to dive towards the ground.

Rizo looked at Mikaela. "Please, Mikaela!" He pleaded. "You have to wake up!" He looked at Krackers. "Can you throw like Mikaela?" He asked. Krackers shook his head. "We can't do it without her!" He shouted over the roar of the chase. They waited a few minutes, which felt like days, occasionally getting tossed about the car.

"What happened?" A weary voice came from the floor. Mikaela sat up, rubbing her head.

"You passed out," Krackers told her. "Can you still throw? Because we really, really, *really*, need to get out of here."

"How long has it been?" Mikaela asked.

"Only a few minutes," Rizo assured her. "Now, can you still throw?"

"I don't know, why?" Mikaela said, then jerked back as if she'd been shocked. "Oh no, no, no. It's all coming back to me now. We're being chased... the plan-"

She stood up and saw the Netrhaphalin on their tail. She turned and grabbed the knife. She threw it a few times, and Rizo was relieved to see that she could still throw accurately.

"Okay," he took a deep breath. "Is everyone ready?"

"Yes!" Kyrie called.

"Yes," Mikaela said.

"Okay," Rizo threw one glue bottle. "One!" Mikaela's throw was perfect. Glue went flying everywhere, and two hovers crashed. "Two!" Rizo threw another tube. Mikaela threw another perfect hit. Krackers pulled the knife back as three hovers crashed in mid-air. "Three!" Another throw, another hit. This time, however, the Netrhaphalin avoided the worst of the spray and no one crashed. "Four!" One got splattered head on and fell out of the sky. It blocked the other hover, however, and that gave the Netrhaphalin an idea. They lined up, a line of seven cars, so that only one of them would get 'glued' at a time. "Five!" Rizo threw the last bottle. Mikaela Threw the knife perfectly. As the glue sprayed into the first hover, it stopped abruptly. Rizo watched in slow motion as the rest of the hovers slammed into it and fell. It was a seven car pile-up.

Unfortunately, the Netrhaphalin hovers were very close to the hover Rizo was in. Kyrie had to swerve to avoid one car, but she ended up soaring towards another one.

"Kyrie!" He called. "Look out!" Kyrie pushed a leaver as far as it could go. It was too late. They slammed into the Netrhaphalin, then shot away so fast it made Rizo sick. However, the nauseated feeling he was experiencing might have been due to the bomb in the hover.

While they had rocketed away, a Netrhaphalin had thrown something into their hover before he fell. As they had been flying down to the street, Rizo had heard a weird noise. He had turned and saw a bomb right in the middle of the hover. His eyes had widened. He began to feel sick.

"Take cover!" He yelled, grabbing Mikaela and Krackers and dragging them behind a seat with him. He saw Anala's eyes widen and Kyrie yank her away. But it was too late. The bomb exploded. Mikaela was ripped out of his hands and flew through the air. The last thing

Rizo thought as he shot straight into a building was *We're going to die.*

And then everything went black.

Recovering

Chapter 10

June 8, 2473

Rizo heard voices.

"How are they?" One voice asked.

"The girl woke up. The youngest one. She didn't get too much of the blast. But the boy and the middle and older girl did. The two girls are in intensive care. A lot of internal bleeding and possible broken bones. The boy managed to get under some cover, so he isn't that bad."

"Any concussions?"

"No, they're lucky. Unlike Riva."

"Hey, I think the boy is getting up. Look at his heartbeat."

Rizo stirred. He opened his eyes and saw two unfamiliar faces peering down at him. A man and a woman. He ached all over.

"Who are you? Where am I?" Rizo asked in a horse whisper. He was in a bed in a bright room with some machinery surrounding him.

"I'm Cadwyn, and this is Dr. Nikita," the man said. Dr. Nikita waved from the other side of Rizo.

"My sister- my friends-" Rizo croaked.

"Here, have some water," Cadwyn told him, handing him a glass. "Your sister, Anala, is awake. If you're her brother then... Rizo, right?"

Rizo nodded. "What about the others? And where am I?"

"You're at the Salvation Hospital," Dr. Nikita informed him. She had a light British accent. Rizo was surprised. He had not heard an accent for quite some time, as the Netrhaphalin forbade travel between language districts. Even the international Gryffin scientists didn't have accents. "The older girl, which I presume is Kyrie, is still unconscious. So is the middle girl, Mikaela. Anala told us everything. Krackers is fine, but very tired. He's asleep. He's the one who helped get you to the hospital."

"But- the-" Rizo started.

"Parrots can fly," Cadwyn reminded him. "He just spread his wings and avoided hitting anything."

"Oh," was all Rizo could say. "You know, Mikaela, she was knocked unconscious before that happened. She came back, it wasn't that bad, but I don't think being unconscious twice in a day is very good. Also, what time is it?"

"One thing at a time, my goodness," Dr. Nikita said. "Don't worry, I'll check on Mikaela again. And it's eight o'clock in the morning, June 8."

"I was out that long?" Rizo asked.

"I'm afraid so," Dr. Nikita told him. "Now rest." She swept out of the room, leaving Cadwyn and Rizo looking at each other awkwardly.

"But I feel fine!" Rizo protested.

"I know, buddy," Cadwyn said. "But you should get some food and water. You must be starving!"

"I am," Rizo admitted.

"I'll get you some food right now. When you're feeling better, can you fill out this form? Just kidding. If you don't rest, Dr. Nikita will have my s- my head."

"Why?"

"I'm her assistant. She's a top doctor, and she doesn't want me pulling her rank down."

"Huh?"

"Yeah, weird, I know. But Dr. Nikita Anggan's one of the best. I'm lucky. I just can't Ever. Mess. Up," Cadwyn said ruefully. He left. Rizo closed his eyes. His head was spinning. Why was the Salvation Hospital helping fugitives? Who were these people? How was Anala? Where was she? Having so many questions and no answers made Rizo's head hurt. He tried to rest.

A few minutes later, Cadwyn came in.

"Eat up!" He said cheerfully. He set a platter full of some weird mashed up stuff on Rizo's bed. Rizo picked at it disdainfully.

"Hey, can I see Anala?" Rizo asked, pushing his food away.

"Oh, yeah, your sister wanted to come in and say hi, but Dr. Nikita wanted you to get some food and rest before you did anything," Cadwyn replied.

Rizo shoveled some food into his mouth. "I've eaten!" He announced. "can I see her now?" He nearly gagged while he said those words. The food tasted even worse than it looked.

Cadwyn laughed. "Eat *all* of it," he said. "I really don't want to cross Dr. Nikita."

"Why?"

"It's just not a good idea, trust me," Cadwyn said, a little bitterly. Rizo got the feeling that Cadwyn didn't want to talk about Dr. Nikita anymore. Rizo forced the rest of his meal down in silence.

"Now can I talk to her?" He asked hopefully.

"Okay, fine," Cadwyn laughed. "You sure are eager to see your sister. I mean, I totally understand. I have a sister, too. Her name is Riva. I miss.... Never mind. I'll get Anala over here." A few minutes passed, and the door burst open.

"RIZO!" Anala cried. "I was SO SCARED that you'd NEVER wake up but here you are! Don't EVER do that again!" She hugged him fiercely. Cadwyn winked and exited, sweeping the remains of Rizo's meal away.

"How are you?" Rizo asked, inspecting his sister.

"Oh, I'm fine," Anala shrugged. "I got up in an hour. I've been waiting SO LONG for you to wake up. I mean everyone, really, but mainly you. It's been SO BORING! I had Krackers to talk to, but he was like, 'I'm so tired, stop shouting and go away! Goodnight.' I really hope Mikaela and Kyrie are okay, don't you? I mean-"

"Anala, slow down!" Rizo exclaimed. "Have you seen them?"

"I have, and they looked HORRIBLE. They're in something called the ICU. Have you met Dr. Nikita? She's CREEPY."

"Yes, but-"

"I KNOW what you're going to SAY. You're going to say something about not saying bad things about other people but I DON'T CARE."

"I'm not going to say anything about that. Do you know why these people are helping us?"

"Sort of," Anala lowered her voice. "I overheard one of the nurses saying that they're fixing us up and then handing us over to the Netrhaphalin."

"We need to get out of here," Rizo whispered. "Where is Krackers? Can you get him right now?"

"Yes..." Anala said slowly.

"Get him and bring him here, right now. And be as quiet as you can."

"Got it. See you soon, boss," Anala bounded out of the room. Cadwyn came in soon after.

"Dr. Nikita will be here soon to check on you," he said. "How was your sister?" Cadwyn moved to press a few buttons on the machine on Rizo's right. A pad on his wrist started to take his blood pressure.

"She was herself," Rizo said. "Very loud."

Cadwyn laughed, then got serious. "You're lucky," he said. "I wish I could see my sister all the time." He typed a few things on to the computer next to the machine, looking grave.

"How old is she?" Rizo asked.

"Riva's eighteen and in intensive care here. She got in a hover car accident."

"Oh, she's lucky she's alive," Rizo said. "That's how my parents died."

"I'm sorry," Cadwyn said. "I've been worrying about Riva too much. I didn't think- Is that why you're here? Were you in the same hover?" He looked up from the computer, concerned.

"No," Rizo shook his head. "That happened a long time ago. When I was little."

"Riva is-" Cadwyn started. He was cut off by Dr. Nikita entering the room.

"Riva is *fine, for now*," Dr. Nikita finished Cadwyn's sentence for him. "Cadwyn? Why are you talking to Rizo? You're supposed to be helping me." Dr. Nikita pushed past Cadwyn and took over the computer.

"I was- I was- waiting for you," Cadwyn stammered.

"Well, if you don't follow my orders from now on, your sister will-" Dr. Nikita abruptly cut herself off. "Just hush up." Rizo frowned. What had Dr. Nikita been about to say? Your sister will what? Was she talking about Riva?

"What will happen to Cadwyn's sister?" Rizo asked. Dr. Nikita glared at Cadwyn. "Nothing," she growled.

"Then I don't have to help you," Cadwyn said.

"Yes, you do," Dr. Nikita lowered her voice so only Cadwyn could hear her. Rizo strained to listen, but he only caught a fraction of their conversation.

"Did you tell... Riva?" Dr. Nikita hissed.

"Maybe... doesn't matter," was Cadwyn's reply.

"It does! I'm... you better...or else."

"Okay, okay! But... Riva...can't turn her in... Netrhaphalin."

"I can... Riva is part of... the Netrhaphalin will want...she's toast... I tell. So you... a better helper... her sake. Otherwise... everyone... know... part of the Rockets. So there." Dr. Nikita turned and acted as if she had not been threatening Cadwyn a minute ago.

Rizo's head was spinning. Riva was part of the Rockets? Was that why she was in intensive care? Did the Netrhaphalin chase her like they had chased him and his friends? Could she help them contact the Rockets?

"Rizo?" Dr. Nikita asked, snapping her fingers in front of his face. "I asked you a question." Oh, this was *bad*.

"Sorry, sorry," Rizo said. "I wasn't listening. I kind of zoned out for a minute." Dr. Nikita squinted at him, as if she could see exactly what Rizo was thinking.

"How are you feeling?" Dr. Nikita asked impatiently.

"Um, fine, yes, completely okay," Rizo said. Dr. Nikita squinted at him again, then sighed. She turned and left, with Cadwyn at her side. In a few minutes, Anala came in with Krackers.

"So what's the plan?" Anala asked.

"There's been a change, actually," Rizo said.

"Great," Krackers rolled his eyes. "What is it?"

Rizo glanced around before he whispered. "I found out that Cadwyn, Dr. Nikita assistant, has a sister that's in the Rockets. She's in intensive care right now, and I think that Dr. Nikita is using her to get to Cadwyn. He has to help her or she'll go straight to the Netrhaphalin and tell them about his sister, Riva."

"Okkkaaayyyy," Krackers said slowly. "How exactly is this relevant to our situation? Oh wait..."

"I think we should help her. Then *she* can help us contact the Rockets," Rizo explained, cutting Krackers off.

"Why can't we just go to the American Museum of Space?" Anala asked. "It's not that far away, right?"

"So here's the thing..." Krackers said uneasily. "When I called a medical hover, they used telecubes to teleport us to this hospital. So I have no idea where we are right now."

"You didn't think that was WORTH MENTIONING?" Anala asked.

"I just woke up!" Krackers protested. "I just-"

"Quiet, you guys," Rizo said, before they could start arguing. He got out of the bed he had been lying on and picked up the paperwork Cadwyn had left on the table. It read: SALVATION HOSPITAL FOR HOVER- RELATED INJURIES, KANOA, OREGON. He held it up for them to read.

"They had to take us this far," Krackers groaned. "and to a place named after Kano. Great. Just *great.*"

"Calm down," Rizo said. "We have a plan now, don't worry. We need to find the Rockets, and we have a way find them now. All we have to do is have a little talk with Riva."

Plans

Chapter 11
June 8, 2473

"Did you say that Kyrie and Mikaela are in the
ICU?" Rizo asked Anala. He was pacing in his room,
despite the fact that he was very sore, covered with
bruises, and should probably be resting in bed at the
moment. Anala was sitting on his bed, and Krackers was
perched on her shoulder.

"Yes," Anala nodded. "Hey, what does ICU stand
for anyway?"

"It stands for Intensive Care Unit, but nowadays the
patients in there don't really need intensive care. It's
more like the More Serious Injuries Care Unit, but even
that name is often debatable. Modern medicine is good

enough to save most people in a day or two," Krackers explained slowly, as if Anala was a five-year-old learning that two plus two equaled four. "You didn't know that?"

"Krackers, be nice," Rizo said firmly. "And shut up. If-"

"Don't say shut up. And be *nice*," Krackers interrupted, mimicking Rizo's tone.

"Be *QUIET*," Anala snapped, imitating Krackers. He flapped his wings noisily in her face to annoy her. "Hey, quit it!" She knocked him off her shoulder, and he flew to the window sill and perched there, looking dignified.

"Thank you, Anala," Rizo said. "*As I was saying*, Riva, Mikaela, and Kyrie are all in the ICU, then we can see all of them and talk to Riva. Then we can get out and go to the Rockets and be safe and problem solved."

Krackers looked skeptical. "Assuming everything goes as planned," he corrected Rizo. "So far, how many things have gone the way we planned? Oh right. Zero."

"There's no need to be sarcastic," Rizo told Krackers sternly. "I think everything will go well."

"I do, too!" Anala exclaimed. "Let's go to the ICU which is the Insensitive Care Unit!"

"We *know*," Krackers said irritably. "And it's the *intensive* care unit."

"I know YOU know! I just WANTED to SAY it. PARDON ME for ANNOYING your BEAK, your HIGHNESS," Anala said with mock sincerity.

"Let's go, enough chitchat," Rizo rolled his eyes. "Anala, where is the ICU?" They exited Rizo's room softly, then turned a few corners, following Anala's directions.

"It's just around that corner," Anala pointed down a hall, after a minute of walking. A nurse was passing through it, humming to herself.

"Okay, don't-" Rizo started.

"Hi! Nurse Alivia! Remember me? Anala? We have the same first letter in our names, isn't that cool? Anala, Alivia, Anala, Alivia!" Anala went out to greet the nurse, waving ecstatically.

"-talk to her," Rizo finished with a sigh.

"We're coming to see our friends. They're in the ICU, which means-" Anala started yammering.

"She knows what the ICU stands for, Anala," Rizo said. "Sorry about my sister. She's really excited to see our friends."

"I AM NOT- mmurphh" Anala was muffled as Rizo covered her mouth with his hand.

"I'm *really* sorry," Rizo told the nurse. "We'll just be in and out, don't worry."

"I see," Alivia said, tilting her head at them. "You need permission to go into the Intensive Care Unit. And you have to be accompanied by a nurse."

"Well, could you come with us?" Rizo asked.

"It's really important, we have to see Riva," Anala said before Rizo clapped another hand over her mouth.

"Riva? Why?" Alivia looked suspicious.

"Uh, um, Cadwyn told me to check on her. He said Dr. Nikita doesn't let him visit his sister," Rizo lied.

"Oh, poor Cadwyn," Alivia said. "That's true. Dr. Anggan keeps Cadwyn wrapped around her little finger all day." Rizo was amazed that his lie made sense. He knew Cadwyn missed his sister, but he didn't know that he could never see her.

"So, can we go in?" Rizo asked.

"Cadwyn told you to?" Alivia asked in response.

"Um, yeah, sure," Rizo said. He felt bad lying to Alivia, but he was desperate. They had to see Riva.

"All right then," Alivia motioned for them to go to the left. "If Cadwyn told you to."

"He did," Anala assured her. Alivia led them into the ICU. Rizo found Kyrie and Mikaela almost instantly. They were on beds facing each other. The Intensive Care Unit was a huge room, yet most of the beds in it were empty.

"Kyrie! Mikaela!" Anala bounded over to them. It looked like both of them were awake and recovering. Rizo hung back, staying by Alivia's side.

"Riva's over there," Alivia told Rizo, pointing to a bed. Riva was awake, staring at the ceiling blankly. "She was hit in the head *hard*. She just looks at the ceiling all day. Your friends are fine, though. They just need a little rest. Neither of them have broken bones, but they both had internal bleeding and the older one had to have a surgery to repair her liver. They'll be out of here in no time at all. They just have to rest." Rizo nodded, not really listening.

"Wait- what?" He exclaimed after what Alivia had said sank in. "Kyrie had a *surgery*? How are we going to pay for that?"

"Let her parents figure that out," Alivia shrugged. "They probably have insurance, don't they?" Rizo doubted that was true. If both your parents were the leaders of an underground, rebel organization, you didn't have things like insurance, or a citizenship, or anything that told other people (or Netrhaphalin) that you even existed. Instead of answering Alivia, he simply nodded to her, excused himself, and walked over to Mikaela.

"Are you okay?" Rizo asked her.

"I'm fine," she snapped. "I don't need your sympathy." She was sitting upright in her bed, scowling as usual.

"Maybe not," Rizo told her. "But you do need the information I have. See that girl over there? Her name is Riva and she's part of the Rockets. I figure she's our key to contacting them."

"That girl looks like she's half brain-dead," Mikaela scoffed. "Besides, I thought we could just go to the American Museum of Space. It's not too far from here...." She trailed off as she realized she actually didn't know where they were.

"That's the thing," Rizo told her. "We're in Kanoa, Oregon, in the Salvation Hospital for Hover- Related

Injuries. So, we can't really get to the American Museum of Space *that* easily."

"Stupid telecubes," Mikaela growled.

"Also..." Rizo went on slowly. He was sure Mikaela was not going to like the other bombs he was going to throw at her, but he had to tell her. She would be madder if he didn't. "Also we need to pay for all of this service and it's going to cost a lot and we don't have insurance and also, also, then they'll hand us over to the Netrhaphalin because they know who we are and we have to go, like, right now even though Kyrie is still recovering from a surgery. Also, also, *also*, I think we should help Cadwyn because Dr. Nikita is blackmailing him. So yeah," Rizo finished quickly.

"First of all," Mikaela sighed eloquently, as if Rizo was a foolish toddler. "We've already broken the law. Who cares about paying anything? Second of all, whatever there is between Cadwyn and Dr. Nikita is none of our business and, may I add, not our responsibility. Third of all, we already have an escape route through that girl, Riva. So stop worrying."

"But- but-" Rizo stuttered.

"*One thing at a time,*" Mikaela advised. "What happened to you? Did you turn into a nervous, worried, fluttering butterfly all of a sudden?" She cocked her head at him, sounding amused.

"No! I'm no butterfly," Rizo protested. "But yes, I'm worried."

"Well, you can sit here talking about everything that's on your mind all day, or you can go over to that Riva girl and get some information," Mikaela said bossily. "Would you rather be a cowardly weakling or someone who does something about his problems?"

"I'll go over, okay, okay," Rizo said. "You don't have to be mean about it." Before Mikaela could tell him that she was not being mean, and, in fact, nice, Rizo speed-walked away towards Kyrie. He explained their situation, and Kyrie agreed that talking to Riva was the best course of action.

Rizo found Riva gazing into space in her bed.

"Hi, Riva," he greeted her.

"Do I know you?" She asked, confused. She was slumped into her pillows and had a glazed look in her eyes.

"We haven't met," Rizo said, which seemed to satisfy Riva.

"I see," she said.

"Cadwyn says hi," Rizo told her.

"Cadwyn... my brother? Or my dad? No, that's Elliott. Everything is so fuzzy. Why are you standing upside down? Elephants. Monkeys. Monkeys! You're a monkey! That's why you are upside down! What were you saying? Cadwyn. Cadwyn. Cadwyn. It sounds right and wrong. Everything is right and wrong. I-"

"Cadwyn is your brother," Rizo cut Riva off.

"My brother," Riva mused.

"Um, Riva- um," Rizo started.

"Yes? Is the sky green again?" Riva looked at him expectantly.

"No, no," Rizo shook his head. "But- We will be at the red planet yet; all we have to do is shoot for the stars."

"I've heard that before," Riva said wonderingly. "I think I'm supposed to say- Bananas and star ships. Wait! I know! I have to say: Yes, I think we can pull it off with lots of hard work. I have heard it's quite nice there.   It will take a lot of rockets to get us there, though."

"So you *do* know *them*," Rizo said triumphantly, then lowered his voice. "How can we find them? The Rockets?"

"Gems and opals," Riva murmured dazedly, before her eyes snapped into focus and she sat up. "In the Jewel Theater on Second Street- Kanoa, Oregon. Find the boy who sells popcorn and tell him Riva sent you. After you do, tell him that the sky is falling for me." Riva slumped back into her pillows, sighed heavily, and continued staring at a fixed spot on the ceiling. "Monkeys and mangoes," she muttered.

Rizo left her, feeling equal parts elated and disturbed. What did she mean by 'the sky is falling for me'? And had she known what she was talking about? What if she had been blabbing nonsense? If she had been telling the truth, how were they going to get Kyrie out of here? She hadn't looked well at all.

He made his way back to Kyrie and asked if she was well enough to steal a hover and fly it to the Jewel Theater that night.

"Of course!" She had scoffed. "I recovered yesterday. I'm just acting with all the groans and moans. I didn't feel anything at all during and after the surgery.

Just a little sore. But I played it up so they'd keep us here. I had a feeling it would be important."

"Are- are you sure?" Rizo asked, concerned. "Can you deal with a high- speed chase like we did a few days ago?"

"Hopefully," Kyrie replied, with less confidence then Rizo would've liked. "Look, Rizo, we have to get out of here now. You said it yourself. If I think I can do it, then I can do it. We'll escape tonight. Now go and tell Mikaela our plan." Rizo nodded, and crossed the room. Mikaela appeared to be listening to Anala chatter on about how she missed good food, but was actually having a conversation with Krackers.

"Anala, how about you go and talk with Kyrie," Mikaela suggested when she saw Rizo coming.

"Oh, sure!" Anala scrambled over to Kyrie and filled her in on why oranges were better than apples.

"What's up?" Mikaela asked. "Are we getting out of here tonight?"

"Yes," Rizo responded. "At midnight, me, Anala, and Krackers are going to come for you. We're going to crack that window over there-" Rizo paused his explanation to point to the window above Kyrie's head.

"Steal a hover and go straight to the Jewel Theater. Then we're going to park the hover far away from the theater so the Netrhaphalin can't find us as easily. We'll go into the theater, spend the night there, and then talk to the boy who sells popcorn. Easy. Done."

"Assuming it goes as planned," Mikaela said, raising an eyebrow.

"That's exactly what Krackers said," Rizo commented. "But I think luck is on our side this time."

"You think?" Mikaela still looked skeptical.

"Yes, I don't just think, I *know*," Rizo proclaimed. "You mark my words."

"I will," Mikaela told him. "But just because you think something is going to go well doesn't mean it will."

"I know! But what other choice do we have?" Rizo asked.

"All right," Mikaela sighed. "I'll go with your plan. It's not like there are any better plans out there. See you at midnight."

Rizo walked out of the ICU feeling energized and ready for their escape. He knew luck was on their side. He could feel it. As his whispered the plans to Anala and

126

Krackers, he felt joy and pride and elation. They were going to make this work.

His plan was rock solid.

It was just too bad that nothing ever went as planned.

Disruption

Chapter 12

June 9, 2473

Rizo had been watching his clock for at least an hour, just waiting. And finally, *finally*, it happened. The thing he was waiting for. The digits on the holographic clock by his bed flipped. 12:00. He jumped off his bed quietly and opened the door. There was a soft creak, and Rizo froze. When no one came running, he tip-toed down the hall to Anala's room. She was wide awake.

"Let's go!" She whispered. She opened her window silently and Krackers flew in. Rizo led them towards the ICU, but stopped when he saw a nurse going into the unit. Here was the flaw in his plan. Nurses visited the ICU throughout the night to check on the more severely injured patients. He glanced at Krackers, who looked resigned to being caught.

"What are we going to do?" Rizo moaned softly. He had been so sure, *so sure*, that this was going to work. He had thought his plan was rock solid. How were they going to escape now? Things couldn't get any worse. Or so Rizo thought.

Dr. Nikita rounded the corner. *Please don't see us,* Rizo pleaded silently.

"What are you kids doing here?" Dr. Nikita asked sternly.

"Nothing-" Rizo started.

"Don't lie to me," Dr. Nikita narrowed her eyes menacingly at them. "You *are* known criminals. Who's to say you aren't doing something sinister?"

"We were- walking!" Anala bust out. "A midnight stroll! Yes, exactly! Don't you just LOVE walking at night? I do-" Rizo could see that Anala was slipping into a hysteric blabbing- whatever mode and needed to be stopped.

"Oh, brother," Krackers said, rolling his eyes grimly. He launched himself at Dr. Nikita and flapped his wings in her face. "Go!" He cried. "I'll catch up!" Rizo didn't need telling twice. He grabbed Anala's hand, pushed past the shrieking doctor and burst into the Intensive Care Unit. He made a beeline for Kyrie, ignoring the startled nurses. Mikaela jumped out of bed and ran over to where Rizo was struggling to open the window behind Kyrie.

"Where's Krackers?" She asked.

"It's a long story," Rizo told her. She frowned, but helped him open the window. They all clambered out as the nurses watched in bewilderment. Dr. Nikita marched into the room with claw marks all over her as Mikaela was climbing out the window.

"Don't let them escape!" Dr. Nikita roared. The nurses stumbled forward, and Rizo shoved Mikaela through the window. Mikaela turned and grabbed his arms, pulling him through. Anala and Kyrie, who had already gone through, helped pull him as well. Dr. Nikita ran over and tugged at his shirt.

"Help!" Rizo called. Mikaela pulled harder. Just as Rizo felt as if he was going to be torn into two, Krackers flew into the room and viciously pecked Dr. Nikita on the ear. She roared in pain and tried to grab Krackers out of the air. He evaded her and pecked her again. Rizo burst through the window and landed in a shrub. Krackers flew out the window, and Kyrie slammed it shut. They ran. Dr. Nikita tried to follow them and whacked her head on the glass. She fell over and appeared to have knocked herself unconscious.

There were a few hovers parked near the hospital. Krackers found a nice big one parked up high so that people couldn't get into it. However, the person or Netrhaphalin who had parked it clearly hadn't had a parrot in mind. It was a convertible, much like the other one they had stolen, and whoever had parked it had left the top down.

Krackers simply flew up, hacked the car's navigator/computer (Rizo couldn't remember), and landed it. Kyrie scrambled on first and took the controls from Krackers. Rizo and the others were close behind. As soon as they were all in the hover, Mikaela slammed the doors and closed the top of the car. Kyrie entered in the coordinates for the Jewel Theater and flicked a switch. The hover flew away soundlessly. No hovers appeared and started pursuing them, which was good. Rizo had had enough of high-speed chases.

"I though you said this was all going to go perfectly," Mikaela said, coming up behind him.

"It kind of did," Rizo pointed out.

"It did if you count alerting the whole hospital," Mikaela said, raising an eyebrow.

"It was still the best escape we've had so far," Rizo argued.

"Oh, yeah?" Mikaela asked, looking behind her. "What if I told you that Dr. Nikita is chasing us right now?"

"No way!" Rizo whipped his head around. Sure enough, Dr. Nikita was chasing them, yelling and shaking her fist. "I thought she was unconscious!"

"I guess not," Mikaela said dryly. "Kyrie! We're being chased by a vengeful doctor!"

"Ha, ha, very funny," Kyrie said from the front seat.

"No, I'm serious," Mikaela called. Kyrie took a look backwards and blanched.

"Oh, nuts," Kyrie muttered. She didn't move. "I- I can't-"

"Step aside!" Mikaela took over the controls. Rizo dragged Kyrie away towards the backseat.

"Are you okay?" He asked.

"I thought I was, but-" Kyrie faltered. "I can't do this."

"You can't do what?" Rizo asked.

"This!" Kyrie waved her arm around the car. "Running away and getting caught- I can't- my head-" She rubbed her temples. "and I have a horrible headache."

"Just rest," Rizo told her calmly. This was Kyrie's breaking point. He knew she wasn't as reliable now. Before, she could be trusted to make cunning split-second decisions, but it was her injury and the tiring days of running away that must have taken a toll on her. Rizo glanced at Anala. When was she going to break? Had she broken already? Had she broken when they had been taken by the Netrhaphalin? He couldn't tell.

He chanced a look behind him. Dr. Nikita was still angrily pursuing them. She wasn't going to stop. Behind her, a few other hovers were gathering, most likely Netrhaphalin patrol cars.

"Mikaela! We have to exit the car!" He called to her.

"How?" She called back. "We're almost to the theater. Just another ten kilometers!"

"We have to get out now!" Rizo said. "Krackers! Take over the controls! Swoop low and left to let us off without them seeing us, then program the car for a random place! Then gun the engine and fly out the window!" Krackers nodded and flew to the front of the car.

"Places! Jump on three!" Krackers called. Rizo tugged Kyrie and Anala towards the door. Anala was bouncing up and down with excitement. Mikaela joined them, her face set with determination.

"One!" Krackers swooped down. "Two!" He cut hard to the left. "Three!" Rizo flung the door open. All of them jumped out and landed hard in some landscaping, then scrambled behind some plants to hide.. Krackers gunned the engine, rolled down the window, and flew out of the hover. He caught up with them a minute later. They hid in the shadows while Dr. Nikita and the Netrhaphalin chased after the empty car.

"Why are we always doing car chases?" Mikaela groaned. "When we do our next chase, can it be somewhere less stressful? Two in a *week*. What bad luck. You said everything was going perfectly." Mikaela glared at Rizo. "We could have been caught. Again!"

"That's not my fault!" Rizo protested. "I don't like car chases either!"

"Whatever," Mikaela sighed. "Let's start walking to the theater."

"Do you even know the way?" Rizo asked her.

"Yes, I'm not a dimwit. I memorized the route while we were flying," Mikaela replied sharply.

Rizo and the others fell silent and followed Mikaela as quietly as possible. They only had one scare, while they were passing by a Netrhaphalin branch station. A Netrhaphalin had been patrolling the streets near the station, and Mikaela had motioned them to hide behind a bush until it was gone.

They walked for what felt like hours, but were really only minutes. Rizo had a lot of time for self-reflection during the walk. He contemplated everything that had happened since the Netrhaphalin had found them. There were some questions about the present such as, *Where had Hope gone?* and *Was Dr. Duarte okay*? that Rizo wanted the answers to. He also had more pressing questions about the future, too. Would the Rockets help them? What would they do if they didn't? Could they go back to the Gryffins yet? These were just half of all the questions whirling around in his head.

The other half of his questions were about all of his plans. Why had none of them gone as planned? All of his supposedly water-tight plans had gone wrong, one way or another. But plans were essential. He couldn't just wing everything. Then everything would fall apart even worse than it would have with a plan, right? *Right?* Rizo had a feeling that he would never know the answer to the previous question. He was too cautious to ever wing anything. Life was a series of plans. It would be chaos to deviate from those plans, surely.

It was almost a relief when Mikaela announced that they were almost at the theater, as it took Rizo's mind off all of his questions. For a minute, anyway. As he rounded the bend, he saw the Jewel Theater. It was huge. Flashing lights surrounded the theater, moving in time to the soft music coming out of the outside speakers. This image gave Rizo even more questions to think about. Why would a shadowy, underground organization make one of their meeting places the flashiest, look-at-me-I'm-awesome theater? It sort of made sense. If you made your meeting place a dark warehouse, Netrhaphalin authorities would be sure to check it out. However, if you exchanged information through a theater that tons of people went to every day- well, it was excellent cover.

"COME on, RIZO!" Anala called from the front of the group. "LET'S go SAVE THE WORLD!"

"Shush!" Rizo told her as he ran up to Anala's side. "Be quiet!"

"I HAVE been QUIET," Anala protested. "FOR the LONGEST TIME! But NOW I can't hold it back! I want to shout EVERYTHING to the WORLD!"

"Anala..." Rizo groaned.

"Fine, I'll be quiet, FOR NOW," Anala told him. "LET'S- let's go!" Anala bounded ahead of the group. Rizo shook his head. In his opinion, Anala acted like a nine year old most of the time. He didn't know when or if she would grow up. Anala reached the front doors of the theater and tugged them open. Or tried to tug them open. They were locked.

"Can we pick the lock?" Rizo asked Mikaela.

"Have you been living under a rock your whole life? Locks are soooooo last century," Mikaela scoffed. "Now they have scanner keypads. You put your hand in the keypad to the left of the doors, see? If your hand is programmed into the keypad, the doors will open."

"I have been living underground for practically my whole life," Rizo argued. "And I like reading history books. Not modern ones."

"Well, this is the present," Mikaela told him. "Not 2053 anymore. So get with it." She gazed around the area intently, searching it for any lurking Netrhaphalin hidden in the shadows. Not that there were many shadows around the Jewel Theater. The lights were so bright, anyone could see them for kilometers around when they were in the air. Rizo wished he could ever actually see a movie. He had heard it was fantastic, and that when you put on the special goggles, you felt like you were really in the midst of the action.

"Can we hack into the scanner?" Rizo asked.

"Those things have triple the security of a NETLINK," Mikaela said scornfully. "It took you hours to hack a NETLINK. By the time you're done, the theater will be open. We'll just wait until morning."

"Where should we wait?" Rizo looked around. There were no huge ferns or trees to hide under.

"Krackers? Can you do a cursory sweep of this area?" Mikaela looked up at the parrot expectantly.

"Oh, fine," Krackers huffed. He flew up and circled around them.

"There isn't much," Krackers reported. "But I think we can hide under this really huge floating building a few blocks from here."

"Excellent," Mikaela said. "Let's move, people!"

As they walked towards the building, Rizo had his most alarming thought yet. What if Riva hadn't understood his question? Was this a dead end?

If it was, and they couldn't find a place to hide, well, they were doomed.

Refuge

Chapter 13

June 9, 2473

It was morning. The Jewel Theater was open. Because it was a weekday, there didn't seem to be many people going to it. Mikaela was leading the way, as usual. If Kyrie had had her head in the game, she would lead them. However, she was still a mess. Now she followed Mikaela sullenly, without making observations or even looking at her surroundings. Her eyes were fixed blankly at the pavement below her feet.

Anala was full of energy, as always. Currently she was skipping by Mikaela's side, chattering on about how hungry she was.

"I haven't eaten in DAYS!" Anala was saying. "Do you know how HUNGRY I am?"

"You ate yesterday," Mikaela pointed out dryly. "You shouldn't be *that* hungry."

"Well, I AM," Anala told her. "And that food tasted like garbage. More proof that Dr. Nikita is evil." However, as they reached the theater, Anala's complaints slowed to a stop. As Rizo held the door open for them, Anala walked through silently, ignoring the flashy posters proclaiming that the *Maestro's Wish* was playing that week.

They made a beeline for the popcorn stand. A boy around eighteen was manning the stand, alert and waiting for customers. The stand was red and held a few fancy machines. He was impatiently tapping the red counter, as if he had nothing else to do. Mikaela frowned slightly, the way she always did when she saw something that had been better before the Netrhaphalin.

The Netrhaphalin had taken away the fancy automated machines that everyone loved and replaced them with popcorn stands. They had said that they were giving more people jobs, but Rizo knew the truth. The Netrhaphalin were just taking away everything good in their society, leaving humans in the past. Dr. Duarte would always shake his head when conversations were held at the table about things like that. Then he would say something like, "We got so far, and now the (Something that Rizo didn't want to repeat) Netrhaphalin are taking us back to the ancient times."

"Uh, hi," Rizo approached the boy. "Um, we would, um, like to, um-"

"Hi, what popcorn would you recommend?" Mikaela cut Rizo off.

"I'd recommend the butterscotch drizzled popcorn, little lady," the boy said, pausing his tapping, evidently pleased to have a customer.

"Uh, thanks," Mikaela said. "do you happen to have any, say, red popcorn? I've heard it's very popular around here."

"No..." the boy said, tilting his head at her. "I mean, I like the color red. I have heard that the Mars popcorn is nice. I don't think we sell it, though."

"You don't?" Mikaela raised an eyebrow. "Are you sure?"

"Well, we do-" the boy lowered his voice. "but only for special customers."

"Don't worry," Mikaela told him, then took a deep breath. "We will be at the red planet yet; all we have to do is shoot for the stars."

The boy gasped. "Yes, I think we can pull it off with lots of hard work. I have heard it's quite nice there. It will take a lot of rockets to get us there, though."

"Riva sent us," Mikaela whispered.

"Riva?" The boy looked worried.

"She told us to tell you that the sky is falling for her," Rizo told the boy.

"You're sure?" the boy asked. "Come to the back room with me. I think we have some of the popcorn you're looking for there." He beckoned them to the back room. An equally alert older woman was waiting there, making popcorn.

"Mom, there's some people who we need to talk to," the boy said to the woman, gesturing at Mikaela, Rizo, and the others. "Can you man the station for me?"

"Sure, Ryder," the woman said. "But first, can I introduce myself? My name is Rachel. I'm Ryder's mother. And you are?"

"Rizo Tyan," Rizo informed her. "This is my sister, Anala, and our friends, Kyrie and-"

"Sharon," Mikaela cut in. "And this is Krackers." She patted the parrot on her shoulder. Rizo shot her a look. Anala looked puzzled, but thankfully did not say anything.

"Huh," Rachel said. "I thought you looked familiar, but if your name is Sharon, then, never mind. And Kyrie! That name sounds familiar. Hmm, maybe you remind me of one of those girls Ryder is always chasing."

"Mom! I don't *chase* girls!" Ryder squawked, flustered. "Seriously! Go to the front!"

"Okay, okay, don't worry," Rachel said, laughing. She winked at them and disappeared into the front room.

"Sorry about that," Ryder apologized. "My mom is an extrovert and loves to meet new people."

"And loves to embarrass you, huh?" Kyrie asked with a mischievous smile.

"Yes, that too," Ryder sighed.

"Don't be sorry, it's fine," Mikaela said, despite the smirk on her face that she was trying to hide.

Ryder shook his head and tapped a few buttons on a popcorn machine, and a platform emerged from the floor. He jumped on it, and motioned for the others to do the same. They followed him, and he pushed a lever on the platform. It descended into the ground for a few minutes, then stopped. They were obviously in an underground network of tunnels, much like the ones Rizo had grown up in.

"Nova!" Ryder called. "Nova! We have visitors!" A beautiful girl Rizo's age emerged from a door on his left. She had long platinum-blond hair and startling blue-green eyes.

"Visitors," the girl, who Rizo thought was Nova, said in a wondering voice. "Here."

"Hi," Rizo greeted her. There was a serenity in this girl's expression that Rizo had never seen before. He tilted his head at her. She smiled at him, and Rizo felt all float-y inside. *Come on, Rizo,* he told himself sternly. *You do not have time for romance now.* He felt silly even talking to himself like that. He really needed to focus.

"This is Rizo, his sister Anala, Kyrie, Sharon, and Krackers," Ryder told her, pointing to them in turn. "Guys, this is Nova. She's thirteen."

"Sharon? At first I thought maybe Mikaela. But of course she died a long time ago."

"That's what I thought, too," Ryder admitted. "If she had lived, I mean. But this is Sharon." Rizo glanced

145

at Mikaela. Her face had a frozen expression on it, one that was unreadable. Was she the Mikaela they were talking about? And if she was, why did they think she was dead?

"They have news about Riva," Ryder told Nova.

"They do?" She asked. "Mom and Dad will want to hear this. One minute, please." She ducked back into the room she had come from with a swish of her sky-blue skirt.

"So, how'd you find us?" Ryder asked. "Not many people know about us."

"We're sort of fugitives," Mikaela explained. "And we needed help. And Kyrie knew about you. I don't know how she knew, but we got here anyhow."

"Wait, slow down," Ryder said. "You're fugitives? Why?"

"We're fugitives for living where we lived," Mikaela growled.

"Where did you live?" Ryder asked.

"It's a long story," Mikaela told him. Ryder realized he wasn't going to get any more information out of her and turned to Kyrie.

"How did you know about us?" He asked.

"You've seen my father," Kyrie said simply. "In one of your meetings."

"Meetings? We don't do-" Ryder stopped, his eyes wide. "Are you Kyrie Duarte?"

"Yes," Kyrie looked up; her chin held high. Her old self was coming back by the minute, Rizo could tell. Rizo was pretty sure it was coming back due to the anger that immediately rippled through Ryder. "I am."

"So you're a Gryffin," Ryder mused. "And you came to us for help? Why didn't you-" He paused, and gasped. "Were you detected?"

"Yes, we were," Kyrie told him. "I don't know what the state of the group is, and if it's safe to go back. That's why I came here. If we weren't in a dire position, I wouldn't have come. But I decided that it was better to stay with a bunch of peace-loving, delusional scientists then to get captured by the Netrhaphalin."

"You take that back!" Ryder exploded. "We are peacemakers, yes, but we are not delusional. There are people still on Mars, and maybe other planets. The Netrhaphalin couldn't get *all* of them. We are rational people who do not think they can take the world back. *That* idea *is* delusional."

"I will take my statement back when it stops being true," Kyrie told him haughtily. Ryder was about to make a snappy comeback when Nova re-entered the hall with a man and a woman.

"Please, come inside the common room with us," the woman said. "We want to hear about everything." She beckoned them into the room. The room was well-lighted and furnished with cozy rugs and soft couches.

"Have a seat," the man said. "Let's introduce ourselves. I am Quamar, and my wife is Dr. Calypso, but she prefers to be called Callie. Also, she hates titles. I believe you have met my daughter, Nova. We are the leaders of the Rockets. I think I recognize some of you, but I'm not quite sure. Who are you?" He made a face, as if he had said something wrong.

"I'm Sharon," Mikaela jumped in. "This is Rizo, his sister Anala, Kyrie, and Krackers."

"You're not S-" Anala started before Rizo muffled her. He didn't know why Mikaela was keeping her identity a secret, but he knew it was probably important. "Don't say that, Anala," he whispered in her ear.

"Yes?" Calypso asked. "You don't need to cut off your sister, Rizo. I would like to know what she was going to say."

"I was going to say," Anala announced importantly. "That you are not so nice." She pointed at Ryder. Rizo breathed a sigh of relief. Anala had understood his message. "Kyrie is recovering from a hover accident and you are not going to say mean things about her."

"But she started it!" Ryder protested.

"Ryder," Quamar told him sternly. "We are supposed to be peacemakers. That means not saying mean things to other people, despite what they say to us." Despite his words, his glare faltered under Ryder's defiant gaze. Kyrie gave Ryder a triumphant smirk, as if to say, *I told you that you all were a bunch of peace-loving softies.*

"Now," Calypso said. "I'd like to know how you know about Riva, and why you have come to us for help."

"I'll explain," Kyrie said. "The Gryffins have been detected. We were captured, but then we escaped, thanks to you, and-"

"Wait- thanks to us?" Quamar asked. "What did we do? Or are you being sarcastic?" He made a confused expression, and Nova winced.

"You shut down all of their communications," Kyrie said. "I assume accidentally, given the nature of your organization, but you did."

"We did- how long ago was this?" Calypso asked, concerned.

"Three days," Rizo replied.

"Did we- I don't think-" Quamar sputtered weakly.

"We had a test that day," Nova spoke up quietly. "Remember? It went wrong, but we didn't think that it did anything to the Netrhaphalin...."

"You're right," Calypso told her daughter. Nova just nodded. Rizo liked how she quietly soaked in information and spoke only when necessary or when she made an observation that she felt was important. Mikaela had been quiet while they were growing up, but never like Nova. When Mikaela was quiet, she was usually disinterested. When Nova was quiet, she seemed to absorb everything happening around her.

"Anyway," Kyrie continued. "While we were escaping our hover got blown up, and we ended up in the hospital. We met Riva there. Rizo, can you explain that part? You were the one who talked to her." Kyrie looked expectantly at Rizo.

"Sure," Rizo said. "But first, I want to know who Riva was in the Rockets, and why she was important."

"Quamar? Should we tell them?" Calypso looked at her husband.

"It's important. We have to," Quamar said with a sigh.

"Okay, fine," Calypso said to Rizo. "Riva was our above ground operator. She's Rachel and Ryan's- Ryder's parents- niece. She was basically our spy in this area. Did she tell you to go here? I mean, most of our contact points are in Space museums, particularly the American Museum of Space. This is our headquarters. We lost contact with her a week ago. We didn't know what had happened to her, but sometimes she can't come and meet with us, so we assumed...." Calypso trailed off.

"Riva is in the ICU at the Salvation Hospital for Hover- Related Injuries. She had a severe concussion, and doesn't really know what she's talking about most of the time. She told us about the Jewel Theater when I told her the phrase to identify the Rockets, and she told me to tell you guys that the sky is falling for her."

"That's what she said?" Quamar asked worriedly. "Are you sure?"

"What does it mean?" Anala asked.

"It means it's over for her," Ryder whispered sullenly. He looked down dejectedly.

"Wait," Nova looked directly at Rizo. "How did you know that Riva was in the Rockets?"

"That's a long story," Rizo evaded her question.

"It's a story that needs telling," Calypso said dangerously.

"Keep the peace, Callie," Quamar put a calming hand on his wife's shoulder.

"Fine, I'll tell," Rizo sighed. "I overheard a doctor-Dr. Nikita Anggan, talking to Riva's brother, Cadwyn. She was blackmailing him into helping her. If he didn't help her, she would turn Riva in to the Netrhaphalin. That's the short version, anyway."

"Did you say Dr. Nikita Anggan?" Calypso asked. She sat back, looking pale. Which was really pale, because she have very light skin to begin with.

"Yes," Rizo nodded.

"That traitor-" Calypso looked ready to bite something. "I can't believe-"

"Callie," Quamar said in a warning tone. "Please."

"How do you know Dr. Nikita?" Anala asked curiously. "Did I mention that she's SUPER SCARY? I mean, she is TOTALLY CREEPY. She was CHASING US in a CAR! She looked SO MAD but also SO SCARY. Like, ONE HUNDRED PERCENT SUPER-DUPER SCARY."

Calypso gave Anala a small smile. "Dr. Nikita studied with both me and Dr. Duarte when we were in school. We were all kinds of different doctors, but we wanted to start an underground group together. Dr. Duarte wanted to take our world back, but I wanted to leave this world to make a colony on Mars. It's been done before the Netrhaphalin took over. But Dr. Duarte argued that freeing humanity here would be better. I do want to free them, it's just that it's so dangerous. The Netrhaphalin are not to be trifled with. Dr. Nikita had a different idea. She wanted to find a way for both the Netrhaphalin and humans to live peacefully together. Dr. Duarte disagreed and eventually left us to create the Gryffins. Meanwhile, Dr. Nikita reluctantly agreed to help me, and we started the Rockets. At first, we collaborated with the Gryffins, but Quamar didn't like their practices. We stopped meeting and cut ties with them," Calypso paused to take a breath.

"In the meantime," she continued. "Dr. Nikita hated life underground. She left us and became a doctor. The Netrhaphalin let her go free in the world because she gave them valuable information about us in exchange for her freedom. I still don't know why she chose to side with them."

"The Netrhaphalin are ruining our world," Mikaela said. "How could Dr. Nikita side with robots?"

"Exactly my question," Calypso said.

"Also, why don't you at least try to stop the Netrhaphalin?" Rizo wanted to know. "They don't feel, they just want to rule us, their creators. They want to take over us. We programmed them to serve us, not the other way around. Even if you don't want to destroy them, don't you see that they're taking our resources? They're forcing us to live underground just to be free. Now, if these were people, I would be more hesitant to destroy them. But they are not human. They are robots! They're only intelligent because we made them intelligent. And they're using that intelligence to wipe us out. They're restricting the number of babies born to each family. They're imprisoning us for no reason. I don't mind a few Netrhaphalin on the planet, but they are multiplying by the minute while destroying us. The *have* to be stopped."

Rizo paused. How were the Netrhaphalin multiplying? In factories? And if they were multiplying in factories....

"How are the Netrhaphalin multiplying anyway?" Mikaela asked, voicing Rizo's thoughts. "Because if we destroy whatever is doing that..." she trailed off.

"Then we're one step closer to taking down the Netrhaphalin," Rizo finished.

Information

Chapter 14

June 9, 2473

"Oh no," Quamar said, looking worried. "Do not tell me that you want to destroy a Netrhaphalin factory." Immediately after he finished his sentence, he clenched his teeth in a nervous expression. Nova frowned disapprovingly while Calypso rolled her eyes.

"That's what they are? Do you know about them?" Mikaela pounced on Quamar's words.

"Argggggggg," Quamar buried his face in his hands. "Yes, we do know a little about them." Nova and her mother exchanged a pained look behind Quamar. Rizo wondered how someone as sharp as Calypso could stand Quamar and how they had ended up together in the first place.

"You DO?" Anala asked. "And you didn't think that was WORTH MENTIONING?"

"I would've, except I know what you were going to do with the information I gave you," Quamar explained. "You're going to go there and destroy the place." He gave them a raised eyebrow that said, *look, I figured out your plan! I'm so clever.*

"Well, now it's inevitable," Mikaela told him. "So, spill. If you don't, we'll get the information somehow." She leveled Quamar with her gaze, and he shrank back. Nova seemed embarrassed by her father, who was turning out to be very disappointing by Rizo's standards. Calypso was much more competent, in his opinion.

"Please, Sharon," Calypso said. "I want to decimate the Netrhaphalin as much as you do. But you might get hurt! So many people have gotten hurt...." Calypso trailed off, looking sad.

"I know," Mikaela said with an expression as hard as steel. "I'm doing it anyway. So don't try to stop me. If you do, I will just knock you unconscious."

"That's actually true," Anala added helpfully. "She's done it to me before for being annoying. I mean, I don't think I deserved it, but HONESTLY, she could have given me a WARNING."

"She did," Krackers muttered. "You just were yelling too much to hear her." Rizo shot him a quelling glare. If Krackers was going to defend Mikaela, Rizo was going to defend his sister.

"Fine," Quamar sighed, resigned.

"No!" Calypso burst out. "Please, Sharon, you are making a terrible mistake! You will die, I know! Please don't do it!"

"Well, it's either that or stay here just waiting. We really are waiting until we can go back to the Gryffins, and we may not even go back to them. They were horrible. At least we can actually do something this way," Mikaela pointed out.

"But it's *dangerous*," Calypso said, as if she would convince Mikaela to stay put if she emphasized the word more.

"Well, *that's* comforting," Krackers snorted.

"I am going to do this," Mikaela said, glaring at Calypso. "And, like I said, you are not going to stop me."

"Us," Krackers corrected. "I'm going with her, too. And you are not going to stop *us*."

"I'm going with, uh, Sharon," Kyrie said. "Anyone else? Rizo? Anala? I would ask you guys, but you obviously don't want to do it." Kyrie looked pointedly at Quamar and Ryder.

"I'll go," Rizo said. "But I don't want Anala to come. I want her to be safe."

"That's NOT FAIR!" Anala exclaimed. "Please, Rizo! I'll be super careful, I PROMISE!"

"No," Rizo told her firmly. "You are staying here. If you get killed, I will be very mad at you *and* I will also be very sad. That is something I definitely want to prevent. Bottom line- you are staying here."

"But Riiizzzzooo," Anala whined.

"Anala." Rizo glared at her.

"This is going to be SO BORING," Anala complained. "Rizo, you owe me one."

"Why is it going to be boring?" Rizo asked, confused.

"You will probably be gone for DAYS! You don't know where it even is or how much the Rockets KNOW!"

Anala cried. "And the only person I'm going to be able to talk to is your boring girlfriend!"

"She's not my girlfriend!" Rizo could feel his face reddening. "And Nova is not boring." He didn't dare look her way, in case her face was- was anything, really.

"Nova is not the only kid here," Ryder told Anala gently. "Don't worry." He grinned.

"Huh?" Anala looked at Ryder, puzzled. He winked at her mysteriously and cupped his hands around his mouth.

"Roci! Roci!" Ryder called. "Rocina! Come here right now!"

"Coming!" Someone responded. A young girl around ten years old bounded into the room. "Oh wow," she said. "New people!"

"Rocina," Ryder said, bringing the girl forward. "These are our guests, Rizo, his sister Anala, Sharon, Kyrie, and Krackers. Everyone, this is my kid sister, Rocina."

"Oh, hi!" Rocina waved at them. "We never have visitors, I'm so excited!"

"Rizo, Sharon, Kyrie, Krackers and I are leaving for a bit," Ryder explained. "But Anala is staying. Can you show her around? She can have one of the guest rooms."

160

"Sure!" Rocina bounded up to Anala. "Hi! I'm Rocina, but you can call me Roci. Do you have any nicknames? Like maybe Nala? Or Ana? Do you want to see your room? Come on, you'll love it!" She grabbed Anala by the hand and started pulling her out the door.

"All RIGHT!" Anala said cheerfully.

"See you, sis!" Rizo called after Anala. "Have fun!" He turned back to all serious faces in the room. She bounded out of the room, already happier.

"Little sisters out of the way, let's get to the more important stuff. How are we going to do this?" Rizo asked. "Can a Rocket come, too? Like maybe... Nova?" He smiled in her direction. She smiled back, and Rizo had to remind himself to stay focused again.

"Maybe," Nova said shyly.

"Nova Lynn Robins! Absolutely not," her father snapped. "These Gryffins can do whatever they want, but *you* are not going with them."

"I'll go," Ryder offered.

"Ryder!" Calypso exclaimed. "Not you! We need you! No Rockets are going, and that's final."

At the same time, Kyrie snapped, "No way!"

"But I want to go," Ryder protested. "I think it could be fun." Ryder smirked at Kyrie, who was scowling at him.

"What if we don't want you to come?" Kyrie asked, gritting her teeth.

"I'm coming anyway," Ryder grinned wickedly.

"You have to ask your parents," Calypso told him with a sigh.

"All right!" Ryder exited the room, excited.

"If he can go, why can't I?" Nova asked.

"Because you are the future of this organization," Quamar told her sternly. "and we cannot afford to lose you."

"Please?" Nova asked.

"No," Calypso replied in an 'and *that's final'* voice. Nova fell silent and shot Rizo a *well, I tried* look.

Ryder came back, grinning his head off. "I can go!"

"Great," Krackers and Kyrie muttered, almost simultaneously. "Just great."

"We have to lay down the law here," Mikaela told him coldly. "One- You two are not going to fight," Mikaela glared at both Ryder and Kyrie. "Two- Ryder, you are not going to interfere with our plan. If you even think about sabotaging our plan, I am going to make you regret it." Ryder made an innocent face at Mikaela, and her scowl intensified. "Three," she continued, just failing to hide her growl, "It's not my fault if you die."

"That's very comforting, Sharon," Ryder said in a sincere voice. At the same time, Krackers asked, "Mikaela, could you make that speech a little less cheerful?" He had obviously forgotten that Mikaela had told everyone her name was Sharon and immediately realized his mistake, wincing slightly.

"I'm stating the facts as they are," Mikaela snapped, ignoring his sarcasm. "And my name isn't Mikaela, you potato head!"

"I'm sorry, I forgot," Krackers whispered apologetically. Mikaela looked at him disdainfully, then wiped all the emotion off her face.

"Mikaela?" Nova asked. "What makes you say Mikaela?"

"Nothing, nothing," Krackers shook his head. "Nothing."

Nova pinned him with her gaze. "You did say something," she said. Rizo realized that so far, the conversation he was in included a lot of quiet communication via just looking at one another. Almost half of the conversation had been held silently, which made Rizo wonder if he had missed anything important. *Does everyone else have a secret language that I don't know about?* he wondered. He sighed. He was terrible at figuring out body language and interpreting other peoples' emotions. To avoid offending anyone, he often tried not to read that much into the situation, in case he got something wrong.

What if Nova and Calypso were rolling their eyes at me earlier, not Quamar? Rizo wondered. He really hoped that wasn't true. He had thought he had done a fair job of reading all of the glares, eye rolls, and stares bouncing around the group during the conversation but... what if he was wrong? What if Nova thought he was a dimwit goof-off? Rizo cleared his head with a little shake. He had enough doubts about the mission to blow up a Netrhaphalin factory. He didn't need more.

"I just got Sharon's name wrong, that's all," Krackers told Nova, without a waver in his voice.

"You said Mikaela," Calypso told him. "And this Sharon looks like the Mikaela I thought was dead. So has she been lying to us or what?" Rizo was startled. He hadn't thought that Calypso would ask such a direct question.

"I can explain," Mikaela said in a chilly voice. "I am Mikaela, but I hid my identity for a good reason. I know the Rockets didn't like the Guardians at all, and neither did the Gryffins. They were a bit direct."

"That's... an understatement," Calypso muttered.

"I didn't want to get everyone riled up," Mikaela explained. "Ryder doesn't like Kyrie just because she's in the Gryffins. And by your standards, the Guardians are way worse than the Gryffins. I didn't want to make waves, that's all." Her explanation would have made sense to a person who didn't know her very well, but it didn't make any sense to Rizo, who actually knew her well.

Mikaela was not afraid of making waves, big or small. She didn't thrive off of conflict, but she wasn't afraid of it, either. Rizo would have to get a better explanation later.

"Okay, I see your point," Calypso relented. Everyone had obviously bought her lie, except Rizo and Krackers. Rizo didn't know if Kyrie believed it, but she hadn't been around Mikaela long. However, Kyrie may have heard about Mikaela through her father, so Rizo didn't really know.

What Rizo really didn't know about was all the terms being thrown around. "What's the Guardians?" Rizo asked. "And why did you describe them in the past tense?"

Krackers shot him a glare that Rizo couldn't interpret. He wasn't sure if it was a *Don't ask questions* glare or a *I'm just mad* glare. Then, knowing Krackers, it could be a *You don't know that? You're so dumb!* glare.

"The Guardians were a group made up of my family," Mikaela told him in a here-is-some-information voice. "They spoke out in public against the Netrhaphalin and blew up one of their stations. After that, the Netrhaphalin came and took away everyone. They missed me. I assume everyone else died." As Rizo watched her, her face never wavered from its stony expression. That was the scariest part of Mikaela. She could hide her emotions so well, you never knew what she was feeling, or even thinking.

"We thought everyone died," Calypso said wonderingly. "Everyone."

166

"Not everyone," Mikaela told her with a half-grimace, half-smile on her face.

"I'm so glad you're alive!" Nova said, elated. "We thought your whole family had been wiped out!" She moved as if she was going to give Mikaela a hug, but Mikaela batted her away with disgust.

"Well, my family wouldn't be dead if you'd have helped them!" Mikaela snapped. "They would be alive, doing real actual things to help to world, not hide from it."

"That's enough," Calypso said with an edge in her voice. Mikaela rolled her eyes. "Fine," she growled. "Back to business. We're going. Can you cowards help us or not?"

"We will," Calypso said. "We'll give you the information about the Netrhaphalin factories."

"Oh, right," Rizo said. He had forgotten that they had valuable information.

"There's one located about a fifty kilometers south from here," Calypso told them. "Next to a Netrhaphalin supply station. It's unmarked on the map and looks small, but it's all underground. We found it while we were looking for a good place to launch a rocket."

"One? You mean there's more?" Rizo asked.
"And did you say fifteen?"

"Duh. Ever heard the expression, 'don't put all
your eggs in one basket? Also, she said fifteen." Krackers
informed him.

"I guess," Rizo said.

"Wait," Calypso interjected. "I said-"

"Anyway," Mikaela sighed, interrupting Calypso.
"Do you have any other information for us?"

"Sorry," Calypso told her. "We don't. But-" Rizo
cut her off, and she sat back, as if she was almost pleased
that she had been cut off and that they didn't have much
to go on. She seemed to hope that they would just get
discouraged by the lack of information and forget about
the mission. *Well, that's not happening,* Rizo thought.

"Okay then, what's the plan?" Rizo asked. They
had to have a good plan if they were going to do this.

"Steal some explosives from the Netrhaphalin, then
use them to blow up their factory," Mikaela told him.
"Easy."

"Easy?" Rizo echoed. "Are you sure? Also, that's
really a... simple plan." It didn't even qualify as a plan by

Rizo's standards. He was only understating his doubts to keep Mikaela from getting mad.

"Excuse me," Mikaela glared at Rizo. "How many of your plans worked so far? None. Which is why I've decided to wing it."

"Wing it!" Rizo couldn't believe it. How could they possibly wing such an important mission? Plans- that was the way to do this.

"Look, you can follow a plan and do whatever by yourself, or come with us," Mikaela told him. Rizo gritted his teeth. "Fine, I'll go with you," he sighed.

"Excellent," Mikaela said, and Rizo wondered if he was the only one who could hear a whiff of sarcasm in her voice. He really hoped she knew what she was doing. Because if she didn't- and her 'plan' failed- well, they were all going to die.

KANO

Annoyance

Chapter 15

June 10, 2473

Calypso had insisted that they stay the night in the tunnels. Mikaela had agreed, since none of them had had much sleep the previous night, and because she was basically the commander of the mission, everyone agreed with her. Calypso had also insisted that she wash their clothes. She had given them other clothes to change into, and had taken theirs away, holding them at arm's length.

Rizo hadn't slept much. He had stayed in the same room as Anala, and she had wanted to talk the whole night. She had gone on and on about how Rocina and her had such big plans for all the things they were going to do together before Rizo finally told her to hush and go to bed.

He had drifted off to sleep an hour later after contemplating the scenarios where they weren't dead by the next day. When his mind had been thoroughly filled with enough horrifying images to last a lifetime, he had finally felt tired and gone to sleep. Needless to say, his dreams were filled with nightmares about all of them dying in terrifying ways.

He woke up to the sound of Anala screaming in his ear, demanding that he get up. She was also bouncing on his bed, which was probably the cause of the pain that kept shooting through his legs.

"Anala! Calm down! You have definitely made your point!" Rizo yelled over his sister's screams.

"Oh, FINALLY," Anala said. "You took FOREVER to get up. Nova even came in here to see if you were okay. She also came here to drop off your clothes, but mostly to see if you were okay." She sat on his legs, looking pleased with herself and gestured to a chair in the room with neatly folded clothes perched on it.

"She did?" Rizo asked. It was really annoying that his face flushed as he said this. Anala would be teasing him about Nova for the rest of his life, or at least a *very* long time.

"Rizo and Nova, sitting in a tree," Anala sang. "K-I-"

"Anala! Please. I don't like Nova in *that* way."

"Uh-huh," Anala said skeptically, not buying this at all.

"Anyway," Rizo said before Anala could say anything more embarrassing, "Is Mikaela up?"

"Your other girlfriend?" Anala teased. Rizo swatted at her.

"You know I don't like Mikaela like that. She's actually pretty scary," Rizo said. "But don't tell her I said that."

"Ha! I know," Anala said. "TOTALLY creepy." She bounced on his legs again.

"Ow! Can you get off me now?" Rizo shoved his sister off his legs and got out of bed. "Also... can you leave so I can change?"

"Sure," she said. "No problem." She sailed out of the room, full of energy, as always.

Rizo changed quickly, folded the barrowed clothes and placed them on the chair. Then he exited the room. Anala was waiting for him outside.

"Come on!" She bounced ahead of him. He followed her more sedately, and took in his surroundings. The tunnel he was in looked like the tunnels the Gryffins lived in. The same old boring gray covered the walls, and it looked like no one had attempted to decorate the place. There were some scribbles on the wall that read: *Ryder was here* and *Rocina too,* but that seemed like the only adornment on the walls. Except for that mark over there.... Rizo stepped closer to the Ryder and Rocina scrawls and found the word ANALA in all capitals, right next to Rocina's name. Rizo shook his head. His little sister had definitely gotten around.

He continued down the gray halls until he saw the common area, which was full of people.

"You sure took your time," Mikaela looked him up and down as he entered.

"What did I miss?" Rizo asked, ignoring Mikaela.

"Nothing," Kyrie reported. "I just got up, and so did Ryder and Krackers. Mikaela's just trying to make us look bad."

"I am not," Mikaela insisted.

"Of course," Kyrie mused disbelievingly. "Of *course.*"

Mikaela glared at her.

"When are we going?" Rizo asked.

"Calypso is trying to talk us into staying the day and leaving at night," Mikaela told him sourly. "She does make a good point." Here Mikaela paused and gritted her teeth. Rizo guessed that Mikaela hated admitting others had good points, and was restraining herself from doing something drastic.

"So are we staying?" Rizo asked.

"I suppose so," Mikaela told him, clenching her fist. "It makes sense."

"Um, so what are we going to do in the meantime?" Rizo wanted to know. Mikaela scowled at him, like he had asked the most obvious question in the world.

"Your favorite things," she scoffed. "Planning and preparing."

"Oh, so we're not going with the 'wing it' plan?" Rizo asked.

"Do you want to?" Mikaela raised her eyebrows.

"No! I'm just checking," Rizo told her quickly. "Can I make a plan?"

"No, we're still winging it," Mikaela smirked. She had obviously been leading him on.

"Really? *Seriously?*" Rizo tried to give Mikaela a wounded expression. Anala and Rocina started laughing hysterically at the expression on his face. Rizo looked around to see if Nova had seen his mess-up, and she was laughing, too.

"Great," he said. "I'm glad I'm a very good entertainer."

"You are," Nova assured him once she had recovered. "You looked like a pouting duck!" She started laughing again. Mikaela frowned.

"I thought so," he mumbled.

"No, really!" Nova told him. "You should be a comedian."

"Anyway," Mikaela said, rolling her eyes. "Rizo's weird faces aside, let's get back to the point."

"Easy for you to say," Nova gasped. "You didn't start laughing. Once you start, it's hard to stop." Mikaela simply glared at her.

"I don't have time for childish things like that," Mikaela snapped. "So don't even try to make me laugh."

"Really don't," Anala advised. "It's not a good idea."

"It isn't," Rizo agreed. He would hate to see Nova get beat up for trying to make Mikaela laugh.

"*Anyway,*" Mikaela said irritably. "Rizo, we're having a briefing in the conference room in five minutes. Be there." With that, she stormed out of the room, her whole body radiating tension.

"Um, did we do something wrong?" Nova asked, concerned.

"That's just Mikaela," Rizo assured her. "Though she does seem a little more ticked off than usual today."

"Yeah, just don't make her mad," Anala advised.

"Um, Nova?" Rizo asked sheepishly. "can you show me where the conference room is? I don't know anything about this place." He smiled at her.

"Sure," she smiled back. "Come this way." Rizo looked behind him and saw Anala making kissing faces at him. He glared at her.

"Be good while I'm gone," he said.

"Have fun!" She giggled.

"Whatever," Rizo said. He shook his head. Nova led him through the halls, pointing out various things he should pay attention to.

"That's the dining room," she pointed to her left. "And that's my room. Then there's Mom and Dad's room, and then, here we are! The conference room!" She pulled the door open, and Mikaela glowered at both of them.   Behind her, Kyrie and Ryder seemed to be having a glaring contest. Krackers was perched on the table, watching them with an amused expression.

"You're late," she said.

"I'm not!" Rizo protested. "I'm right on time!"

"You're late," Mikaela repeated. "You can go now, Nova."

"Um, okay," Nova gave Rizo a fleeting smile and retreated into the hall.

"Thanks for the tour," Rizo told her.

"You're welcome," she smiled, then disappeared down the hall. *Am I too obvious?* Rizo wondered. *Does she like me like I – snap out of it. You might die in a few days. You don't have time for romance.*

Rizo shook his head to clear it.

"Get with it!" Mikaela waved a hand in front of his face. "We don't have time to deal with your romantic problems!"

"What? No. I'm not- no," Rizo stuttered.

"Deny it all you want," Mikaela shrugged. "but we need to get focused. Everyone else is waiting."

"Um, okay," Rizo said.

"Okay!" Mikaela marched up to the table with extreme dignity and immediately took charge. "Ryder! Pass me that map! Rizo! Sit down! We have to figure this out now. Okay, I'm going to go raid the station while you guys provide a distraction. Understood?" She looked around.

"Uh, wait, a distraction?" Rizo cringed. "Also, shouldn't you bring someone with you?"

"Yes, a distraction. Get with the program, Rizo. You're really slowing this down. If I must take someone, I'll take Kyrie."

"Why Kyrie?" Ryder asked. "Why not me?"

"Or me?" Rizo asked.

"Because I don't trust you as much as I trust her, and because Rizo is not going to be much help, plus he's going to fall in love with the first girl he sees there."

"What? No! How do you even think- no!" Rizo protested.

"You did it with Nova just yesterday," Mikaela said, in a here-is-some-information voice.

"I did *not*!" Rizo said indignantly. "Also, why would there be any humans in the station?"

"I don't know! But I don't need you getting romantically involved in this!" Mikaela said. "So shut your trap."

"Fine," Rizo said. His face felt like it was on fire, and he bent down in an effort to hide it.

"*Okay*," Mikaela said slowly. "So you guys are going to make a distraction, and then-"

"A distraction?" Rizo asked, worried.

"Yes! I've repeated this twice already. I'm starting to wonder if you have a concussion, Rizo!" Mikaela glared at him.

"No, I'm more concerned about being caught while making a distraction," Rizo said. "I mean, you and Kyrie are the ones with all the fighting skills."

"What about me?" Ryder asked. "Hello? Anyone? I'm here?"

"We know," Mikaela growled. "We actually don't want you here, ahem. AHEM."

"Duty noted," Ryder said, putting up his hands and grinning at Mikaela. She glared at him.

"*Okay*," she growled. "After we get some explosives, we'll cover our tracks and lead them on to a different trail. Then we'll make our way over to the factory and blow it up. Understood?"

"Can we have more-" Rizo started.

"Of a plan?" Krackers finished for him. "No way. All of the plans we've ever followed have been disastrous."

"They were not!" Rizo said. "They worked out fine!"

"Do you count getting exploded and knocked out fine?" Krackers asked. "Because that's exactly what happened."

"Everyone!" Mikaela called before Rizo could snap back at Krackers. "Are you clear on that?"

"Yes," Ryder and Kyrie said in unison. They glared at each other.

"Yes," Rizo said.

"Fine. Rest. I'll meet you here in the evening. Don't be late." Mikaela stormed out of the room. Krackers swooped out after her and slammed the door.

Looking at Ryder and Kyrie's glares, not to mention the way Mikaela was acting, Rizo had a feeling that this mission would be anything but good.

It was going to go horribly.

No, it was doomed.

Gone

Chapter 16

June 10, 2473

A week ago, Rizo would have been excited to go above ground and breathe fresh air, if only for a minute. Now, after being captured, chased, hospitalized, and chased again, Rizo was hesitant about going back up, going closer to the Netrhaphalin. And that was putting it mildly. Rizo was terrified. However, he had to put on a brave face for everyone and say he was fine and he was excited and it was all going to be good. Why? Because he wanted to make a good impression on the Rockets and didn't want to appear cowardly. If he was being truthful, he also wanted to make a good impression on Nova.

That was the other problem he had to deal with- Nova. She was constantly popping up in his head at the most *annoying* times. He barely knew her, and he was acting like a pathetic, love struck sea slug in front of her. He didn't not want to be a perfect person, but he knew he was acting sickening. It wasn't Nova's fault. It was Rizo's fault, and he knew it. He *had* to snap out of it if he was going to focus on the mission. Unfortunately, his heart and head were not interested in getting their acts together. He knew he should not get distracted by Nova, but he did anyway. It was frustrating. It was annoying. And it was downright infuriating.

The problem was, Rizo couldn't do anything about it. He couldn't just freeze his emotions away. So basically? He was trying very hard to keep Nova out of his mind (which he learned was impossible) and just focus on what they were going to do.

This was proving to be very hard and difficult. This combined with Rizo's fear of the Netrhaphalin and going above ground made him an absolute mess. Not to mention all the teasing about him and Nova. Example:

Anala: Rizo has a girlfriend! Rizo has a girlfriend!
Rizo: Anala! Stop it!

Anala: Don't say 'stop it.' That's not nice.
Rizo: But-
Anala: Rizo has a girlfriend! Rizo has a-
Rizo: STOP IT!!!

This conversation that Rizo had been replaying in his head had been held an hour ago, and he was still ticked off. Little sisters were the *worst*. Rizo wasn't even sure if he was ready for *that* sort of thing. He shook himself hard. He needed to focus. They were going above ground in an hour.

Rizo made himself go over the things he had tucked away in the pockets of his shirt and pants: and anti-sedative, water, a wrench, a friction fire lighter, rope, and a few wires. Mikaela wanted to minimize how much they stole from the Netrhaphalin- not because she felt bad for them, but because she didn't want to take any chances and end up in prison or dead. Besides, the only thing they needed to steal was an explosive. The Rockets said they didn't have any, but Mikaela believed they were lying. She wasn't about to call them on it, however, because they'd been extremely nice and had not only let Anala stay with them, but also helped supply all the things needed for the mission.

Nova had been super nice and had helped them-no, Rizo couldn't think about her right now. He shook himself and made his way to the conference room. He realized that he didn't know what time it was. Hopefully, he wasn't late. Rizo glanced at one of the holographic clocks on the wall.

"Great Gryffins," he muttered under his breath. He *was* late. Mikaela was going to kill him. He raced down the halls, trying to recall the tour Nova had given him. Unfortunately, he couldn't seem to remember much except- except for things he *didn't* need to remember.

"Arggggggggg," Rizo growled, rubbing his temples. When he came to a turn, he ran left, but that was a dead end. He backtracked, and turned right instead of left. Rizo came up dry. He needed to find someone to help him he had to-

"Rizo!" Mikaela scolded him. "Get off me right now or so help me, I'm-"

"Okay! Okay!" Rizo had ran straight into Mikaela and knocked her over. He was officially toast. He stood up quickly, wincing in preparation for whatever was to come. Mikaela stood up, dusting herself off, and glared at him. Her glare could've melted an iceberg, it was so intense.

"You're late," she growled. She wrenched his arm painfully and dragged him over to the conference room. "Don't ever do anything like this ever again." She wrenched his arm harder, then let go and shoved him into the room. Rizo stumbled in, and Mikaela stormed past him.

"Now that *Rizo* is here," she barked. "I will review our plan and set it into motion." She said 'Rizo' like it was a slimy, rotten oyster that had gotten into her food.

"Got it," Rizo said. Mikaela started to say something, then stopped. She took a deep breath and continued, clutching the table as if her life depended on it. *Or as if my life depended on it,* Rizo thought with a shiver. *It must be taking everything Mikaela has to restrain herself from killing or at least maiming me. I guess she just doesn't want to do anything drastic in front of everyone.*

"Anyway, we are going to go out in half an hour, everyone. We are going to make our way to the Netrhaphalin supply station on foot, to avoid another hover chase, then raid it. After that, we are going to blow up the Netrhaphalin factory. Assuming the explosion is successful, the ultimate goal would be to destroy all the Netrhaphalin factories. Then we take down the remaining Netrhaphalin, and then we get our world back. Done, all problems solved." Mikaela sat back in her hover chair, looking pleased with herself. When nobody said anything for a minute, she sighed and tapped the conference table twice. Holograms flickered to life, suspended over the table.

"Okay," Mikaela pointed to the map that had sprung up. She pointed to a red dot in the center of the map. "This is where we are. And this is where the station is," Mikaela paused to point to a blue dot on the map. It was frighteningly far away. Mikaela zoomed the map out with a flick of her wrist. "And this," she thumped her finger triumphantly on a yellow dot a good distance away from the station. "Is our target."

"They're... farther apart than I expected," Rizo said slowly.

"They are really far," Ryder agreed.

"Well, I don't care," Mikaela said stubbornly. "I would still blow the factory up even if it was in outer space."

"Still, Mikaela, you're being a little unreasonable," Rizo argued. "Are going to *walk* to these places? *Walk?* I thought Calypso said that they were only fifteen kilometers away from here."

"She said fifty, you dingbat," Mikaela said scornfully. "And yes, we're going to walk. Everyone knows that hover chases are the worst. I'm not a total idiot as to let that happen again, unlike *some* people." She looked pointedly at Rizo.

"So you admit that you're an idiot, just not a *complete* one?" Ryder asked with a cheeky grin. Krackers smacked his head with one wing.

"I am no such thing!" Mikaela banged her hand on the table, making the map disappear. "I was just trying to- to make Rizo feel slightly better." Rizo didn't buy her explanation for a second. Mikaela never cared about other people's feelings. At least, this new, bolder, angrier Mikaela in front of him didn't.

"Okay, okay," Ryder put his hands up. "I was just asking."

"You are not going to be a problem on this mission," Mikaela growled softly. "Otherwise I will personally feed you to the sharks."

"There's just one problem with that plan," Rizo pointed out reasonably. "Sharks are extinct."

"It's a metaphor!" Mikaela was raging now. "I mean to the Netrhaphalin, you- you! Argggggggg! You all are unbelievable! I don't know how we can defeat the Netrhaphalin with a bunch of sloths like you! No, don't tell me that sloths are extinct! I know they aren't, because I am looking at them right now! The laziest, most annoying slugs of sloths in the history of history! Argggggggg! So help me, I- I- Argggggggg!" Mikaela stomped out of the room, fuming. "This is never going to work!" Rizo heard her muttering ominous threats as she stormed away. Krackers flew after her.

"Um, so, *that* went well," Ryder looked at them uncomfortably. Rizo sighed. If everyone hated each other, then how could they even get a job done?

"Let's meet up in an hour," Kyrie sighed. "Hopefully, Mikaela will have cooled down by then." She got up and left the room.

"Okay," Rizo said quickly. He started to get up.

"Hey, wait," Ryder said, motioning for him to sit back down. "I have a few questions." Rizo couldn't blame him. He had thousands of questions, all swarming around in his head. He nodded.

"Okay, One," Ryder held out one finger. "Is that Mikaela girl always like that?" Rizo nodded. "Oof. That's rough. How did you live with her?"

"She wasn't that bad until we got captured and all," Rizo told him truthfully.

"Huh," Ryder mulled this over. "Anyway, Two, how can I stay on Mikaela's good side?"

"There really isn't any way that I know," Rizo shrugged. "If anything, you should ask Krackers that."

"Uh, okay, um, Three, what's the deal with Krackers? How is he so smart?"

"He's genetically modified," Rizo told him.

"No way, man! So that's why he's such a pain in the rear!"

"He does like to act pretty high-and-mighty," Rizo admitted.

"Talk about an understatement," Ryder muttered. "Okay, Four, why does Kyrie hate me?"

"I don't think it's personal," Rizo shrugged. "Well, you did insult her, so, maybe it is. But I think she hated you first because she's very loyal to the Gryffins and has been raised with the knowledge that the Rockets are useless."

"Can you give me more information about that?" Ryder asked.

"Why?" Rizo looked sideways at Ryder. "Why do you want to know this anyway?"

"Oh, no reason," Ryder said quickly. He drummed his fingers on the table, much like he had been doing at the popcorn stand. A few holograms clicked on and off, but Ryder wasn't concerned. He just kept drumming his fingers absentmindedly.

"Hmm," Ryder's drumming stopped.

"Yes?" Rizo looked up expectantly from where he had been inspecting a small dent in the table intently.

"Do you- are you- well, will you tell me about- about your friends if I tell you how to win Nova over?"

"What? What- no. I'm not that, no- no! I mean- no! I don't- Nova- no!" Rizo stuttered.

"It's okay, we all deny it at first," Ryder said soothingly, though he looked like he knew exactly what he was doing.

"I'm not- I'm not *interested* in Nova!" Rizo exclaimed. "No way!" He really hoped that was true.

Saying the words with conviction did not do anything to help his rapidly beating heart.

"Don't worry," Ryder said, sitting back. "I think you're a bit young for that type of stuff. Anyway, see ya!" He winked at Rizo and left. Rizo sank in his chair, feeling a mess of emotions he wasn't sure he wanted to untangle.

Not to mention the thoughts. Rizo tried to push them away before they dragged him under like a current in a river. However, the question that Rizo had been trying to bury, trying to shove away, resurfaced, and Rizo didn't have the energy to push it somewhere far away. *Am I being obvious? Does Nova know?* Those were the questions that were coming back to haunt him every day. Rizo grabbed at his hair angrily. He didn't want this. And yet... he sort of did. That was *maddening*. Rizo hated when his thoughts were conflicted. He liked things to be predictable, black-and-white. Unfortunately for Rizo, the world was far from just two colors. It had a whole spectrum of rainbow colors and everything else anyone could imagine.

Rizo had to walk to clear his head. Rubbing his temples, he stumbled out of the room and plowed straight into Nova.

"Rizo! Just who I need!" Nova sounded frantic. Rizo wondered if he had done something wrong. *You just ran in to her, of course she's mad*, he scolded himself.

"Listen," Nova said hurriedly. "I haven't told anyone else this yet because I'm hoping you'll know what to do. And I'm coming with you." She walked down the hall briskly, and motioned for him to follow.

"Wait, what?" Rizo asked. "Coming with me where?"

"You'll see, let me explain," Nova said patiently. "I didn't have anything to do with this, I promise. I just found-" She hurried around a corner, making sure no one had seen them.

"Tell me what's wrong," Rizo said, stepping in front of her, gently stopping her from going anywhere.

"I'm so sorry," Nova looked at him, and her eyes were worried and helpless. "I'm so, so sorry."

"Now you're making me worried," Rizo said, frowning slightly.

"I would've stopped her if I could, Rizo. I'm so sorry. Let me help you."

"Just tell me," Rizo insisted. "I will let you help."

"Even if it means disobeying my parents?" Nova asked.

"Yes," Rizo said. "and why would we have to do that? Just tell me. You can trust me." He looked into her eyes, and saw that she did trust him.

"I do trust you," Nova said, taking a deep breath. "Don't freak out. They've gone above to do *it*. She was so mad, I'm sorry. We have to stop them."

"Who?" Rizo asked, though he knew the answer already.

"Krackers and Mikaela."

New Ideas

Chapter 17

June 10, 2473

Rizo ran down the hall hurriedly with Nova beside him. The whole underground base flashed by his eyes as he ran from room to room in search of Kyrie.

"Why aren't we going to the exit?" She gasped.

"We can't do this by ourselves!" Rizo told her. "We need Kyrie!" He turned a corner sharply and bumped into Anala and Rocina.

"What IN THE-" Anala started. She and Rocina had obviously been doing more wall drawing. Rocina was trying to hide some e-markers behind her back. Rizo gave them both hard looks, and Rocina flushed and smiled guiltily.

"I have to go, I'm sorry, get out of my way!" Rizo attempted to push Anala aside.

"Wait, why?" Anala trotted alongside him, eager for information. Rocina followed her, forgetting to hide the e-markers. She was gripping them so hard; a stream of holographic red was flying out of one of them.

"I just do! Now Anala, go with Rocina right now I don't have time for this!" Rizo ran into different rooms, gasping for breath.

"Rizo! TELL me what's HAPPENING!" Anala pulled him backwards, slowing him down.

"Where's Kyrie?" Rizo asked, casing the hall wildly.

"I just saw her glaring at Ryder, why?" Rocina piped up. "Man, she really hates my brother." Rocina seemed mildly offended on Ryder's behalf.

"Can you take me to her?" Rizo pounced on Rocina's words.

"Sure," Rocina turned around. "Follow me." She started down the hall at a leisurely pace, and Rizo asked her impatiently to speed up.

"Oh fine," Rocina grumbled. She sped up slightly, annoyed. She reached a door on Rizo's left and lifted her hand to knock. Just then, Kyrie threw open the door, furious. Rizo glimpsed Ryder in the background, looking flabbergasted.

"Such a coward I- What in the world?" Kyrie asked, glaring at them.

"Mikaela and Krackers have gone to blow the factory up by themselves. We need to follow them!" Rizo blurted, quite forgetting that both Anala and Rocina were listening intently.

"They've gone?" Anala asked quietly. "Well, that's RUDE. Can I help you?"

"I know, and maybe," Rizo replied a bit absentmindedly, before he realized he was talking to Anala. "I mean, you obviously can't come."

"WHAT!" She rounded on him, eyes blazing. "I can be useful, just you wait!"

"I thought we had already settled this," Rizo sighed, his mind racing forward. He had to keep Anala here, out of danger. Then he would track down Mikaela and Krackers and calm Mikaela down. She really needed to work on her anger management issues.

"But you NEED help!" Anala insisted. "I was okay with it at first, when you were going to have Mikaela, but now-" Ryder pushed past a bewildered Kyrie and interrupted Anala.

"What in the name of Edward Duarte is going on here?" He asked.

"Do NOT-" Kyrie started, furious.

"We need Kyrie's help," Rizo said quickly before Kyrie could finish her sentence.

"Not mine?" Ryder gave Rizo an injured expression.

"Well, no," Rizo said.

"That's fine," Ryder said. "I'm coming with you anyway, so don't bother trying to stop me."

"Can I come, too?" Rocina asked, looking up into her brother's face.

"No, Rocina. We've already lost Riva. We don't need to lose someone else." Ryder bent down to hug Rocina. "Please stay."

"Okay," Rocina said, slightly reluctantly. "I'll stay."

Rizo wished he had even a fraction of Ryder's influence on his younger sister.

"Now, go and pretend to play so you have an alibi, and don't tell them what you know," Ryder told his sister, gesturing to the hall. She nodded and quickly disappeared into a room far away from them.

"Okay, let's go," Kyrie said in a commanding voice. She crept towards the exit chamber. Rizo followed her, his mind racing.

"Oh, yes!" Anala bounded after Kyrie happily.

"I didn't say you could come!" Rizo told her severely.

"Well, too bad!" Anala was bouncing on her toes by now, thoroughly excited about the rescue mission she was going to be a part of.

"Anala..." Rizo said, preparing himself for the ensuing screams.
"Please."

"Don't Anala ME!" Anala whirled on him. "I. Am. Going."

"Anala, listen to reason," Rizo tried.

"YOU are the one not being reasonable!" Anala gripped his arm tightly. "I am going, END of STORY!" She shook him slightly.

"Fine, fine," Rizo said, wrenching his arm away from his sister. "You've made your point. Don't get all violent."

"Violent?" Anala glared at him. "That wasn't violent. Knocking someone unconscious is violent. Giving someone a shake on the arm is far from *violent.*" She growled unpleasantly.

"All right!" Rizo backed away from her, holding his hands high.

"Good," Anala looked satisfied. "Let's go."

"We've wasted enough time as it is," Kyrie barked. "Come on."

They had stopped while Rizo and Anala had been arguing, and Kyrie urged them on quickly and silently. After a few minutes of stealth walking, they had gotten nowhere.

Kyrie paused. "Ryder? Where's the exit?" She grimaced painfully while saying this.

"I am useful after all," Ryder grinned. "Come on." He took them in the opposite direction. After a few more minutes, they found a sign marked EXIT. "Shoot, the platform's up." Ryder frowned. "Let's hope my mom doesn't- wait, how did Mikaela get past my mom?" He pressed the button to pull the platform down.

"We'll see," Rizo said grimly. "Let's hope Rachel isn't knocked out."

"Mikaela would do that?" Ryder asked.

"She's done it before," Anala said. Ryder furrowed his brow, concerned. The platform was on the ground by now, and they all got on it hurriedly. Ryder flicked a switch, and they rocketed upwards. When they exited the platform, the back room was seemingly deserted. Anala crept cautiously around the room while everyone else headed for the door that led to the front.

"Look!" Anala pointed. Everyone looked in the direction she indicated and saw Rachel slumped on the ground.

"Mom!" Ryder ran toward the unconscious figure. He felt her pulse. "She's alive. Good thing the theater is closed, otherwise we would have people asking questions. I need to tell Calypso."

"No," Kyrie put up a hand to stop him. "You can't. Then she would start interrogating us. We have to go *now.*"

"But- okay," Ryder glanced at his mother, then started forward. "Let's go." They exited the popcorn stand quietly and moved towards the exit of the theater. A thought struck Rizo. "How will we know where to go?" he asked. "We don't have a map."

"I guess we'll have to go back down then," Nova said, frowning.

"No way!" Rizo said, shaking his head. "We can't risk it."

"Then we'll have to wing it," Kyrie said. "By the way, did I say that I was the leader? Because I am."

"What makes you the leader?" Ryder asked indignantly.

"Because I'm the most trustworthy and competent," Kyrie replied condescendingly, looking down her nose at Ryder before snapping back to her usual self. "No, seriously, I think I should be the leader."

"Do we *have* to wing it?" Rizo wanted to know.

"Yes," Kyrie said. "Unless you want to go back."

"No, no," Rizo shook his head. "Oh well."

"Wow," Anala looked at him, astonished. "I thought you'd put up more of a fuss. Oh, wait, I know why you're acting so tough. It's your girlfriend!"

"Anala!" Rizo shot her a disapproving look. "I don't- I don't know what you're talking about!"

"Uh huh," Anala said disbelievingly. "Right." Rizo swatted at his younger sister.

"Don't get all violent," she said, mimicking Rizo's tone from earlier.

"Enough!" Kyrie said firmly. "How are we going to find Mikaela and Krackers?"

"Well, let me help you," Ryder said, with a smirk on his face.

"What?" Kyrie turned to him, stopping in her tracks.

"*I* brought a map," Ryder told her smugly. He held up a small disk. When he tapped it twice, a holographic map appeared over it.

"Why didn't you tell us sooner?" Kyrie asked angrily. "We spent valuable time worrying about that!"

"Well," Ryder grinned. "I wanted to see you worry first."

"You jerk!" Kyrie grabbed the disk from him furiously and immediately started tapping it. "Let's see," she muttered to herself. "The station is over there. Map, take us to the Netrhaphalin Station of Supplies."

"Certainly," the map replied in a cool voice. "The Netrhaphalin Station of Supplies is 23.4 kilometers south from here. I have outlined your path. Have a safe journey."

"*Twenty three kilometers?*" Ryder looked aghast. "You have got to be kidding me. No way am I walking that far. Let's go by the telecubes."

"Um, and where will we find those, Mr. Unrealistic Ideas?" Kyrie asked curtly.

"There's one not far from here," Ryder said. "It's a patrol station, and it has a cube."

"Aaaaannnnnddd, we have to fight ten dozen Netrhaphalin to get to it," Kyrie said.

"Don't be such a Gloomy Gus," Ryder said reprovingly.

"Well, don't be so unrealistic that what you're thinking wouldn't even happen in movies!" Kyrie shot back.

"What! Movies are pretty realistic," Ryder argued.

"Uh, huh, what about time travel?" Kyrie snapped. "It's been hundreds of years since the idea came up, and we still haven't even figured it out yet!"

As they continued arguing, Rizo watched, appalled about the dysfunctional relationship of the group. Kyrie and Ryder hated each other, Mikaela was angry at everyone, Rizo was annoyed with his sister, and Nova- well, it was only a matter of time before some conflict

204

showed up around her. Peace was not enough. Rizo had to bring them all together if they were going to do anything.

"GUYS!" He shoved himself in between Kyrie and Ryder, who were still bickering. "In order for this to work, you guys have to stop squabbling Every. Single. Moment. Of. The. Day! And in order for that to happen, you have to make friends."

"NO way!" Kyrie stepped back and shuddered.

"Fine, then at least a truce?" Rizo begged.

"Rizo's right," Nova said. Rizo felt little tiny explosions going off inside him. *No, don't think about that right now.* "I think you should make peace."

"Fine," Kyrie stormed towards Ryder and held out her hand. "No more snide comments or arguments from now on. Truce?"

"Truce," Ryder agreed. They shook on it.

"Good," Rizo nodded. "Now, where were we?"

"The part where we have to walk, like, ten thousand kilometers," Ryder said.

"It's not ten thousand you id- Never mind." Kyrie closed her eyes and rubbed her forehead. "This is going to be hard."

"Anyway, you were saying that there's a telecube somewhere nearby?" Rizo asked.

"Yeah," Ryder nodded. "I was going to say that the station has been abandoned-more or less- and that there's a cube there."

"What do you mean, more or less?" Nova asked.

"It's a skeleton crew. I thought you knew this," Ryder frowned at Nova.

"As it happens, no. My parents don't tell me everything," Nova wrinkled her forehead slightly. "Anyways, so basically we'll go, fight a few Netrhaphalin, then teleport to the supply station, and then wait for Mikaela to come and meet up with her."

"Pretty much," Rizo said. He turned and addressed the map. "Can you show us the route to the nearest Netrhaphalin patrol station?"

"Certainly," the map replied. It zoomed in and a red dot flashed, indicating the location of the patrol station. "The place you are locating is 4.9 kilometers from here."

"That's WAY better than 20-something kilometers," Anala pointed out.

"All right, let's go." Kyrie led them in the direction the map indicated they go. Rizo fell back to talk to Nova.

"Man, we got in a lot of fights that were pretty much useless. You must think that we're always like that."

"Well, are you?" Nova asked.

"Well, yes," Rizo sighed. "I'm working on it. I haven't made much progress, though."

"You helped Kyrie and Ryder make peace. That was something," Nova smiled at him.

"I guess," Rizo said, keeping his head down so she wouldn't see his grin.

"How did you find the Gryffins? I didn't know that they let children join." Nova looked up at Rizo.

"They don't- well, at least they didn't let us join. They took us from an orphanage, but we never really *joined*." Rizo looked away.

"An orphanage? Did they select you on purpose?" Nova asked.

"I don't think so," Rizo said. "They were trying to raise a generation away from the influence of the Netrhaphalin, I think."

"Interesting." Nova mulled this over for a bit. "How old were you when- when you arrived at the orphanage?"

"I was four, I think, and Anala was just a baby," Rizo paused. "I know that you want to know the story." When Nova said nothing, Rizo continued with a sigh. "I was in daycare, and it was getting late. When it was almost time for us to get picked up, someone called the daycare, I guess, and then a caretaker, Miss Rosa, she came over and told me. Anala didn't understand, I mean, how could she?" He looked at her, and his voice caught in his throat. "Sometimes my parents- Hanah and Olai- they start to fade from my memory. But I *have* to remember them." A heavy feeling had descended around Rizo, and he desperately wanted to lift it, although he did not know how.

"I understand," Nova said. She couldn't understand, not if she hadn't ever had a loved one die before. But maybe she did know. Maybe an uncle or a cousin or a grandparent had died in her family.

"Have you ever had a family member..." Rizo trailed off.

"No," Nova shook her head. "I can't imagine what it would feel like." *Then how could you understand?* Rizo's mind whispered. Rizo pushed that thought away.

Nova seemed to have a lot of empathy. She could understand, couldn't she?

"I don't want to talk about it," Rizo said. After a moment, he said in a light tone, as if they had not been discussing such a serious topic a moment before, "I take it you don't have any brothers or sisters?"

"No," Nova said wistfully. "I wish I did."

"You can have mine if you'd like," Rizo said jokingly.

"You shouldn't say that," Nova said reproachfully. "You're very lucky."

"I suppose I am," Rizo said thoughtfully. He had never really considered having a sister lucky, but he guessed that he would be a little lonelier without her. "Have you ever had any pets? Dr. Duarte wouldn't let us have any, not that we had any pets accessible to us underground."

Nova smiled. "I once had this hamster named Paws- don't laugh! I was five!"

"I'm not laughing," Rizo said, keeping a resolutely straight face. "Paws is a very- very *creative* name."

"I guess," Nova laughed ruefully. "It died a long time ago. Riva had brought it back for me for my birthday."

"Riva," Rizo echoed.

"Yes, you saw her, didn't you?" Nova asked. "I know what she said, but what was she like? Did she mention us?"

Rizo shook his head. "She could barely remember anything. I was half worried that she didn't know what she was talking about and that we were going to walk into a perfectly normal theater and go to a perfectly normal popcorn stand with no intention of rebelling against anything."

"We don't *rebel*," Nova said reprovingly. "We are supposed to be peaceful."

"Well, then, I guess- never mind. How far have we gone?" Rizo didn't want to make Nova mad, so he abruptly changed the subject.

"LESS than a KILOMETER, silly," Anala said. She trotted back to talk to them. "I TRIED to talk to Kyrie and Ryder, but they were all CRANKY. Like, Great Gryffins, CALM DOWN already. I really hope you guys are talking about interesting things, then I can stop being BORED!

Or if you decide to do some SMOOCH- I mean NOTHING," Anala said hurriedly as Rizo shot her a glare that could melt a glacier. "Then I want to be WARNED in advance," she finished smoothly, running a hand down her hair and flipping it, trying to act like a diva.

"I see," Rizo told her icily. Both Nova and Anala sensed that the conversation was over and fell silent. Rizo was left to think. He hoped that everything would go well. He had a gut feeling that things were going to get better. However, last time he had thought things were going to go well, nothing really had.

So basically, he was at square one. He didn't wish that he had never met Nova- that wouldn't be true- but he did have other wishes.

I wish everything had gone better.

I wish that Mikaela and Krackers hadn't left. That wish opened up the gates holding in wishes he had kept buried for most of his life:

I wish that I had someone to turn to, to give me advice.

I wish that I had someone who loved me and took care of me. Rizo knew Anala loved him, but he had to take care of her, not the other way around.

The last wish was the answer to his previous wishes. The thing that would keep everything from ever happening. If this wish had come true, Rizo might have not known of Nova's existence. That was hard to imagine now. However, this setback could not keep him from wishing it anyway. Nothing could. Rizo took deep breaths and let himself think what he had not let himself think for so long:

I wish that my parents were still alive.

Identification

Chapter 18
June 10, 2473

The hollow ache within Rizo had not faded by the end of their journey. He glanced upwards. Framed by the setting sun, a floating building, much more modern than the one Rizo and the others had stayed in when the Netrhaphalin had captured them, loomed overhead. It was completely detached from the ground, a good ten meters in the air, so that intruders could not get in just by taking jet lifts. There was a small column that connected the building to the ground. It most likely contained the telecube system. It was well fortified, the only way you could get up was through a hover. Netrhaphalin could fly, so it was no problem for them.

For Rizo and the others, however, this was a very big problem. None of them could fly. If they had had Krackers, maybe they could have solved the problem more easily. He could have seen a possible way up.

"And how are we going to get up there?" Kyrie glared at Ryder. "We've spent at least an hour walking here- all for nothing. We'll never catch them now!"

"I didn't say this plan was foolproof!" Ryder shot back. "I just suggested it, and you went with it!"

"Guys! You made a truce!" Nova told them. Kyrie turned in a circle, stomping furiously. Ryder looked around with a helpless expression.

"We need a plan," Rizo told them. "So far, winging it hasn't worked so well. How are we going to get up there?"

"Exactly my question," Kyrie growled.

"Let's case the building," Rizo said. "We'll go in groups. Then we'll meet back here and make a plan of action."

"This sounds like another waste of time," Kyrie said.

"Well, it's better than nothing," Rizo argued. Kyrie didn't say anything. "Look, you and Anala can go together, and Nova, Ryder and I can work with each

214

other." Miraculously, Kyrie didn't argue, and she took off abruptly with Anala trotting by her side.

"Come on," Rizo said, gesturing to Ryder and Nova. They followed him wordlessly. They circled the building, once or twice making observations but coming up dry. It was hard to see in the dark. Rizo began getting frustrated. Why had they even thought this had been a good idea? Right after getting captured and hospitalized, they were going straight back into the fray. Sure, it was sad to see such a dilapidated world at the mercy of the Netrhaphalin, but why had they wanted to go and blow something up? Rizo kept replaying everything that had happened in the past week to see why they had decided to do this obviously dangerous and ultimately stupid thing. He was so wrapped up in everything, he didn't even notice when Anala said that she had found a way to get in.

"Rizo? Rizo! Have you been listening?" Someone was poking him hard.

"Oh, sorry," Rizo looked down at his little sister. "What did you say?"

"I said, I found a way to get in!" Anala was beaming at him.

"That's great!" Rizo exclaimed. "Wait, is this a trick?"

"No, it's not!" Anala looked offended. "This is real!"

"Anala, no one says 'real' anymore," Rizo sighed.

"And how would you know?" Anala shot back. "You've been living under a rock your whole life!"

"Well, so have you!" Rizo argued.

"Stop! Stop!" Nova interjected. "Calm down. We need to focus."

Rizo glared at Anala, but kept quiet.

"What did you find?" Nova asked, taking a deep breath.

"There's a hover behind the station," Anala said proudly. "We can use it to fly up to the building."

"Why didn't I see that?" Rizo grumbled. "Anala just got lucky."

"No need to be mean," Nova said reprovingly. "Please don't argue."

"Sorry," Rizo said, a little ashamed. "Sorry, Anala."

"Nice move," she said with a wink.

"I have no idea what you're talking about," Rizo said, careful to keep his face straight and his voice calm.

"Yes you do," Anala teased.

"Anyway," Rizo said before things got out of hand. "Let's go."

"Agreed." Kyrie walked off in what Rizo assumed was the hover. "Let's go." Her face looked as if it was carved from stone. The others followed behind.

"What's up with her?" Ryder asked Anala.

"I have no idea. She seems mad, but I have no idea what she's mad about," Anala replied.

"Why don't you ask her?" Ryder asked, though his tone was teasing. Anala, however, took him seriously.

"No WAY!" Anala looked horrified. "If she's mad, you don't want to make her even more angry. She can be SO SCARY sometimes."

"I was just kidding," Ryder said with a smile.

"She doesn't really like to kid," Anala said very seriously.

"Got it," Ryder said, in an equally serious tone, though it looked as if he was trying to suppress a smile. "Your sister reminds me of Roci," he told Rizo. Anala bounced ahead of them, towards Kyrie.

"Yeah," Rizo nodded.

"Here it is!" Anala gestured at a small hover near the ground that Kyrie jumped into with help from Ryder (which she grudgingly accepted) and hacked into the car. She lowered it quickly.

"Hop on!" She opened the door, and they all scrambled on. There wasn't enough seats for all of them, so Rizo and Nova remained standing. The hover rocketed forward, and Rizo and Nova fell into both Anala and Ryder.

"Sorry!" Rizo scrambled off Anala, while Ryder helped Nova up. Rizo clung to the side of the hover as it flew upwards. Kyrie stopped the hover at the entrance to the building and whispered, "Act normal and follow me." She climbed out of the hover and stood up sharply. Everyone followed her, exiting the car with the exact same stance. Kyrie walked forward and pressed a button marked VISITORS near the glass door.

"Welcome," a cold voice called from seemingly nowhere. "Please wait." Kyrie stood ramrod straight as she waited and motioned for the others to do the same. A Netrhaphalin soon appeared on a holographic screen that popped up from right underneath Kyrie. She took several steps back, forcing the others to do the same.

218

They were dangerously close to the edge of the platform that jutted out from the building. Rizo didn't dare look down at the drop that would certainly take them to the hospital.

"What is your business here?" The Netrhaphalin on screen asked.

"We have urgent news," Kyrie said. "Pertaining to a few things I think you are very interested in."

"At this time of night? What is it?" The Netrhaphalin asked.

"Who are you?" Kyrie countered.

"Inferior beings like you do not need to know my name," the Netrhaphalin said haughtily. "But for the record, I am Lume. Who are you?"

"Lila," Kyrie lied.

"Lila who?" Lume asked suspiciously.

"Lila Everett," Kyrie said. "May I come inside? This information is to be shared in a more secure room."

"No," Lume said sternly. "Wait. I must talk to my superior first. The screen went blank.   Lume reappeared a moment later with another Netrhaphalin by its side. "This is Beta." He turned to Beta. "These humans want to talk inside. They claim to have important information."

"I see." Beta glared at all of them. "We will see if you are telling the truth. Step on this scanner, please." Kyrie stepped forward and placed her hand on a sensor.

"Slightly raised heartbeat... could indicate lying... searching files for identification... why hasn't it found her yet? These scanners are getting slower every day," Beta grumbled. "WHAT? You- explain this." The sensor flashed red, and Kyrie withdrew her hand quickly with a yelp of pain. The sensor flashed to the results of her scan. In big red letters, the words IDENTITY NOT FOUND flashed across the screen. "Explain yourself!" Beta glared at Kyrie. "Or there will be consequences!"

Rizo shared a look of fear with Nova. If they were discovered, well, all Beta had to do was push them off the platform. That would be a pretty horrible way to die, or at least get severely hurt.

"I'm Lila Everett," Kyrie said in a steady voice. "I have identification. This has never happened before."

"Lila Everett," Beta muttered. "Lila Everett... two in this district! Photos... yes, yes, no, dark hair, no, shorter than this one...." Beta looked up sharply. "Are you from around here?" He asked Kyrie.

"No," she answered. "Look, by the time the system gets me right, they'll get away!"

"Who?" Beta asked, suddenly interested.

"I can't tell you here," Kyrie said. "Inside."

"You cannot enter without identification! Show me your card." Beta pointed to another scanner that had risen from a compartment on the ground.

"My card?" Kyrie asked.

"Yes, *your card*," Beta said menacingly.

"Okay!" Kyrie walked forward, and to Rizo's astonishment, pulled out a small disk and pressed it to the scanner. The scanner glowed green, and a cool voice said, "Identification accepted."

"Finally," Beta growled. "Now, for everyone else."

"Surely one identification is enough," Kyrie protested.

"It should be a simple process," Beta said. "Hands on the scanner. Now."

Rizo stepped forward and placed his hand on the scanner. After a few moments, the scanner flashed red and a searing pain flew through Rizo's hand. He jerked it back, and the pain receded.

"Ouch," he whispered. He massaged his hand, and Nova gave him a look of sympathy.

"YOU don't have a match either!" Beta growled. "Your card, please." Rizo glanced at Kyrie. He didn't have a card, and he had no idea how to get one. She mouthed something at him. *Sing it? No. Wing it. That's more likely, but I don't want to,* Rizo thought. He took a deep breath and glanced at Nova, who was looking at him expectantly.

"I lost my card," he lied. "Everyone except for Lila was going- um- canoeing and we got flipped over and we lost them. Lila is taking us to get some more- um- and she has information for you."

"We don't replace cards," Beta said curtly. "The supply station does that. Now go away."

"We *can* replace cards, though," Lume said helpfully.

"Yes, but it's not our job. Lume, go away. Mara needs help in the hover department."

"Yes, Beta," Lume glided off the screen. Beta looked ready to leave, so Kyrie stepped up her act.

"Can we please just get their cards here?" Kyrie asked. "The supply station is so far away."

222

"No," Beta said.

"Please?" Anala asked, putting on her lost-little-girl-face. "We'll be really quick."

"No!" The screen closed with a snap.

"Great," Kyrie growled. "Now what are we going to do?" Ryder stepped forward and started fiddling with the door, unnoticed my Kyrie, who was ranting under her breath. After a few grumbles along the lines of, 'lousy robots' and 'pesky sons of a slug' she looked up, fuming, and noticed Ryder near the door. "What are you doing?"

"Doing things the messy way." Ryder grinned. He pointed to some trash cans on the side of the platform and walked over to them. In minutes he had found a metal bar, which he took to the door. He gave it a ferocious whack. Nova cringed expectantly, and Anala grabbed Rizo's arm. Rizo prepared himself for the crash of metal hitting the glass door.

It didn't come. The metal rebounded, and Ryder stepped back, clearly confused.

"Force fields. It some of the 'new' technology humans are not allowed to have," Kyrie said when Ryder turned questioningly towards her. "Oh, shoot." Rizo looked at the door. Five Netrhaphalin were heading towards them. The door burst open with a crash.

"Run in!" Kyrie yelled. Rizo grabbed Anala and pulled her towards the door. Nova tried to run forward, but was caught by a Netrhaphalin. Ryder was already in the building, and Rizo threw Anala towards him, then picked up the forgotten metal bar and hit a Netrhaphalin with it. He made his way towards Nova, who was still struggling, and clubbed the Netrhaphalin holding her over the head. It spun around, and she ran towards the door. Rizo saw Kyrie fighting two Netrhaphalin at once near the edge of the platform, and he made his way to her. Ducking a few stray laser beams, he pushed forward. With a well-aimed swipe, he sent both reeling. Kyrie gave them both shoves that sent them over the platform.

"Thanks," she said. "Can I have that?" Rizo handed her the bar, knowing that she could probably use it better than he could. With a few swipes and fancy moves with the bar, Kyrie created a pathway to the door.

"Go!" She yelled. Rizo didn't need telling twice. He ran in and looked around wildly for the others. Kyrie caught up with him and surveyed the room. She headed down the hall, the metal bar at her side, and Rizo followed her. In an instant, hands pulled both Kyrie and Rizo into a small closet full of cleaning supplies.

"Ahhhh- oh." Rizo looked around. The closet was dark, and he had no idea who was who in the cramped area.

"What are you hiding for!" Kyrie whispered. "Let's go to the cubes!" Ryder glanced out of a peephole and pushed the door open.

"What did you do to those guys?" Ryder asked. "I don't see any Netrhaphalin anywhere."

"I shut them down," Kyrie said. "It's pretty hard to do, but there's a vulnerable spot in the back of their head. If you hit that hard enough, they freeze temporarily."

"Do I want to know how you know that?" Ryder asked.

"Probably not," Kyrie told him. "Anyway, do you know where the cubes are? I don't think there will be a sign saying, THIS WAY TO THE TELECUBES anywhere."

"Um, I was sort of hoping you would know where they were," Ryder said uneasily.

"Oh for goodness' sake! I don't know everything!" Suddenly, Kyrie stopped. She pulled Ryder back and whispered, "Two Netrhaphalin up ahead. Leave them to me." Rizo watched as Kyrie creeped up on the two Netrhaphalin, one who Rizo recognized as Beta, and clubbed them over the head with the metal bar she had been holding. Both of them froze, then crumpled.

"Come on," Kyrie said. She motioned them down the hall. Rizo crept along, trying to be as quiet as possible.

After a few minutes of wandering, Kyrie started to take more risks to find the telecubes. There was one very messy run in where the guards had almost set off the alarm, and another where Kyrie was almost captured.

Nova and Rizo were exchanging very worried looks after the third close call, and Rizo crept up to talk with Kyrie.

"Slow down," Rizo hissed at her. "They probably think we left, but if you take any more risks...."

"I know what I'm doing," Kyrie snapped back. "Don't distract me. Now shush." She shot him a look that meant he would be in big trouble if he didn't behave himself. Honestly, Kyrie was scary sometimes. Anala was right.

Rizo had no choice but to shut up and creep alongside Nova. After around fifteen minutes of searching and a few close calls, they finally found the telecube. Kyrie programmed it to deposit them a mile away from the supply station. They filed in, and Rizo was hit with a tingling sensation as he was dissolved and re-formed in a park filled with a lush greenery and fountains.

Kyrie had been the last to exit the station, so she was the last to exit the cube exit. There was a difference between exits and entrances; you could only go one way with a telecube. The Netrhaphalin who went to this park probably went back through the supply station's telecube. After all, it was only a mile away. The park was peaceful, and Rizo felt like he could stay there forever. However, he could feel his adrenaline, which had been surging through his body a few moments before, quickly drain out of him. Rizo suddenly realized how tired he was.

"We have to go to the supply station and see if they've gotten there yet," Kyrie said. "However, we've been up all night. We should get some rest. Ryder and I can go to the station, and you guys can stay here and find a good place to sleep."

"Got it," Nova said sleepily. She yawned. "I don't know about you, but I'm so tired."

"I'm not!" Anala was bouncing around on her tip toes. "It's so nice here! Come on, it's only one in the morning!"

"Exactly," Rizo said. "Let's go find some place to sleep. Good luck, you two." He nodded to Kyrie and Ryder, and they headed off into the night. Rizo stumbled towards a secluded area well hidden by bushes. He brushed some dead leaves off the grass and curled up, exhausted. Nova lay down a little ways away, and Anala fell asleep next to Rizo.

Rizo felt himself being swept away into a dreamless slumber.

Much too soon, he felt someone shaking him awake. Kyrie was standing over him, looking concerned. It was morning already; the sun was well over the horizon.

"What's up?" He asked groggily.

"Not much," Kyrie said.

"What's the news?" Rizo asked.

"Well," Ryder said. "The good news is that it seems like Mikaela and Krackers haven't gotten to the station yet. The bad news is that we are now the most wanted people in this district."

Waiting

Chapter 19

June 11, 2473

Rizo lay down again. After all he had been through, this was definitely not on the top of his Terrible Things That Keep Happening To Me list.

"What's the big deal?" He asked. "We can just hide until Mikaela and Krackers arrive."

"You don't understand," Kyrie said, somewhat exasperated. "I found this near the park fountain." She held up a holographic message that clearly pictured Rizo, Anala, Kyrie, Ryder, and Nova. Underneath that was a brief paragraph explaining that they were very dangerous and any sightings of them were to be reported immediately.

"They popped up overnight!" Rizo exclaimed. "No way! The Netrhaphalin are not *that* fast."

"Obviously, THEY ARE," Anala said. "Why is no one freaking out more? WE SHOULD be TERRIFIED. I mean, I AM."

"We *shouldn't* be terrified," Nova said practically. "That's what the Netrhaphalin want us to do. But if we keep our heads, then we can find a way out of this mess."

"Nova's right," Rizo said, smiling at her.

"Oh, side with her, why don't you," Anala said huffily. "You're only doing it because you're IN LOVE with her!"

"Anala!" Rizo glared at his sister. "I am not!"

"Right," Anala winked at him.

"Honestly! I feel like we've had this conversation a million times already!" Rizo said.

"Enough," Kyrie said, waving her hand dismissively. "We have bigger problems."

"Can't I just have a *little* fun?" Anala whined.

"You've already had it," Kyrie said sternly, though Rizo thought she looked amused. "Anyway, we have to be on the move. We aren't safe here."

Kyrie led them out of the small clearing and out of the park. "Don't act sneaky. Act like we have every right to be here. Then people won't take a second look at you," she advised.

"Kyrie," Ryder argued. "Our clothes are ripped, we have scrapes and bruises everywhere, and we look like we slept on the ground last night. Show me someone who doesn't notice that."

"Stop being unreasonable," Kyrie snapped. "And we did sleep on the ground last night."

"I'm not being unreasonable!" Ryder said. "And I'm stating the obvious!"

"Oh, stop it," Nova said, flapping her hands at them. "Can we just go five seconds without arguing with one another?"

"No one asked your opinion, little Miss Peacemaker," Kyrie snapped, infuriated. Nova's face fell, and she dropped to the back of the group, looking defeated. Anala, who had been watching with wide eyes, gave Nova a look filled with sympathy. Rizo dropped back with her, and she tried to wipe her eyes without him seeing.

"Don't mind Kyrie," he said. "She's just stressed, and Ryder put her over the edge." Nova shot him a look of disgust.

"You all are so mean!" Nova said, swiping at her eyes again. "Mikaela hates me for no reason-"

"Don't take it personally, Mikaela hates practically everyone," Rizo said consolingly.

"Kyrie thinks I'm a peace-loving airhead-" Nova continued furiously, as if she had not heard Rizo.

"No way, she's just annoyed right now," Rizo protested.

"Krackers is so stuck up he can't stick his nose in the air any higher-" Nova raged, wiping her eyes again.

"Well, he's actually nice when you get to know him," Rizo said, a little hopefully.

"And you keep on defending your friends! I guess I'm just the girl who tags along, after all. I thought you trusted me!" Nova rounded on Rizo, tears in her eyes.

"I do trust you, it's just-" Rizo started.

"You trust them more," Nova said in a strangled voice. "I know how these things work." She shot Rizo a look filled with fury and hurt, then stomped over to Anala, who put an arm around her comfortingly. Rizo actually stopped walking. What had he said to make Nova so angry? He really didn't get it. Girls were so weird sometimes.

Feeling disgruntled, he walked faster until he was next to Ryder.

"So that just happened," Ryder said in an undertone. "What did you say to make her so upset?"

"I was kind of hoping that you knew," Rizo admitted. "Is that... normal?"

"No, not at all!" Ryder said. "I've only seen her blow up like that once before, when she was a lot younger. But don't take it personally. She's probably just stressed, is all."

Rizo remembered saying the same thing about Kyrie, and now that he was hearing it, it did sound kind of lame.

"Well," he said slowly. "Do you think she'll ever talk to me again?"

"Probably," Ryder shrugged. "Nova is pretty forgiving. Just let it blow over."

"Should I apologize?" Rizo asked, worried.

"Why not?" Ryder asked.

"I mean, I don't want her to flip out again," Rizo said.

Ryder laughed. "Nova probably feels bad about that. Don't worry, she won't bite."

"Really?" Rizo asked, surprised. Mikaela had blown up only a few times, but when she did, she certainly did not feel bad about it.

"What, Kyrie and Mikaela are super unrepentant?" Ryder asked with a smile.

"Well, Mikaela, yes. I just met Kyrie, though, so I wouldn't really know," Rizo responded.

"You just met her?" Ryder's eyes widened. "I thought you knew her for forever!"

"No, really, she only showed up when we had to evacuate the tunnels," Rizo said. "Haven't I told you this before?"

"If you did, I didn't remember!" Ryder exclaimed. "Whoa. So nobody knows who she really is!"

"What do you mean?" Rizo asked.

"I mean, I thought Kyrie was pretty well known, she's Edward Duarte's *daughter*! But she's still some big mystery, even to you! You don't know what she ever did before you met her!" Ryder exclaimed.

"I still don't understand," Rizo said blankly.

"Oh right," Ryder nodded. "One of my favorite games that I played with Rocina and Nova is to wonder what the famous Dr. Duarte is doing. We used to come up with all these devious schemes. Kyrie and her brother were sort of evil villain adjacent."

"Dr. Duarte isn't that horrible!" Rizo protested.

"You didn't grow up in the Rockets," Ryder told him. "Calypso and Quamar -well, mainly Quamar- really painted him as downright evil."

"*That's* evil," Rizo said, appalled. "I mean, you guys didn't even meet Dr. Duarte!"

"I saw him once," Ryder said. "And he was pretty scary. In his defense, though, I was about eight."

"See?" Rizo said. "You were just a kid. Trust me, Dr. Duarte isn't that bad."

"Whatever you say," Ryder said. "Why don't you go apologize to Nova?"

Feeling as if Ryder had just changed the subject to stop them from arguing, Rizo walked backward towards Anala and Nova.

"Hi Nova," he said.

"Nice of you to notice me," Anala said in a huff.

Rizo ignored his sister. "Look, I'm really sorry about... all that."

"I'm sorry too," Nova sighed. "I shouldn't have blown up like that. You were just trying to be nice." She and Rizo smiled at each other.

"Over here!" Kyrie called from the front of the group, startling both of them. Nova and Rizo whipped their heads around and saw Kyrie pointing to a public restroom. They ran to catch up with her.

"In here," she hissed. They all waited as each of them relieved themselves and cleaned their clothes and hair. Rizo tried his best, but he only emerged looking as if he had fallen into a puddle. Kyrie gave him a disdainful look. Nova, however, came out looking like someone who was going to go to a party, in Rizo's opinion.

After they had finished washing themselves, Kyrie led them back to another secluded part of the park.

"Wait, we're going back?" Rizo asked.

"No, I just have to check something," Kyrie responded.

She made a beeline towards another hologram picturing them and studied it closely.

"They didn't put our names on here," she mused. "That's good."

"Why?" Rizo asked.

"Because then we can use our real names without getting caught," Kyrie said matter-of-factly. "Honestly, do you ever stop asking questions?"

"Yes!" Rizo said. "I've only asked two, really!"

"Whatever," Kyrie said. "Come on, we have to go to the supply station." She turned abruptly and made her way through the park. Rizo followed her silently. He was exhausted. He hadn't had much sleep that night, and he was betting he wouldn't have that much the next night, either.

"I'm so tired," he said with a yawn, to no one in particular.

"I am too," Nova agreed.

"So am I," Anala said. "WHY can't we just have a DECENT NIGHT'S REST for Gryffin's sake!"

"Keep your voice down!" Kyrie hissed from the front of the group.

"Sorry!" Anala whispered back. "I'm just being who I am!"

"Anala," Rizo said warningly.

"WHAT?" Anala asked. "OH MY GOODNESS who cares what I do?"

"I do," Rizo said.

"Well, I don't care that you care," Anala said. "I am going to be whoever I WANT to be, thank you very much."

"Guys, please don't argue," Nova pleaded.

"All right," Rizo said, a little reluctantly.

"Rizo and Nova, sitting in a-" Anala started.

"Anala. Please." Rizo glared at his sister.

"I'll just leave you to it!" Anala chirped in a sing-song voice. She skipped off in Ryder's direction, humming under her breath.

"Sorry about that," Rizo apologized to Nova awkwardly. "My sister is just..." he trailed off.

"Trying to be amusing," Nova finished for him.

"Something like that," Rizo said.

They walked in silence for a while, keeping an eye out for any Netrhaphalin and hoping that Kyrie knew what she was doing. Rizo didn't *doubt* Kyrie, it was more that he hoped that everything would go well. And that sort of depended on Kyrie's choices. Minutes ticked by, and as their trip to the station was fairly uneventful, Rizo began to relax. Maybe they weren't going to have any trouble after all.

"I can't wait to go home," he said to Nova. He missed his quiet, uncomplicated life in the tunnels.

"Me too," she whispered. "I hope my parents are okay. We didn't tell them what we were doing. They must be worried out of their minds."

"Oh," Rizo hadn't thought of that. They probably should have left Calypso and Quamar a note explaining where they had gone. "Don't worry," he told Nova. "I'm sure your parents will understand why you left."

"When I tell them," she said ruefully. "*If* I tell them."

"Don't worry," Rizo said again. "You'll see them soon."

"Hopefully," Nova said.

"No, you will!" Rizo looked straight at Nova. It was hard to think that he had just met her a few days ago, yet they had done so much together, survived so much together. "Trust me, you will."

"Okay." Nova took a deep breath. "I will."

"Good," Rizo told her. "Now don't forget. You will come out of this alive."

"Alive?" Nova asked. "What about unhurt?"

239

"Well- I-" Rizo stammered before he realized Nova was smiling.

"Come on," Rizo said. Kyrie was ducking into some landscaping up ahead, and Anala was close behind her. Rizo and Nova walked faster and joined them in their hiding place. A huge bush had a cramped space that they could just fit in. Kyrie was positioned so that she could see out of the bush without being seen. It was dark inside the small space, and everyone had trouble getting themselves into comfortable positions.

"We have to wait now," Kyrie said. "Mikaela and Krackers will probably come soon."

"How soon?" Anala whined. "I'm getting cramps already!"

"I don't know," Kyrie said irritably. "Ryder, stop stepping on my foot."

"Sorry," Ryder grunted. "I can't see where my feet are."

"Well, pay more attention!" Kyrie snapped.

"Ouch," Rizo hissed as someone pushed him into a tangle of sharp branches. "Watch it."

"Sorry!" Anala hissed back. "Ow!" Nova had accidentally stepped on her foot.

240

"I'm so sorry!" Nova whispered.

"Quiet everyone!" Kyrie said. "Netrhaphalin coming this way!"

They all fell silent and waited. Rizo held his breath.

"Okay," Kyrie said after a few long minutes. "It's gone."

Rizo shifted so that he could see out of the bush and bumped into Nova.

"Sorry," he muttered, shifting back into his original position.

"It's fine," Nova responded.

They sat there in the semi-darkness for hours. This period of time gave Rizo a lot of time to think. Possibly too much time. After replaying the last day and a half, Rizo's mind wandered to a scene where Anala left him and Nova alone for one second- No. He shouldn't think about that.

Rizo forced himself away from that thought and went back to fantasizing the days he had spent underground, without a care in the world. Well- not really. He had had other things to worry about. However, those things seemed like mere trifles compared to the worries he had now.

How long had it been since they had entered the bush? Surely not an hour. But wait- was the sun setting? No, it couldn't have been that long.

Rizo shook his head, trying to clear it. He should be getting some rest right now. Rizo shifted to a more comfortable position and tried to sleep.

At first, rest seemed impossible. Rizo felt like he should be awake, in case anything exciting happened.

However, after a few minutes, he dozed off. His dreams were plagued with images of the Netrhaphalin capturing them and were accented by blue-green eyes.

Rizo was dreaming of Anala shutting up for once when a light touch on his shoulder woke him up.

"What happened?" Rizo asked, straightening.

"Mikaela and Krackers," Nova whispered. Kyrie was emerging from the bush, and Ryder was crawling out after her. Rizo, Anala, and Nova filed out and turned to face Mikaela and Krackers. They both looked a bit worse for wear- but Rizo knew that he looked the same way.

"Mikaela," Kyrie said cautiously. "Krackers."

Meeting

Chapter 20

June 11, 2473

"You don't sound happy," Kyrie noted.

"I'm not thrilled," Mikaela replied.

"But you're not mad?" Kyrie asked.

"I'm not mad," Mikaela said.

"But?" Kyrie prompted her.

"This is going to be interesting," Mikaela said. "I'll cut straight to the point. Are you here to join us or stop us?"

"Join you," Kyrie said. "It was really uncool of you to leave us."

"Not to mention knocking out my mother," Ryder said, obviously still angry about that.

"I'm sorry about that," Mikaela said, without any empathy in her voice. "I didn't really want to do it. Rachel was just in the way."

"You didn't have to resort to drastic measures," Ryder pointed out.

"Do you really want to have this argument?" Mikaela sighed.

"Well, I don't *not* want to," Ryder said in a cold voice.

"Can we just go on with the plan now?" Krackers asked, rolling his eyes.

"Hush up," Mikaela snapped at him. "I want to ask these guys some questions first."

"Humph." Krackers flew off Mikaela's shoulder and perched on a tree branch. He began preening himself while sticking his beak in the air.

"What questions do you have for us?" Rizo asked.

"Well, for starters, how did you get here faster than us?" Mikaela asked.

"Telecubes," Kyrie replied coolly.

"Telecubes?" Mikaela raised an eyebrow. "How did you manage to get ahold of one?"

"We broke into a station and borrowed one," Kyrie said, as if this feat had been as easy as pie.

"Impressive," Mikaela said, with a hint of scorn in her voice. Rizo wondered if he was the only one who could hear the note of actual respect in that word. Judging by Kyrie's repressed smirk, Rizo thought that she must have heard it, too.

"Any other questions?" Kyrie asked.

"Yes, actually," Mikaela dipped her head slightly. Rizo couldn't believe how few words had been spoken between Kyrie and Mikaela, though they were obviously having a very different conversation under the polite one Rizo was hearing.

"Why is *she*-" Mikaela nodded at Nova. "here? I thought she would like to stay safe with her mother and father." Mikaela said this all in a light tone, though Nova still looked hurt.

"I can be useful, you know," Nova said in a slightly wavering voice. Mikaela waved this off with a flick of her hand.

"Anyway," Mikaela continued, as if Nova hadn't said a thing. "How long have you been waiting here?"

"Long enough." Kyrie glanced at Nova, who was obviously distressed. "And don't dress down Nova. She, unlike some people, has the sense to stick with her team. And she doesn't get angry over Every. Single. Thing."

"I understand this train of conversation, thank you very much," Mikaela said, in a colder voice than before.

"Well, I'm glad," Kyrie said. "You needed to."

"Excuse me?" Mikaela lifted an eyebrow. "I thought that *you* thought that the Rockets were useless."

"I did," Kyrie lifted her chin. "And some of them are. But Nova and Ryder are at least nice."

"And useful," Ryder interjected, sounding offended. Rizo glanced at Nova. She looked like she was hovering between gratitude and anger towards Kyrie.

"Well, that's good," Mikaela said, though she clearly didn't mean it.

"Mikaela, I think you need to learn something," Kyrie said with a sigh.

"What?" Mikaela demanded.

"You don't have to hate everyone," Kyrie said. Mikaela opened her mouth to protest, and Kyrie put out a hand to stop her. "No, you pretty much do. Don't deny it. But don't you see? If you always hate everyone, then

246

everyone will always hate you. And friends can be useful. Ryder helped us get into that station. And Nova helped us work together, as a team. Can't you see? You hate the Netrhaphalin, and that's why you're trying to take them down. But if everyone hates you, then they'll try to take you down. Please, Mikaela. Would it hurt you to hear someone out for once?"

"I hear people out when they have something worth hearing," Mikaela growled.

"That's not the same thing," Kyrie said.

"I didn't hate you," Mikaela looked at Kyrie. "I thought you could understand me. But you don't."

"I do," Kyrie said quietly. "But before I tell you why, let's get into a more private space. Then we're not at so much risk."

"All right," Mikaela growled. She walked quickly towards a small building on the side of the station. She tugged the door open, and everyone went inside. The building was obviously an abandoned storage unit. It was dark inside, and smelled like smoke. Krackers began coughing.

"Now, what were you going to say?" Mikaela asked.

"I said, I understand," Kyrie said. "I told you that my mother died because we couldn't get medical care for her. What I didn't tell you was that my mother didn't only get radiation through her work- she always wore protective equipment- mom also got it through one of her many close calls with the Netrhaphalin. She was one of our spies who would venture out into the world to collect supplies. A few times, she was caught. After the third time, the Netrhaphalin tried to kill her using a radiation technique. She escaped, but she was never the same. She died a month later."

Rizo looked at Kyrie, and saw that her face was bent, no doubt concealing the distress on her face. How horrible that must have been, to see the destruction and cruelty of the Netrhaphalin first hand.

"I see," Mikaela said. She actually sounded a bit sorry for Kyrie, if that was possible. "You *do* understand- a little."

"We all understand, to some degree," Kyrie said gently. "Can't we be friends? Please don't hate us."

"I'll try to be polite," Mikaela said, slightly harshly. "But only if you give me reasons to."

"Mikaela," Kyrie said warningly. When Mikaela glared at her defiantly, Kyrie sighed. "I guess that's the best I can do. Now let's go steal some explosives."

"Wait, you're actually going to help me?" Mikaela asked, somewhat sarcastically.

"Of course," Kyrie said calmly. "I wouldn't lie."

"So how are we going to do this?" Rizo asked.

"You and Anala put up a fuss," Kyrie said. "Mikaela and I will go in. Nova and Ryder, stay here. That way if we get caught, you can come try to rescue us."

"You're putting our potential rescue in the hands of *Rockets*?" Mikaela asked disbelievingly.

"They are useful," Kyrie said. "Put the lazy, peace-loving stereotype away."

"Well, that stereotype is accurate for some people," Mikaela argued back.

"I know, but still," Kyrie said sternly. "You said you'd try."

"Oh, fine," Mikaela said. "I'll try."

"Good," Kyrie nodded approvingly. "Let's go. Rizo and Anala, make a huge distraction and don't stop until we come and rescue you."

"Will that be, um, necessary?" Rizo asked. "The... rescuing part?"

"Probably," Krackers said. "By the way, you haven't told me what I'm going to do during all this."

"Stay with Ryder and Nova," Mikaela suggested. "The more competent rescue people and parrots, the better."

"Oh, fine." Krackers flew into the corner of the storages unit with a few grumbles as Ryder protested, "We *are* competent, you'll see!"

"Rizo and Anala, go for it," Kyrie said.

"Wait- what?" Rizo asked. "What are we supposed to do?"

"Anala can figure that out," Mikaela said with a shrug. "She's pretty good at making a fuss."

"Rizo, you heard her, LET'S GO!" Anala tugged on Rizo's arm.

"Um, okay." Rizo glanced at Nova.

"Good luck," she whispered.

"Thanks," Rizo whispered back.

"COME ON!" Anala pulled Rizo quietly out of the storage unit, then walked until the station was a few buildings away.

"EVERYONE! LISTEN UP!" Anala yelled. "I NEED TO TELL YOU SOMETHING!" A few heads popped out of windows, looking for the source of all the yelling.

"YEAH! LISTEN TO ME!" Anala yelled. "THERE IS SOMETHING I WANT TO TELL YOU! YES, YOU! GATHER AROUND, EVERYONE!" Rizo covered his ears. His sister was really quite loud. Now more people (and Netrhaphalin) were trying to see what the fuss was all about.

"I KNOW SOMETHING THAT YOU WILL REALLY WANT TO KNOW!" Anala shouted.

"Stop yelling at once, or you will be accused of breaking the law," a Netrhaphalin called from the supply station.

"I DIDN'T KNOW THAT I WAS BREAKING THE LAW," Anala yelled back.

"Well, now you do," the Netrhaphalin said.

"WELL, I DON'T CARE," Anala shouted. "YOU ARE JUST A LOUSY ROBOT!"

"You did not just say that!" The Netrhaphalin flew towards them, furious.

"YES I DID!" Anala yelled. "What's your name anyway?"

251

"Excuse me?" The Netrhaphalin looked momentarily taken aback.

"WHAT'S YOUR NAME?" Anala yelled.

"I am Amil," the Netrhaphalin said with great dignity.

"OH, YOU HEARD ME," Anala said. "I HEARD A RUMOR THAT ROBOTS DON'T HEAR VERY WELL. I HEARD THAT THEY HAD TO HAVE HEARING AIDS."

"Excuse me!" Amil seemed scandalized. "Where did you hear that?"

"SOMEWHERE," Anala said, waving her hand airily. "MONKEYS AND BANANAS."

"Are you crazy?" Amil asked, now looking a bit confused.

"Yes," Rizo said, taking advantage of the situation. "My sister was hit on the head very recently, and I tried to take her to the nearest Netrhaphalin station. Needless to say, she has been very... funny and refuses to go in."

"Let me call a few more Netrhaphalin," Amil said. "That way we can deal with your sister."

"DO NOT DEAL WITH ME, YOU STINKY HORRIBLE HUNK OF JUNK!" Anala screamed hysterically. By now, Anala had attracted quite a crowd of onlookers.

"I DON'T WWWAAAANNNNTTTTT TO GO! DON'T MMMMMAAAAAAKKKKKKEEEE ME!" Anala howled.

A few more Netrhaphalin arrived on the scene.

"I am Peto," one of them said. "I am in the Department of Information. What is your sister's name?" Peto looked at Rizo expectantly.

"Anna," Rizo lied. "ANNA," he repeated more loudly. Anala caught his eye and nodded slightly. She understood that she had another name now.

"Anna who?" Peto asked.

"Anna FREEMAN," Rizo said loudly. Anala nodded again.

"Coming through! Coming through!" Five more Netrhaphalin were making their way towards Anala, who was yelling something about hyenas. The Netrhaphalin were now trying to load her on to a stretcher, and she was putting up a fight, now screaming about aliens. She kicked at them and tried to run away, yelling.

"We need back up!" One of the Netrhaphalin yelled. "She's a danger to society!"

"On it," Peto said. He pulled out a NETLINK and called someone on it. "This is Peto. Requesting a backup squad. Thanks, bye."

Three more Netrhaphalin shot out of the supply station. Anala put up more of a fuss, hitting onlookers and Netrhaphalin alike. The backup squad hovered above, looking for a place to land.

Anala started throwing rocks at the Netrhaphalin. One hit an onlooker, and Peto raced to their side, desperately trying to keep the damage to a minimum. The person collapsed into Peto, and he tried to prop them up and failed.

Anala was throwing rocks at the backup squad in the sky, and one of them had collapsed. Peto pulled out his NETLINK again, looking disgusted at his co-workers' performance. "All Netrhaphalin, report to disruption scene immediately. I repeat, immediately." Ten Netrhaphalin soared out of the building and joined the action. Rizo glanced over to the storage unit. He hoped that Mikaela and Kyrie would go in soon. As far as he knew, the station was empty.

A few moments later, two figures entered the building, unseen by anyone except Rizo. He caught Anala's eye and signaled for her to keep going. She amped up her performance, yelling and screaming and throwing things.

The Netrhaphalin were getting to her, however. Rizo shot a worried glance at the supply station. Mikaela and Kyrie had better hurry up or risk getting caught.

A few minutes passed. The Netrhaphalin had been refraining from using lasers because they thought that Anala was out of her mind. However, they were getting a bit edgy as Anala put some of them out of commission. Rizo really hoped that Mikaela and Kyrie would just hurry up. He didn't want to see Anala get hurt.

A Netrhaphalin came up to him, looking a bit battered and stressed.

"You her brother?" It asked, jerking its head in the direction of Anala.

"Yes," Rizo answered evenly. "I was already questioned by Peto, you know, the one in the department of-"

"Yes, yes, I know," the Netrhaphalin growled. "He needs to be rebooted. He got collapsed, and he crushed his NETLINK. I have to question you again."

"Oh, all right," Rizo said, panicking inwardly. What if he forgot what he had said to Peto? If there was some record of what he had said somewhere, then he would be in big trouble. "What's your name?"

"Why do you need to know?" the Netrhaphalin asked suspiciously.

"No reason, no reason," Rizo said quickly. He felt it necessary to know because if he was ever questioned by yet another Netrhaphalin, he could say that he had told everything to this one, in hopes that he need not repeat his story again, thus giving him less chances to mess everything up.

"Well, it's Rerl," the Netrhaphalin said proudly. It seemed like all the Netrhaphalin took much pride in their names, as if it made them even more superior to everyone else. Rizo wondered why this was.

Rizo glanced nervously back at the supply station. There was still no sign of Mikaela and Kyrie. He turned back to Rerl.

"So, were you going to ask me any questions?" Rizo asked.

"Why, yes," Rerl said. He looked nervous himself. "What is your sister's name?"

"Uh," Rizo said, trying to recall what he had said before. "Anna. Anna Freeman."

"Anna...." Rerl said thoughtfully. "Hey, Jami!" He called to another Netrhaphalin. "What's the protocol for all information?"

"You don't know?" A Netrhaphalin, whom Rizo assumed was Jami, called back. "Honestly, who put a rookie just out of training in an important job?"

"Quia did!" Rerl called back.

"Quia is a rookie itself!" Jami exploded, making his way over to Rerl. "Why did you take orders from it? It's just one letter up from you!"

"Exactly!" Rerl said. "Quia is higher than I am, so I thought that-"

"Well, you thought wrong!" Jami said. "Get up in the air, you, now!"

Rerl flew up, looking disgruntled. Rizo was bewildered. He had no idea what 'one letter up' was supposed to mean. He glanced back at the station. He still didn't see Mikaela and Kyrie. However, something made him take a closer look. The front door opened, and both of them emerged, clutching huge objects.

Good, Rizo thought. *They did it. Now all we have to do is get out of this mess.*

Inter-Robot Miscommunication

Chapter 21

June 11, 2473

Rizo glanced back at Anala. She was in full hysterics, sobbing about lions, jaguars, and sharks, all of which were extinct. He glanced back at Mikaela and Kyrie. They were still making their way towards the storage unit. He and Anala were going to have to wait it out until they could come and rescue them. Rizo was actually surprised that Anala had been able to draw all the Netrhaphalin out of the station *and* keep them focused on her. Although, if they were all like Rerl, it was definitely possible. Rerl was the least competent Netrhaphalin Rizo had ever come across.

Rizo turned back to the chaos. Jami was shouting orders while Rerl and a few others flew around in a craze, shooting a few laser beams into the fray.

"I told you!" Jami bellowed. "DO NOT shoot lasers into the disruption! You already hit Luda!"

"Just trying to help!" Rerl exclaimed. "Honestly, Jami!"

"Shut your mouth," Jami said scathingly. "Good-for-nothing lousy robot."

"Excuse me!" Rerl glared at Jami. "Take that back!"

"Calm down!" Jami instructed him. "If you can't take an insult well-"

"That was beyond insulting!" Rerl said. "Admit it!"

Following Rerl's and Jami's exchange, Rizo gathered that calling a Netrhaphalin a 'robot' was a very insulting thing to them.

"Go away," Jami said, angry. "Go back to the station *now.*"

"Humph." Rerl flew off, obviously furious.

"Quia! Follow Rerl! You too, Qsio! And you, Rube! All rookies clear out! Leave this to the professionals!" Jami called.

With a few grumbles, five Netrhaphalin flew back towards the station. Mikaela and Kyrie had made it out just in time. Even though they were inexperienced, Rizo had a feeling that Rerl and the others were still dangerous.

"Circle the target!" Jami yelled. "Some of you, keep the crowd back!"

The Netrhaphalin did as they were told, pushing the observers away and cornering Anala at the same time.

"Ana- Anna!" Rizo called, almost forgetting to call his sister by her alias.

"Help!" Anala shrieked. The Netrhaphalin were closing in on her. "HELP! Please, no, don't, PLEASE!"

Anala sounded desperate. Rizo could no longer see her, as she was surrounded by a mass of metal bodies.

"Don't hurt her," an observing mother pleaded, clutching her own daughter.

The Netrhaphalin ignored everyone. Anala's screams grew louder, more desperate. "PLEASE! NO! PLEASE! I DON'T-" Her cries abruptly stopped as Rizo caught a glimpse of blue light. Rizo watched in horror as the Netrhaphalin parted, revealing his sister, crumpled on the pavement, either unconscious or... Rizo didn't want to think about it.

"NO!" He looked at the nearest Netrhaphalin, who happened to be Jami. "What have you done to her? *What have you done?*"

"She's only stunned," Jami said calmly, with superiority in its voice. "We have different settings on our lasers, you know. Or maybe you don't. Humans are so small-minded."

"Is she hurt?" Rizo asked, ignoring Jami's dig at humans.

"I do not know," Jami said, in a maddeningly calm voice. "I have never been stunned. I do not think I ever will be, for that matter."

"Will she be alright?" Rizo asked, struggling to keep his voice steady. How could this insufferable robot act this way? Netrhaphalin were really horrible. They had no feeling, no conscience. How could they just act like nothing had happened?

Rizo glanced at his sister on the ground and felt like throwing up. Her face was twisted in agony, as if the blue laser had been a dagger. The Netrhaphalin were dragging her into a hover nearby. Anala's head rolled listlessly from side to side.

"Please, can I just see my sister," Rizo asked beseechingly.

"Let the boy through," Jami said commandingly. Rizo bent down and examined Anala. She had cuts and bruises all over her body. Her hair, matted and dirty, trailed across the street. He checked her pulse. It was weak and feeble.

"I'm so sorry," Rizo said. "I shouldn't have let them hurt you like this."

Anala did not even stir. If Rizo hadn't just felt his sister's pulse, he would have thought she was dead.

"Move aside," Jami said curtly. "Your visiting time is over."

"But-" Rizo started.

"Move," Jami instructed him. Rizo looked up miserably. He was not letting *them* take his sister away. Rizo was about to look back at his sister when he saw something that made him keep his head up. Kyrie and Mikaela were approaching stealthily, with Krackers flying silently behind them. Nova and Ryder were following them- Ryder seemed excited, while Nova looked worried.

Kyrie held up her hand, and all of them stopped. Krackers hovering right behind Jami.

"I won't step aside," Rizo said defiantly, pulling Anala away.

"Just you wait, boy," Jami growled. "I'll-" But what Jami was going to do, Rizo never found out, for Kyrie yelled, "NOW!" and attacked Jami, hitting him on the head with a rusty metal bat that she had probably found in the storage unit. Jami promptly collapsed, his body falling into a limp mass of limbs. Rizo dragged Anala out of the way of the fight that exploded, with Mikaela, Krackers, Ryder, and Kyrie de- mobilizing as many Netrhaphalin as they could. Nova helped Rizo half-drag, half-carry Anala out of the fray and towards a few trees well out of the Netrhaphalin's sight. Rizo gave Nova a grateful smile.

"Thanks," he said, shifting Anala into a more comfortable position.

"What did they do to her?" Nova asked, staring, horrified, at the pained expression on Anala's face.

"Stunned her," Rizo replied. "Do we have any access to water? It would help Anala...." He trailed off as Nova shook her head.

"Should we help them?" Nova asked, jerking her head to indicate the others.

"I think they'll be fine," Rizo said, lying down in the grass. "I'm exhausted."

"I was so worried when you all were out there," Nova said, looking at Anala.

"I was worried, too, for Anala," Rizo said. He and Nova were quiet for a minute. A scream broke the silence. Rizo sat up and looked at Nova. Her face mirrored the panic in his.

"I'll go," Rizo said, jumping to his feet. "You stay with Anala."

"No, I'll go," Nova said. "You've been through so much already."

"No! Stay with my sister!" Rizo said harshly. "Look, if you go, I'll go too, and then no one will be with Anala."

"You *wouldn't*," Nova breathed, fire in her eyes. "I can't believe you don't care about your sister!"

"I do care, but- okay, really, they need help, just stay here!" Rizo ran off. He knew Nova wouldn't leave Anala, no matter what.

When he saw what their situation was, he was shocked to find that it had escalated so quickly- and not in their favor, either. Mikaela was on the ground, apparently stunned- or worse, and Kyrie and Ryder were cornered. Krackers was holding off five Netrhaphalin, drawing them away from the others. Rizo watched as a laser narrowly missed him.

He turned, and saw Kyrie and Ryder dodging blue lasers, which were being fired everywhere. The metal bat, which Kyrie had used when she had first came on the scene, lay deserted on the street. Rizo picked it up and crept towards the nearest Netrhaphalin. He slammed it into the back of its head, and it crumpled. He hit another one in the same place, and it too, collapsed. Three more Netrhaphalin were still tormenting Kyrie and Ryder. Rizo tried to hit one of them, but it dodged out of the way and grabbed the bat. Rizo tugged the bat back towards him. The Netrhaphalin pulled back. When Rizo didn't let go, it flew upwards, trying to drag the bat away from Rizo.

Rizo clung to the bat for dear life. Slowly, the Netrhaphalin rose upwards, determined to stop Rizo. Rizo was lifted off the ground. Kyrie overpowered the Netrhaphalin she had been fighting and it crumpled to

the ground. She made short work of the one who had
been shooting lasers at Ryder, then turned to Rizo, who
was now a good distance from the ground.

He didn't know why he was holding on to the bat.
He didn't know why he hadn't released it when the
Netrhaphalin had tried to pry it out of his grasp. Perhaps
he had thought that the Netrhaphalin would use it
against him. Whatever the case, he couldn't let go now.
He was more than ten meters high at the moment, the
drop would certainly hurt him.

"Kyrie!" Rizo called. "Help!"

"Don't worry!" Kyrie called back. "I'm coming!
Ryder! Take Mikaela to safety, over to Nova, then come
back and help Krackers!"

"On it!" Ryder replied. He carried Mikaela away,
towards where Anala and Nova were. Kyrie grabbed an
arm from one of the crumpled Netrhaphalin nearby and
threw it up. Narrowly missing Rizo, it hit the Netrhaphalin
holding him in the eye. The Netrhaphalin dropped out of
the sky, hissing curses, then steadied itself. Rizo was now
dangling two meters off the ground. Kyrie threw another
metal limb she had picked up from the ground. This time,
the Netrhaphalin swerved out of the way.

"Jump!" Kyrie called to Rizo. "You won't get any lower!"

The Netrhaphalin expanded suddenly and grabbed Rizo's arm. Rizo kicked at the Netrhaphalin fruitlessly. He thrashed around, trying to get the Netrhaphalin to let go.

Kyrie tossed another limb at the Netrhaphalin. Rather than dodge the projectile, the Netrhaphalin shot a red laser beam at it, and the leg crumbled to dust. Kyrie threw two more metal body parts at it. One exploded under the Netrhaphalin's deadly stare, but one hit its target. The Netrhaphalin loosened its grip on Rizo's arm. With one last jerk of his hand, Rizo broke free from the Netrhaphalin. The ground came ever closer, and Rizo's descent ended with a sickening crunch and a groan. It was a few seconds before Rizo realized that he was the one groaning. He had landed on his hands and knees, and his wrist was aching horribly. Bolts of pain shot through his body, and he collapsed, breathing heavily.

After a few long seconds on the ground, he chanced a look up at the Netrhaphalin. It was shooting red laser beams at Kyrie, who was dodging them expertly. Krackers and Ryder were running (and flying) towards her, concerned.

"Get back!" Kyrie yelled at them. "The red lasers are fatal!" Ryder stopped in his tracks, but Krackers flew forward, striking the Netrhaphalin on the back of his head. It dropped out of the air for a moment, then righted itself and turned on Krackers. Krackers flew upwards and away, circling high above the Netrhaphalin, out of reach of its lasers. The Netrhaphalin, torn between going after Krackers or Kyrie, hovered in midair indecisively.

Ryder took advantage of the situation to chuck some debris at the Netrhaphalin, missing by a couple of centimeters. This still provided a good distraction, however. As the Netrhaphalin whirled around to face its new attacker, Kyrie lobbed a metal limb at it. It crumpled and fell out of the air with a loud crash.

Immediately, Kyrie and Ryder ran towards Rizo, who was clutching his wrist. During the final fight, Rizo had been forcing himself to ignore the pain shooting through his wrist up through his arm. However, now that the fight was over, the pain came back, stronger than before.

"I- I think it's broken," Rizo gasped, holding up his injured arm. Kyrie inspected his wrist.

"It doesn't look good," she agreed. "Let's get you to a safer spot. I daresay we'll have a ton of these pesky robots on our trail if we don't get to a shelter soon."

"Did you get the explosives?" Rizo croaked. He didn't want to hear that after all that had happened, the mission had been unsuccessful.

"Yes," Kyrie said firmly. "But the important thing right now is to get you patched up. Ryder, can you give me a hand?" Ryder helped Rizo to his feet, and they both made their way over to where Nova and Anala were.

"What happened?" Nova asked frantically when she noticed Rizo wincing and supporting his injured hand. "Why is Rizo hurt?"

"I fell," Rizo told her between grimaces. "Don't-worry- about- it." He lay down on the grass and closed his eyes.

"What happened?" Nova demanded, turning to Ryder. "Tell me!"

"It's a long story," Ryder said wearily. "But we're pretty sure that Rizo broke his wrist."

"Oh dear," Nova said. "how did it happen?"

"It's a long story," Ryder repeated. "We don't have time right now. We have to get to safety. How are Anala and Mikaela?"

"Still stunned," Nova reported. "I don't know when they'll wake up. It could be hours. And you, Kyrie, and I are the only ones who can really transport them. I don't think Krackers can carry much- besides, we need him for defense- and Rizo's in no position to carry anything."

"Sorry, what?" Kyrie had just arrived, with Krackers behind her. "I didn't catch all that. How are Mikaela and Anala?"

"They're still stunned," Nova sighed, a bit exasperated. "Nothing new."

"We have to move," Kyrie said. "I'll take Anala, Ryder, you take Mikaela. Nova, help Rizo get along. And Krackers, you scout ahead and behind for us," Kyrie finished.

"On it," Ryder said as Krackers wordlessly soared into the air. Ryder hefted Mikaela's limp body off the ground, and Kyrie did the same to Anala. Nova helped Rizo up. Rizo hadn't even noticed that his leg hurt until he put weight on to it.

"Ow," he gasped as he collapsed onto the ground. Now that he peered closer, he could see that his ankle was swollen. "It's my ankle," he told Nova. "It doesn't hurt *that* much." Rizo tried to put on a brave, just-shake-it-off face, but he couldn't help grimacing as he stood again. Nova supported him, and he limped behind Kyrie and Ryder.

"Guys, you may not have noticed, but we look really suspicious right now," Krackers informed them as he swooped down. "No Netrhaphalin are following us, but two of you are carrying unconscious people and Rizo looks like he's been in a hover crash." Rizo stiffened at these words.

"Don't say that," he growled.

"Oh, sorry," Krackers said indifferently. "Didn't your parents die in a hover crash?"

"Yes." Rizo gritted his teeth. "Now go away." He didn't want to think about his parents right now. He had enough to deal with already.

"Well, that's nice," Krackers said, flying off.

"No arguing, please," Kyrie said in a weary voice. "We have to get to some shelter soon. It's pretty late."

"I know where to go," Ryder said quietly. "Follow me." He called Krackers down and told him something, then resumed walking deliberately between streets.

Rizo glanced at the sky. It was a dusky gray-pink and purple, a gorgeous sunset that didn't match their situation at all.

After a while, the sky was a red-black, streaked with light pollution and scattered with a few dim stars. They still hadn't found a shelter, and both Kyrie and Ryder were exhausted.

"You do know where we're going, don't you," Rizo wondered after what felt like hours of trudging through deserted streets and dark alleyways.

"Yes," Ryder assured him. "Nova should know where we're going. It shouldn't be long now."

"Me?" Nova seemed confused. Then her mouth dropped open. "Ryder! What are you thinking? We can't go there!"

"Where?" Rizo asked. "I don't know what you're talking about!"

"Riva isn't there anymore! You won't be able to get inside!" Nova said. "Plus, Dr. Nikita knows that Riva is with the Rockets!"

"We have to try," Ryder said. "and I can get in. Riva programmed my hand into the scanner the last time I was there."

"I still think this is a bad idea," Nova said crossly. "There's too much risk."

"Nova, tell me one thing we did today that *wasn't* risky," Ryder said.

Nova opened and closed her mouth. "Fine," she relented. "I get your point."

"Good." Ryder didn't say anymore.

"What are you talking about?" Rizo asked. "I don't understand."

"A safe house," Nova explained. "Riva lived there, but now she doesn't. It's downright reckless to go to it."

"How much farther do we have to go?" Rizo asked. Risky or not, the safe house sounded amazing. They would get a bed to sleep on, food and water to feast on- Rizo couldn't wait to get there.

"We're a few blocks away," Nova said. "Honestly, what is Ryder thinking? What if we get ambushed?"

"Calm down," Rizo said. "I bet we'll be fine."

"Humph." Nova crossed her arms, and Rizo winced as he had to put weight on his injured ankle.

"A little help here?" He asked. Nova supported him with a tiny huff of annoyance.

"It's not much farther," Ryder told them after a few minutes of silence.

"Thank goodness," Kyrie said. "My arms are about to fall off."

"Hey, mine are too!" Ryder said.

"I'm sorry," Rizo croaked. "I would help except-" he gestured to his ankle and wrist.

"No, you need to rest," Kyrie said. "You helped us a lot today."

"All right, here it is," Ryder said. He looked up at a house ten meters in the air. Ryder then placed his hand on a panel. A platform emerged that Ryder gestured for them to stand on. It rose slowly, until it was level with the house. They exited the platform, and it descended and sank back into the ground. Ryder then unlocked the door with his hand. As the door swung open, Rizo caught a glimpse of a kitchen and a living room beyond it. Ryder clapped, and the lights turned on, revealing a cozy house with two windows pointing out towards the street. Kyrie and Ryder lay Mikaela and Anala on nearby couches and went into the kitchen, looking for something to eat. Rizo sank onto a couch beside his sister and leaned back with a sigh.

They were safe.

For now.

Stunned

Chapter 22

June 12, 2473

    Rizo woke up on the couch, his ankle and wrist throbbing. A glance at the windows told him that it was morning already. His stomach was growling. He hadn't had much to eat for days, and he was starving. Anala and Mikaela were still lying on the couches, blissfully unaware of what had happened.

    Rizo winced as he put weight on his foot.

    "Ow," he groaned.

    "Let's get you all fixed up, shall we?" Ryder entered the room with a cup full of a steaming drink and braces for Rizo's wrist and ankle.

"Found these in a drawer," Ryder said, holding up the braces. "And these, too." He pulled out a few cold compresses and handed them to Rizo, who immediately applied them on to his injuries. "Hungry?" Ryder asked. When Rizo nodded, Ryder set down the braces and went to the kitchen. He came back with a freshly baked scone.

"Kyrie just cooked these up," he explained. "All the fresh stuff was rotten, so she found some canned dough and made these. They're amazing. She and Nova are in the dining room."

Rizo hurriedly put on the ankle and wrist braces and made his way over to the dining room, taking the scone from Ryder in the process. He bit into it. Ryder was right. They were amazing. However, Rizo was so hungry that he thought that even stale bread would taste great.

He glanced around the room. Like the rest of the house, it was special in that it was somewhat anti-Netrhaphalin, not to mention a bit shady. A *Mars Mission* poster was hanging on the wall, and a *We Want Freedom* poster was hanging on another. Both had hologram masks that could make them look acceptable to Netrhaphalin who stopped by for a courtesy look-over.

"Hey, Rizo!" Kyrie called from behind a mountain of scones and a jar of jam.

"Hi," Rizo replied, sitting down on a chair. "The scones are amazing."

"Thanks!" Kyrie said brightly.

"Yeah," Ryder agreed. "How did you even know how to make them? I thought no one knew how to cook anymore."

"We didn't have robots to cook for us underground!" Kyrie laughed. "Dad always said it was too risky. Which was ironic, because he also brought a modified Netrhaphalin underground with us, so...." Kyrie shrugged.

"Ryder, seriously," Nova said. "We didn't have cooking robots either! Where have you thought all your food came from all this time?"

"Oh." Ryder's ears turned red. "Uh... magic? I mean, food just sort of... appeared!"

"Ryder!" Nova scolded. "Come on! You never even thought that we were supplying you with food every day?"

"I never really thought about it," Ryder said defensively. "It was an honest mistake, guys! Anyone could have thought that!"

Nova rolled her eyes. "Yeah, right," she said sarcastically.

They all laughed at how flustered Ryder was. Rizo couldn't remember ever being this cheerful.

"What time is it?" He asked.

"Ten o' clock," Kyrie replied promptly.

"Wow, I'm *still* tired," Rizo yawned. "How are Anala and Mikaela?"

"Stunned," Kyrie reported. "I don't know how we'll get them out of it. I thought they would be awake by now." She frowned. Instantly, a feeling of gloom replaced all the happiness in the room. Rizo regretted bringing Anala and Mikaela up, but he had wanted to know how his sister was and what he could do for her. Another thought occurred to him.

"Where's Krackers?" He asked.

"Outside, cleaning out the bird feeder," Ryder smirked. "He wanted us to take the birdseed out of the feeder for him, but we refused."

Rizo peeked out of the window and saw an indignant- looking Krackers trying to eat in a dignified way. He stifled a laugh.

"I know, it's hilarious," Nova giggled, then abruptly stopped. "Um, what are we going to do now that we're pretty safe?"

Rizo looked at Nova curiously. Why had she changed the subject so quickly?

"I'm not sure," Kyrie said. "Before we do anything, we should find a way to wake Anala and Mikaela up." A thoughtful silence descended upon the group. Rizo was the first to break it.

"Kyrie," Rizo started. He had an important question that he hadn't had time to ask before. "How did you have an identification card?"

"Oh, that," Kyrie smiled wistfully. "My dad always ensured that Jared and I had a card with an alias to keep us safe in situations like that."

"He didn't give *us* cards," Rizo said.

"He wasn't planning to take you outside for a while," Kyrie said. "And you did have ID cards, just he burned them because they were dead giveaways to the

Gryffins. Everyone knew you guys had been taken, and everyone was trying to track you for a long time."

"But *you* did go outside?" Nova asked curiously.

"A few times," Kyrie shrugged. "Once my mom...died, Dad wouldn't let us outside for the longest time, unless it was absolutely necessary. But he thought he had time until he had to get cards for all of you. Obviously, he was wrong."

"How come we never saw you until we were detected?" Rizo wondered.

"I was busy," Kyrie said simply. "When Mom died, I had to take over for her, and Jared was doing a lot of covert operations outside. You were Dad's responsibility, not ours. We had more on our minds."

"Huh," was all that Rizo could say. He couldn't believe that Dr. Duarte had been planning to keep them cooped up in there for so long. Yes, the Netrhaphalin were ruthless and cruel, but Rizo knew he would have gone mad if he had had to stay underground for too long.

"Dr. Duarte always sounds so creepy," Nova shivered.

"He is not!" Kyrie snapped, fire in her eyes. "You barely even know him. I'm his daughter, hello? Who knows him better? Me, not you! Don't talk about things you don't understand. Especially Dad. That goes for you, too." She glared at Ryder, who put his hands in the air, trying to look harmless.

"Sorry, sorry," Nova mumbled, looking down. "You're right."

"Go easy on her, will you?" Rizo asked.

Kyrie shot him a glare. "Don't start something you'll regret," she growled.

"Fine," Rizo relented. "But don't be a Mikaela about it."

"What's that supposed to mean?" Krackers asked. His feathers looked distinctly disheveled, although his haughty stare was the same as ever.

"Nothing," Rizo said quickly. If Krackers told Mikaela what he had said, she would be on a warpath.

"Really..." Krackers said questioningly. "Nothing. I... see." Krackers' tone indicated that he knew exactly what Rizo had meant and that he was planning to tell on him.

"Anyway," Rizo said, eager to change the topic of discussion. "Can we have a plan for *once*? After all, the next part of the mission is the most crucial and dangerous part. Have you realized we actually have to *blow something up*?"

"Plans haven't worked very well," Kyrie pointed out. "We've been through this."

"I *know*," Rizo said. "But still. I'd feel more secure."

"Well, that's kind of the least of our problems," Ryder said, shrugging in an easygoing yet apologetic manner. "Not that I have a say in the whole mission. Though I wish that *someone*, ahem, *ahem*, would let me talk about at least *some* of my ideas, because they're *actually* very good."

"I've gotten the gist of this conversation, thank you very much," Kyrie said with a sigh.

"Well?" Ryder looked at her expectantly. "Can I actually help? I mean, I have helped before, but on *your* orders. I have some useful ideas, you know."

"No," Kyrie said firmly.

"Why not?" Ryder wanted to know.

"Because," Kyrie said crossly.

"Because what?" Ryder wheedled.

"Because I don't like or trust you," Kyrie said matter-of-factly.

"I'm offended," Ryder said indignantly. "I've proved myself to be trustworthy. I've helped *a lot.* Kyrie, please?"

"No," Kyrie said, getting up and carrying her plate to the kitchen.

"But wwwhhhhhhyyyy?" Ryder whined, following her.

"Because," Kyrie snapped again. She and Ryder continued bickering, as usual.

"Well, we all know how that's going to end," Nova said, shaking her head.

"Yep," Rizo agreed. "Those two. And I thought they were supposed to be the authority figures around here."

"Honestly, I'm not surprised," Krackers said loftily. "Humans are extremely unreasonable and agitating. Parrots are *much* better."

"Oh, stop it," Nova said. "That's not true."

"It *is,*" Krackers argued.

"Well, even if it is, parrots are even *more* unreasonable and agitating," Rizo said.

Krackers ruffled his feathers importantly and flew into the living room, and Nova exchanged a mischievous look with Rizo.

"Who stuck a feather up *his* beak?" She asked, a smile playing at the corners of her mouth.

"I have a feeling that was us," Rizo said, grinning back at her.

"Come on, let's go see what we can do for your sister and Mikaela," Nova said, picking up her plate and carrying it to the kitchen. Rizo followed her. After depositing them into a dishwasher, they ventured into the living room. Anala and Mikaela were still lying motionless on the couches.

"I'll go get some cold compresses," Nova said worriedly, whisking back towards the kitchen. She returned a few seconds later with two cold disks in her hand. She gave one to Rizo, who applied it to some of the bruises that covered his sister, while Nova did the same to Mikaela.

After a few minutes, Nova checked on Rizo's progress, pursing her lips. "You know, you should put Anala in a more comfortable position. Look, her arm is squashed, cutting off her circulation. That's not good."

285

"That's a good point," Rizo said, nodding. Nova had again demonstrated her knack of noticing tiny details.

Nova gently shifted Anala into a better position.

"There," she said, inspecting her handiwork. "Now, what's next?"

Rizo and Nova spent the next few hours cleaning the house, brainstorming with Kyrie and Ryder on how to wake up Anala and Mikaela, and aggravating Krackers. Still, while they sat on the couch, staring blankly at the motionless forms of Anala and Mikaela, Rizo wondered how much they had actually done. Had they accomplished that much? It was hard to tell. Yes, they had spiffed up the house and tried to revive Mikaela and Anala, but all those things suddenly seemed small. They hadn't made much headway in anything. Rizo sunk into a stew of hopelessness. They couldn't really do anything right now. Even if they did do something, it felt pointless.

"Hey!" Nova snapped her fingers in front of Rizo's face. "Snap out of it! We're safe now, there's no need to be such a Gloomy Gus!"

"I don't know," Rizo said slowly. "We're not *really* safe, and everything we do is useless."

"Come on, Rizo!" Nova said. "We survived the Netrhaphalin, which were wwwwaaaaayyyyy scarier than I thought they would be! We *deserve* to have a little fun!"

"Nova...." Rizo groaned. "Please. You know what, I feel like a nap." He got up from the couch and entered the bedroom Ryder had said was his earlier. Rizo didn't really want to take a nap, he had just had to get away from other people. Even Nova, who was probably feeling pretty hurt at the moment. Rizo felt a twinge of guilt. Nova really hadn't deserved such abruptness.

He lay down on the bed, thinking. Why had things worked out the way they had? And how could they wake his sister up? Poor Anala. He hoped that she wasn't in pain. Despair and guilt washed over him, like waves pounding on an already crumbling cliff.

Why hadn't he kept his sister safer? She was his responsibility now that his parents were dead. It was his fault she was like this. All his fault.

He had never been the best brother. He hadn't ever defended his sister like he should have. He hadn't helped Anala when she had thrown tantrum after tantrum when she had been learning to read. He hadn't helped her when she had struggled with her endless schoolwork.

287

He hadn't even tried to save her from the Netrhaphalin. He was a failure. His parents would be so disappointed if they could see him now.

Rizo battered himself with angry thoughts until something broke inside of him.

He became furious.

He didn't want to be here. Rizo punched his pillow into a better shape, then lay down on it, feeling like kicking something. He hated that his whole life had been flipped over because of Dr. Duarte. Why had this happened?

Why?

Midnight Conversation

Chapter 23

June 13, 2473

Rizo didn't know when he had fallen asleep. All he knew was that he had been thinking angry thoughts and had somehow drifted off into a dreamless slumber. And now he was awake. It seemed like it was late at night. The hologram by his bed read 1:00 am. Everyone had obviously gone to sleep. The house was quiet, and Rizo was hungry. He had skipped dinner. Well, early morning or not, Rizo was going to get something to eat. He wandered into the kitchen, stumbling around in the dark. He clapped, and was instantly blinded by the sudden brightness. He found some food and sat down to eat it, thinking.

How where they going to achieve everything they had set out to do? Without Mikaela and Anala? Kyrie was great, but she couldn't do everything by herself. Suddenly everything they had planned to do seemed impossible. They were crazy to think that this was going to work.

Rizo knew that he had thought this the day before, and that it hadn't done him any good, but it was hard *not* to think that they were crazy.

"Rizo?"

Rizo looked up. Nova was standing there, looking sleepy.

"I thought you were here," she said cheerfully, sitting down next to him. "Man, you look like your head's about to explode."

"It is," Rizo said.

"Why?" Nova asked.

"Because, everything seems so... impossible," Rizo explained.

"It really isn't," Nova smiled. "Honestly. Sometimes I feel like you're too grounded."

"What's that supposed to mean?"

"You think too much about reality. Sometimes it's fine to let your mind wander."

"I don't know how to do that."

"Exactly. You think that it's impossible. Just try imagining something different, completely out of this world."

"You don't make any sense," Rizo said, shaking his head.

"No, *you* don't," Nova laughed. "Rizo, there are thousands of places to go and see. So many realities to weave. You don't deserve to miss out. So try."

"I can't," Rizo said, assuming Nova was joking. "I appreciate the gesture, but really. No one could do that."

Nova pulled back, looking offended. "*I* can do it," she said stiffly. "I'm not joking. It's real. As real as it could be. You have no idea how many things I've done in my head."

"Wait, you're not just trying to make me feel better?" Rizo asked, genuinely confused. He had thought that Nova was just making all of this up. *Though if Nova had been making all of it up, she had a pretty good imagination*, Rizo thought. *Man, girls were confusing. Why can't they just say what's on their mind?*

I don't understand why they have to go in a roundabout way.

"No, it's real. And I thought I could make it real for you, too. I guess not," Nova sighed. "You seem like you want to leave this reality right now."

"I do," Rizo said.

"But you can't," Nova said. "If you could just imagine-"

"That's a waste of time," Rizo cut her off.

"That's what it is," Nova said. "And it's not a waste of time!"

"But-" Rizo started, worrying that he had done something wrong.

"I'm off to bed," Nova said, getting up and hurrying away.

Rizo watched her figure disappear back into the shadows, then lay his head on the table. What had he done wrong? He had really thought she had been joking. But she hadn't been. She had been trying to help him. He had officially blown it. Rizo trudged back to bed, feeling a mix of confused emotions.

After hours of tossing and turning, he finally fell into a sleep troubled by nightmares. Flashes of Nova yelling, "You don't understand!", Anala crumpling in slow motion, while Rizo stood, helpless, watching in horror, and worst of all, Kyrie announcing that Anala was dead. At this last vivid scene, Rizo awoke with a jerk. Anala couldn't be dead. What could he do? He thrashed wildly for a minute, before realizing that he had been dreaming. He blinked and looked around. His clothes, which Kyrie had washed while they wore some extra clothes they had found in the house, were neatly folded by his bedside. He put them on and left his room. Kyrie was toasting bread while debating with Ryder about whether water was wet.

"But water *makes* things wet, it's not wet *itself*," Ryder was arguing.

"That makes no sense," Kyrie snapped back. "Hi, Rizo. Don't you *love* how Ryder is letting me do all the work? It's really nice of him, don't you think?"

"Um-" Rizo wasn't sure how he was supposed to answer that question.

"Well, I'd just mess everything up," Ryder said charmingly. "In that way, I am being nice, because then you don't have to clean up after me. Remember, I haven't the faintest idea on how to cook. My mom gave up teaching me when I almost burned the popcorn machine down."

"See, this is why *I'm* in charge," Kyrie said, rolling her eyes at Rizo. "Things only burn down and blow up if I *want* them to. Could you get out the jam?"

"Sure," Rizo said, eager to escape the warzone. He walked over to the cabinet, then grabbed the jar of jam. "Here."

"See," Kyrie said. "People in the Gryffins are taught to be *helpful*, unlike those lazy peace lovers in the Rockets."

"Excuse me," Nova's voice was sharp. "We are not lazy."

"Guys, please just be nice to one another," Rizo said, before Kyrie could make a snappy retort.

Both girls glared at each other, but didn't say anything. Kyrie carried the toast and jam to the table. They sat around it in silence.

"So," Rizo said. "How are we going to wake up Mikaela and Anala?"

"That's the thing," Kyrie sighed. "I was doing a bit of research yesterday, and it seems as if the stunning laser puts the people into kind of a coma that only the Netrhaphalin can lift."

"Oh, no," Rizo groaned. "Why are those robots such jerks?"

"I believe the idea is that it keeps the people nice and harmless until the Netrhaphalin want to question them," Kyrie said.

"I know *that*," Rizo said impatiently. "But how are we going to wake them up?"

"I honestly don't know," Kyrie said. "I suppose we could ambush an Netrhaphalin and take the device they use to revive stunned people. It's supposed to be a small piece of metal that sends the precise amount of electric shock into a person's body so that they wake up but just enough so that they don't die."

Nova shuddered. "Creepy. It sounds like there's a lot of ways that can go wrong."

"So can we ambush a Netrhaphalin?" Rizo asked.

"I suppose," Kyrie said. "It would be hard, though. Rizo, your arm and ankle are still healing, so you can't go- Ryder, you come with me. You're the oldest, and Nova can stay behind so that she can help Rizo if any trouble comes."

Rizo glanced at his injuries, which were still in braces. He had forgotten about them, but now that they had been brought up, they started aching. A lot.

"But I want to go," he said.

"That's absolutely out of the question," Kyrie snapped. "Next thing you know, you're in the hospital. Ryder and I should get going. It's going to take a while to stake out the place and then overpower a lone Netrhaphalin. If we're not back by dark, then something bad has happened."

"By dark?" Rizo asked. "That's hours and hours from now!"

"I'm being realistic," Kyrie said. "Now, Ryder, we should pack quite a few things. A heavy bat, some water and food...."

They spent breakfast going over stuff they would need. After they had packed all the necessities, Kyrie and Ryder set out, leaving Rizo and Nova behind.

"What are we going to do?" Rizo asked.

"I don't know, use your imagination," Nova said. Both of them fell silent, no doubt remembering their awkward conversation at night.

"Are there any books here?" Rizo asked. He glanced around. There was a shelf that was partially full of books. He limped over to it and checked them out. There were only a few children's and teens' books, the rest were boring adult books like *How to Make Your Garden Look Amazing* and *The Comprehensive Guide to Interior Décor.*

Rizo picked a book called *Jay's Bird* and sat down. As he listened, watched, and read, he realized that this was a toddler book. Disgusted, he put it back on the shelf and picked *The Adventures of the Dragon.* This turned out to be a brain-numbing book, but at least it took his mind off the other things worrying him.

He paused his reading to see what Nova was doing. She was playing a game against herself, flicking the hologram into different places and shapes. Rizo felt bad and walked over to her.

"Do you want to play a game?" He asked.

"Oh, sure," Nova said gratefully. She wiped the hologram clear of the game she had been playing and scrolled through the list of games they could play.

"Let's see, there's *Build a City, The One and Only, Snarky Sayings, Crush that Robot-*"

"Yeah, let's do that one," Rizo said. "Maybe it will give Kyrie and Ryder good luck."

"Okay," Nova said, choosing the game Rizo had wanted. Rizo snapped his fingers, and a chair floated towards him. He sat down, and the hologram started dealing out weapon cards to him.

"You know, I can't believe that the Netrhaphalin haven't banned this game," Rizo said.

"Oh, they have," Nova said confidently, considering her cards. "We just got our hands on some of the old holograms that still had *Crush that Robot* on them."

"So did the Gryffins," Rizo said. "Do you want to go first?"

"Sure," Nova said, moving her player a few steps forward.

The game continued, and Nova ended up winning after a few rounds.

"Good game," Rizo said, smiling.

"Do want to play again? Something else, I mean," Nova asked.

"Sure," Rizo said. There was nothing else to do.

They played games for a long time, then ate lunch. Then they spent the afternoon making excuses for why Ryder and Kyrie weren't back.

"I'm sure they'll be back soon," Nova said.

"They're just... stopping to eat," Rizo said uneasily.

"That's right," Nova agreed.

Rizo anxiously paced from one end of the room to another.

"Sit down," Nova said, flapping her hands at him. "You're making me nervous."

Rizo sat down, then started shifting his weight from one hand to another.

"Oh, it's no use," Nova fretted. "I'm so worried."

Rizo took a book from the shelf and began to read it. It was the dullest story imaginable, about a plant growing, but it kept his mind off the danger Kyrie and Ryder were in.

"Oh dear, oh dear," Nova kept muttering while she picked things up and set them down again.

"I do think we'd better look for them," she finally said.

"It's not dark yet," Rizo pointed out.

"Stop being so melodramatic," Krackers groaned from his perch on the sofa.

"I hate just waiting," Nova said. "What if they're being tortured by the Netrhaphalin? What if-"

"Nova," Rizo said in a stern voice. "This is one of the times when an overactive imagination is *not* helpful."

"I can't help it," Nova wailed. "What if-"

"Nova," Rizo said warningly.

"All right, all right!" Nova said. "I just can't *stand* it!"

"Neither can I," Rizo said. "But please, just calm down."

"Okay," Nova said in a shaky voice. "*Okay.*" She took a deep breath, muttering, "I will be calm. I *will* be calm."

Rizo sat in silence for a long while. It felt like hours and hours before there was a knock at the door. Both Rizo and Nova jumped up to answer it.

"Ryder?" Rizo flung open the door. Ryder was standing there, supporting Kyrie, who was bleeding heavily and appeared to be unconscious.

"Get her inside," Ryder grunted.

"What happened?" Nova asked frantically, running and grabbing some cold compresses. Rizo helped Ryder carry Kyrie inside, then shut the door.

"We got it, but she got badly hurt. Fell from a ten-meter drop onto some cactus landscaping," Ryder gasped, clutching his side. He looked badly bruised, but overall uninjured. He handed Rizo a small disk.

Nova was tending to Kyrie, dabbing at her scratches and one bigger gash on her arm.

"How did she get that?" Nova asked, pointing to the gash.

Ryder winced. "We were fighting, and I threw some glass, and it hit her. Sorry we took so long. It was hard trying not to be noticed while supporting Kyrie."

Nova simply nodded and applied some bandages to the cuts all over Kyrie.

"Can I wake them up?" Rizo asked, nodding to Mikaela and Anala and holding up the disk that could revive them.

"Better wait until Kyrie wakes up," Ryder advised. "That thing can hurt people."

Rizo nodded, but he felt impatient. He knew he shouldn't, Kyrie had just gotten beat up in order to help his sister, but he did. Krackers flew over.

"Let me see that," he snapped. Rizo blinked. He had forgotten the parrot had even been there.

The parrot grabbed the disk and started prodding it and muttering to himself.

Rizo handed Nova a tube of something that proclaimed itself to be "The Best Bruise Remover Ever-Watch Them Fade Before Your Eyes!"

She took it and dabbed some of the paste on to Kyrie's face, which looked bluer and more purple than her usual natural tones.

"I think I can work this thing," Krackers said confidently. Rizo knew Krackers was extremely self-confident all the time and therefore did not find his tone reassuring at all.

"You think?" He asked.

"I know how to work this, don't worry," Krackers said airily. "I know it looks difficult, but I can handle it." He set the device on the table and began to preen himself.

"Oh. My. Goodness!" Nova glared at Krackers. "Stop acting like that *all* the time! If you do that wrong, Anala and Mikaela could die!"

"Calm down," Krackers told her in a bored voice. "It's going to be all right." He spoke as if Nova was a mere toddler struggling to understand that one plus one equaled two. Rizo glanced nervously towards Nova. He really hoped she wouldn't just let Krackers walk all over her. He was a real pain.

"I am just as intelligent as you are, thank you very much," Nova snapped. "There's no need to act as if I'm three."

"Just as intelligent," Krackers mused. "We'll see about that."

"You are- are- just the worst!" Nova exploded. "Out. Out! Go eat from the bird feeder or get captured by the Netrhaphalin, see if I care! But you are not going back in this house again! This is Rocket property, you scumbag!" Nova threw the nearest thing at Krackers, which happened to be the tube of bruise remover. It hit him in the eye with surprising accuracy.

"Ow," he said, flying to safety.

"Out. OUT!" Nova grabbed Krackers by his tail feathers and opened the window, holding his claws firmly so that he couldn't scratch her. Furious and fed up, she flung Krackers out of the house and slammed the window shut. He flew through the air wildly before regaining his balance. He didn't even attempt to come back into the house, he simply flew away.

"Good riddance," Nova said, giving Krackers one last glare before turning around. She froze at the shocked expressions on Ryder's and Rizo's faces.

"I might have... uh, gotten carried away," she mumbled, flushing red.

"What are you talking about?" Rizo asked. "That was awesome!"

"You think?" A small smile played on Nova's face for a moment before she got down to business again.

"Now that we've gotten that hooligan out," she said conversationally. "I think we'd better see how we can help Kyrie."

Rizo picked up the bruise remover from where it had landed after striking Krackers.

"That parrot totally got what he deserved," Rizo said to Nova in a whisper.

"I guess," she said, a little ruefully. "I may have gone a little overboard. What if he tattles on us? The Netrhaphalin would probably pardon him if he tells them where we are."

Rizo was alarmed by this possibility. Thankfully, before he could truly think through what the consequences of Nova's blow up were, Kyrie groaned and shifted. Rizo bent closer, all other thoughts flying out of his head.

"Kyrie?" Nova asked softly.

"Owwwww," Kyrie moaned. "Everything hurts." She seemed to snap awake a little more and tried to sit up, but lay down quickly with a small wince.

"Take it easy," Ryder said gently. For once, Kyrie didn't make a retort.

"Kyrie, how do we use this?" Rizo asked impatiently, holding up the disk that could either wake up- or kill his sister.

"Let her rest," Ryder scolded Rizo. "Your sister and Mikaela can wait."

"But they're probably hungry! They haven't had water in days!

"It's only been a day," Ryder corrected him. "I do want to wake them up, but I don't want to rush it and do it wrong, either."

Rizo sat down, grinding his teeth in frustration. Couldn't everyone see that Mikaela and Anala really needed to get up? Nova glanced at the window, then at the door. When Rizo looked at her questioningly, she mouthed the word, *Krackers*. Rizo frowned, remembering how Nova had put them in danger. He glanced at the window as well.

"Rizo," Kyrie croaked. "Give me the disk." He handed it to her, ignoring Ryder's protests.

"She's still extremely injured!" He exclaimed disapprovingly.

"You have to push this button here, then switch the light to green," Kyrie said. "Although... I don't see why the Netrhaphalin would put such information out to the public... unless...." Kyrie trailed off. "The green light probably kills the person. And the red light probably *revives*," she mused. "So it should be red."

"Wait, why?" Rizo asked.

"Because, think about it," Kyrie said. "Humans have no need for this device unless they have a stunned person lying around. And the only people who are stunned are people who are breaking the law. The Netrhaphalin don't care if someone dies. Death is nothing to them, because they can just get fixed. So it would make sense that they would try to trick people into doing their dirty work for them."

Rizo sat there, weighing his options. Kyrie's logic did make sense, but this was a huge gamble. If they did this wrong, Anala could die. However, if they didn't wake her up at all, she would still die, because she wasn't eating or drinking.

"I can't wing it," he said. "There's too much at stake."

Kyrie ignored him.

"Put the red light on her finger," Kyrie said, as if they had already decided to proceed. Rizo was forced to conclude that this was probably the best option. However, he still had a nagging feeling that red was not a color that indicated survival.

"Kyrie-" he started.

"Just do it, Rizo," Kyrie said in an unnaturally strained voice.

With shaking hands, Rizo did as he was told.

"Now flip that switch," Kyrie said, pointing to a lever on the device.

Rizo took a deep breath. The moment of truth would come soon, he told himself. In a moment, he would know whether Anala would live- or die.

He flicked the lever and closed his eyes.

Waking Up

Chapter 24

June 13, 2473

Rizo kept his eyes closed as the device grew warm, then cold. Opening his eyes slightly, he saw his sister thrashing on the couch, obviously in pain. After a few seconds, she lay, still and quiet.

"How is she?" Rizo asked desperately. "Is she-" He couldn't bear to say the words.

"I think she's still breathing," Nova said uncertainly, which did not boost Rizo's spirits.

"Anala has to be okay," Rizo said louder, as if in a dream. He turned around so that he would not have to see Anala.

"Rizo?" Rizo whirled around. Anala was blinking slowly.

"Ow, that HURT," she groaned. "I mean, what did I miss? Where am I? How did I get here? The last thing I remember, I was surrounded by Netrhaphalin. Oh my goodness, I'm STARVING. And THIRSTY. Rizo, can I have something to eat?"

"All right," Rizo said, overwhelmed with relief and happiness. Anala was fine! Rizo shuddered, thinking about what might have happened if Kyrie had followed what she had read. What might have happened if Rizo had refused to follow her logic and set the light to green instead.

Shaking his head to get rid of those thoughts, he went to the kitchen to get some food for Anala. He grabbed two leftover scones and returned to the living room, where Mikaela was waking up drowsily.

"Here," Rizo said, handing them a scone each.

"Thanks," Mikaela said grudgingly.

"Thank you!" Anala chirped enthusiastically. Mikaela shot her a disgusted look.

"Where's Krackers?" She asked.

"Away," Ryder said evasively.

"Away where?" Mikaela narrowed her eyes. "Where is he?"

"I kind of... threw him out," Nova said quietly.

"You didn't think that maybe he might squeal to the Netrhaphalin about this?" Mikaela asked angrily. "Not that I think Krackers would do that, but it's still a liability!"

"It only crossed my mind after he flew away," Nova said.

"Awesome." Mikaela lay down, breathing slowly. "I get stunned for one day and *this* happens."

"Hey, Kyrie got seriously hurt in an effort to wake you up," Ryder said. "Why did we even do that? It *may* have been worth it if *someone* would say thank you."

"Thanks, Kyrie," Mikaela said with a sigh. "So you can only wake up a stunned person with this, huh?" She picked up the disk and inspected it closely.

Rizo nodded.

"RIZO!" Anala looked at her brother, sitting up. "YOU KNOW, being stunned REALLY HURT. I had all types of HORRIBLE nightmares. In one of them, you were throwing books at my head, but instead of hitting me, they just went through my head, because I was A GHOST. Can you IMAGINE THAT?"

"Uh, no, I can't," Rizo mumbled, massaging his ears.

"Well it was SO WEIRD but-" Anala continued.

"Please stop," Mikaela said flatly. "If you continue, you could blast all of our eardrums off or, worse, alert the Netrhaphalin that we're here."

"Oh, FINE." Anala folded her arms crossly and turned her back to Mikaela.

"Anyway," Rizo said, steering the conversation towards safer waters. "What's next? An explosion?"

"That's right," Mikaela said, with a slight smile on her face.

"Where's the factory?" Ryder asked.

"Where's your map?" Nova asked. "We marked it on there."

"Oh, right." Ryder fumbled in his pockets for a second, then pulled out a disk. He tapped it a few times, and holograms zoomed in and out until they came into focus. "It looks like it's quite a few kilometers from here," he reported.

"The exact number, please?" Mikaela asked crisply.

312

"Seventeen," Ryder told her.

"That's not bad," Nova remarked.

"You're FORGETTING SOMETHING," Anala announced, pointing at Kyrie. "She needs to get better, and Krackers has to come back."

"That's right," Mikaela said, biting her lip. "Kyrie's a really good fighter. And it would be convenient if Krackers came back, too."

"Let's not pull a stay for a long time until Mikaela gets fed up again, please," Ryder said. "We don't need to go on more spontaneous rescue missions."

"Krackers and I never needed 'rescuing'," Mikaela said stiffly.

"Fine, rendezvous missions," Ryder said, grinning. "Better?"

"Only marginally," Mikaela said disdainfully, although Rizo thought he had seen a smile flit across her face for a split second. Unbelievable. Was Mikaela finally putting aside her prejudices against the Rockets? This thought was quickly diminished as Mikaela snapped, "You just made things harder for us. Way to ruin anything." She stomped away and looked out of the window, looking for Krackers.

"What a nice, delightful girl," Ryder said quietly, gazing after Mikaela. He turned to Rizo and grinned conspiratorially. "A pity those qualities are buried *very* deep down."

Rizo shook his head. He didn't understand how Ryder could get away with saying stuff like that.

"Rizo?" Nova asked. "I need you to come help with something.

"Okay," Rizo said, walking to her side.

"Kyrie needs a lot of bandages," Nova said. "Every time I patch something up, a new cut grabs my attention. Could you get me some more cloth strips? They're in the kitchen."

"Sure," Rizo said, hurrying towards the kitchen. After he found the bandages, he hurried back and gave them to Nova.

"You know," he said. "I can't believe we've survived this long without any adult supervision."

"Ryder's technically an adult," Nova pointed out.

"I know, but he doesn't act like it," Rizo countered. "I mean, he's started more fights than he has actually stopped."

"Oh, *that* kind of supervision?" Nova asked. "I thought you meant an adult protecting us or something."

"Oh, I guess that would be pretty good, too. I wonder if Kyrie can get anyone else to help us. I mean, she's sort of out of commission at the moment," Rizo said. "Doesn't she have an older brother?"

"You mean Jared?" Kyrie asked softly. "I guess I can get him over here. He could tell us what's happening in the Gryffins and when it's safe to come back. This could be a huge operation. We really can't do it alone. Maybe Dad could even help if he isn't still scrambling or... captured. You know, that's actually a great idea."

"Well, how do we reach him?" Rizo asked. Even though this was great news, he felt like they were constantly trying to reach somebody that could possibly help them.

"It's simple," Kyrie said. "Get my shoe."

"What?" Rizo asked.

"Get my shoe. You took it off me when Ryder carried me here," Kyrie repeated.

"Okay," Rizo said slowly. He was seriously considering asking if Kyrie had hit her head. Nevertheless, he found her shoe and gave it to her. She pulled up the sole and help up a small square device. She then held it close to her face and whispered something that Rizo couldn't hear. Kyrie pressed a red button twice and repeated her words, then pushed the button again.

"I've called him," she said. "Jared should be here as soon as possible, or at least be able to send me a message." Kyrie threw her shoe at Ryder. "Ryder, start doing something useful."

"I'm looking for Krackers," Ryder protested, even though he had been doing no such thing.

"*Mikaela* is looking for Krackers," Kyrie clarified impatiently. "You are being useless."

"Well, what do you want me to do?" Ryder asked.

"You and Mikaela should go to find Krackers," Kyrie instructed him. "If you're not back in an hour, I'll send Nova after you."

"What about me?" Rizo asked.

"You're injured," Kyrie said. "The only reason you feel well is because Nova and I have been slipping you painkillers every few hours."

"What?" Rizo asked, not knowing whether he should be thankful or angry.

"Wow, Nova, I didn't know you could be that DEVIOUS," Anala said, wide-eyed.

Nova turned red. "Kyrie did most of it," she mumbled.

"But Nova did it when Ryder and I were out," Kyrie said.

Rizo looked at Nova, astonished. "Nova! I didn't think you had it in you! Actually, you did a great job. I had absolutely no idea that I was taking painkillers."

"Thanks... I guess?" Nova said uncertainly.

"Enough revelations," Kyrie said briskly. "Ryder and Mikaela, get going."

"But it's nighttime!" Ryder protested. "Come on!"

"Nevertheless," Kyrie said warningly.

"Oh, fine," Mikaela said. "I'll annoy him for you."

"Thank you," Kyrie said cheerfully. Ryder shot her a look as he followed Mikaela outside. "How could you do this to me?" He asked Kyrie beseechingly.

"You deserve it," she responded as Mikaela shut the door behind them.

"Now that we've gotten him out of our hair," Kyrie said. "I've got to get down to business. If someone knocks on the door, ask if it's Max. I'm not expecting anyone named Max, but if that someone is trying to trick us, then they'll think that we *are* expecting a Max and say yes. If they say that, then don't open the door under any circumstances."

"Kyrie, your logic is making MY HEAD HURT," Anala complained.

"Anyway, press that button." Kyrie ignored Anala and pointed to a red button that had certainly not been on the wall before. "I installed an ejection mechanism," she explained. "For an undercover resistance house, this place has such little security. Anyway, that will throw them off the ledge to the ground and we can escape."

"How?" Rizo asked.

"Through the only resistance-y thing that's in this house," Kyrie said. "The bookshelf. If you turn the book *When Mangoes Fly* ninety degrees, then flip *Dragons of the West* upside down and remove *Moon Rocks* from the shelf, a keypad will be revealed. If you enter the right code, then an escape route will open up."

"How did you figure that out?" Nova asked.

"Ryder told me," Kyrie said. "The first day we came here. Anyway, you'll have to help me into the escape tunnel because I can barely walk."

"What do we do if the guys doesn't say that he's Max?" Rizo asked.

"Then ask who he or she is. If they say Charlie Maine, then let them in. If they say anything else, then press the red button and deploy the escape tunnel," Kyrie said, then thought to add, "Unless they say that they're Ryder and Mikaela, of course."

"Can you repeat that?" Anala asked innocently. "I didn't catch most of that."

"You did," Kyrie snapped. "Don't mess with me."

"Okay FINE," Anala said sourly. "I'm trying to LIGHTEN the MOOD around here."

"I-" Kyrie froze. "I just heard a knock," she whispered.

Nova and Rizo glanced at each other and cautiously approached the door.

"Hello?" Rizo asked uncertainly. "Um, are you Max?"

"No," an unfamiliar voice answered. Rizo peered over at Kyrie, whose face was blank.

"Then who are you?" Rizo asked.

"Charlie Maine," the voice replied. It was deeper this time, however, and Kyrie attempted to sit up, but collapsed with a groan. Rizo wrinkled his forehead. The second voice sounded familiar.

"Uh, come in," Rizo said, aware that he might be dooming them all to a painful death or at least a painful capture. He opened the door and gasped.

"Dr. Duarte?"

Family Drama

Chapter 25

June 13, 2473

Rizo looked past Dr. Duarte. What looked like a younger version of Dr. Duarte was standing there.

"Are you Jared?" Rizo asked.

"Yep," he replied. "Wow, it is chilly at night. Let me in."

"How did you get here so fast?" Nova asked.

"We have a telecube," Dr. Duarte said, closing the door behind him. "We had to walk a bit, but other than that, it was a smooth journey. How did you escape? All of us had gone to another place with our telecube and destroyed the rest of the tunnel before we realized that we had left all of you behind. And who is that?" Dr.

Duarte looked suspiciously at Nova. "And where are Krackers ad Mikaela?"

"It's a long story," Kyrie said from the couch.

"What happened to you?" Jared asked.

"A run-in with our favorite robots," Rizo said. "Among other things."

"Sit down," Nova said. "We have a lot to tell you."

Dr. Duarte and Jared sat down, still looking confused.

"It all started when we got captured by the Netrhaphalin," Kyrie explained. "Well, all of us except Krackers."

"Wait, how-" Jared started before Rizo cut him off.

"But don't worry, we escaped," he said.

"But then we got into a HIGH-SPEED HOVER CHASE, can you BELIEVE it?" Anala chimed in.

"And then the hover we were in blew up," Kyrie said.

"I can't believe-" Dr. Duarte began.

"So then we got taken to a hospital and met your ex-colleague, Dr. Nikita," Kyrie continued.

"WHAT?" Dr. Duarte bellowed. "Nikita is working at a hospital? That traitor!"

"And we realized that she was going to HAND US OVER TO THE NETRHAPHALIN," Anala said.

"And so we escaped again," Rizo said. "But then we got into another mini hover chase because Dr. Nikita was super mad."

"Wait, you're forgetting Riva," Nova interjected.

"Oh, right, so Kyrie told us that we couldn't meet up with you guys because you were probably still scrambling so she told us about the Rockets and said that they would probably help us," Rizo explained. "But we had a hard time finding them until we realized that Dr. Nikita was blackmailing one of her assistants into helping her because he had a sister who was in the Rockets."

"And then we found them and then we learned about the factories," Kyrie said.

"Wait, what? I'm really confused," Jared said.

They spent a good part of an hour explaining, and when they had finished, Dr. Duarte shook his head.

"You really aren't useless after all," he said. "I assume you called us so that we can help you?"

"Correct," Kyrie said. "Rizo and I are out of commission and Krackers is potentially missing. We need your help."

"Okay, we can do this," Jared said. "I can't believe how much my little sister has done!"

"Jared," Kyrie leveled her brother with a stony gaze. "I'm only *one* year younger than you!"

"So when are Krackers, Mikaela, and this Ryder character coming back?" Jared asked, changing the subject.

"I don't actually know," Kyrie said, lying back down. "They could be gone forever."

"Kyrie!" Nova reprimanded her. "They're our friends!"

"That's questionable," Kyrie sighed. "At least with that jerk Ryder."

"Kyrie, come on! Without Ryder, Anala wouldn't be awake, and neither would Mikaela. Without Ryder, you would be in the hands of the Netrhaphalin!" Nova argued.

"Without Ryder, I wouldn't have this gash on my arm!" Kyrie countered. "I know he's a Rocket, but that doesn't make him better, Nova!"

"Enough arguing," Rizo said. "Please, for our sake, if not yours."

"Thank you, Rizo," Dr. Duarte said. "Kyrie, stop making a big fuss."

"Me? Nova's the one who started it," Kyrie complained.

"*You* started it," Nova shot back. "with that nasty comment about Ryder."

"I did not!" Kyrie said.

"Girls," Dr. Duarte said sternly. "Please."

"Yeah, learn some manners, Kyrie," Jared taunted his sister.

"Shut your-" Kyrie started.

"Jared, Kyrie!" Dr. Duarte stood up, glaring at his kids. "What would your mother think if she saw you right now?"

Both of them immediately fell silent.

"Thank you," Dr. Duarte said, shaking his head wearily.

"Mom didn't make threats like that," Jared said to his father. "What would she think if she saw you using her to scare us?"

"Charmaine-" Dr. Duarte paused. "Let's just stop arguing. It's been a long day."

"Dad, come on! Not that excuse *again*," Jared started.

Sensing a war, Rizo beckoned for Anala and Nova to follow him into his room.

"I thought that this would be a good idea, but now I'm not quite sure," Nova said, sitting down on Rizo's bed. "I mean, just listen to them."

They all fell silent for a minute as they listened to Dr. Duarte shout, "Both of you! I don't believe your antics!"

"See," Nova said helplessly. "I mean, we can't kick them out, but it's going to be hard to work with them."

"I agree," Rizo said, and Anala snorted with laughter. "What's so funny?" He asked.

"Nothing," Anala giggled. She glanced at Nova, then back at Rizo.

"Cut it out," Rizo said, swatting at his sister.

"Stop, both of you." Nova stood up. "We don't need *another* argument right now."

"All right," Rizo said. They all sat in silence for a long time, listening to the war raging on in the living room. It was somewhat comedic, just listening, as Kyrie,

Jared, and Dr. Duarte all dredged up grievances from the past.

"Jared put his underwear on my bed when I was five!" Kyrie screeched. "And you didn't do anything about that!"

"That was because you put salt on my birthday cake instead of sugar!" Jared yelled back.

"I did not! Dad mixed up the labels!"

"That *never* happened," Dr. Duarte interjected.

"It did," Kyrie protested. "Don't deny it!"

Nova and Anala were giggling hysterically. Rizo grinned at them.

"What a disaster," he said. A few minutes later, Nova wrinkled her forehead.

"Did you hear that?" She asked.

"Hear what?" Rizo asked.

"I think someone's knocking on the door," Nova said.

"It could be Ryder, Mikaela and Krackers," Rizo said. "I'll go get them."

He got to his feet and went to the door.

"Who is it?" He asked.

"Ryder," someone answered. Rizo opened the door, and Ryder, Mikaela, and Krackers, who looked extremely ruffled, paled when they heard the shouting match.

"Is... this a bad time?" Ryder asked.

"Pretty much," Rizo said. "Follow me. I'll explain." He led them into his room.

"Dr. Duarte came, along with Kyrie's brother, Jared. They got in an argument, and it hasn't shown any signs of stopping yet."

"Some family reunion," Ryder said, shaking his head.

"Well, how did you find Krackers?" Nova asked.

"I'm *right here*," Krackers said condescendingly.

"I don't care," Nova snapped, clearly still annoyed with him.

"We found him a few blocks down, cleaning out another bird feeder," Ryder said, laughing. "There was a family that was watching him. They thought he was hilarious. We had to explain that he was our pet who had escaped." Mikaela cracked a smile.

"It *was* funny," she conceded.

"Mikaela!" Krackers squawked indignantly. "I'm your friend!"

"It was still funny," she said, shrugging.

"I had to eat somehow!" Krackers explained with as much dignity as he could. "This house is all out of birdseed!"

Krackers looked defiantly at all of them as they laughed uproariously. Ryder was banging his fist on the ground, and Mikaela made no attempt to conceal her amused smiles. Anala was clutching Rizo, she was laughing so hard.

When they had finally stopped laughing, Kyrie, Jared, and Dr. Duarte were still arguing.

"I think it's time to break them up," Nova said.

"The problem is, how?" Ryder glanced around the group. "I mean, I personally find Dr. Duarte pretty scary."

"He's not *scary*, just... intimidating," Mikaela said.

"Exactly," Ryder said. "Anyway, my point is that breaking up a family fight is easier said than done."

"Well, it's either that or we get nothing done and sit here for the REST OF ETERNITY," Anala pointed out.

Rizo gritted his teeth. "I think we should just go and do it."

"What, no plan?" Nova teased him.

"Not this time," Rizo said. "I have a feeling that this is one of those times when plans can go horribly wrong. Not that I have anything against plans, it's just this situation in particular."

"Oh," Nova said. "I thought for a minute that you had given up your habit for good."

"It's not a habit," Rizo said a bit defensively. "It's sort of a preference." Inwardly, Rizo didn't know how he felt about the whole plan thing since he had woken Anala up.

"Whatever you say," Nova said.

Rizo decided not to comment on Nova's words and instead led the way to the war zone.

"Um, Kyrie? Dr. Duarte?" He asked tentatively.

Mikaela rolled her eyes. "You can be so *naïve* sometimes," she groaned. Sticking her fingers into her mouth, she whistled so shrilly that Rizo nearly jumped out of his skin.

Dr. Duarte, Kyrie, and Jared all turned to look at her. Mikaela glanced at Rizo, as if to say, *It's your turn now.*

"Um, how are we going to get anything done if you fight all the time?" Rizo asked. "You guys arguing won't get us anywhere. And if you've forgotten, we have a Netrhaphalin factory to blow up."

The Duartes all had the grace to look a bit ashamed.

"All right," Dr. Duarte sighed. "On behalf of our family, I apologize. We did come here for a reason, after all."

"FINALLY," Anala said.

"Let's get down to business," Mikaela said in a serious tone. "Kyrie and Rizo are both out, which leaves just Me, Nova, Ryder, Anala, and you two." Mikaela indicated Dr. Duarte and Jared.

"And me!" Krackers said indignantly.

"Actually, we may be able to help Rizo," Dr. Duarte said. "Kyrie said you had a sprained wrist and ankle, so I brought some Quick Fix." Dr. Duarte produced a small bottle of pills.

"One of these should speed up your healing process," he said. "However, you'll have to lie in bed all day until the pill stops working. Kyrie and Rizo should both take one."

"Okay," Rizo agreed. "It's nighttime, I'll be sleeping for a while anyway."

"It makes the most sense to blow it up tomorrow night anyway," Mikaela said.

"Okay, it's settled then," Dr. Duarte said. "Rizo, take this pill and immediately go to bed. Don't get out unless absolutely necessary and only for a short period of time. Only when I clear you can you start participating in this operation. Understood?"

"Yes, sir," Rizo said, taking a pill and heading for bed. As he lay down on his bed, he felt an exhausting sensation sweeping over him. Immediately, his whole body began to ache. Rizo shivered. Modern medicine was helpful, but right now he was pretty uncomfortable. He thought about the people who the Netrhaphalin had experimented on. The Netrhaphalin had been trying to perfect direct brain inferences on humans so that they could control them. Most of the experiments had gone horribly wrong, often killing the humans, so the Netrhaphalin had finally given the idea up. Those people must have been in much more pain than Rizo was in now, but everything still hurt. Badly.

Rizo tried to go to sleep. That would hopefully speed up this process. However, listening to Nova and Anala excitedly review plans didn't exactly help. Plus, he had learned from experience that you never slept when you wanted to, you just had to wait for it to happen.

He waited and waited. It seemed that sleep would never come. However, his eyes began to flutter and his mind became foggy. He was going down a tunnel with only black at the end.

He took a deep breath and let the darkness swallow him.

>>> 9 hours later...

Rizo felt as if tiny needles were stabbing at him from all directions. He felt like he was going through a blender, his limbs were flailing wildly. It took him a while to realize that someone was shaking him. He pulled away. The shaking hurt.

"Ow, go away," he groaned.

"Rizo!" Nova called, as if from a long ways away.

"I can't... Nova?" Rizo asked groggily.

"Get up! Dr. Duarte said you should be able to by now, and we need you!"

"Okay," Rizo said, sitting up with a wince. "As long as I don't have to do anything like running."

"No, we need you to hack something!" Nova said. "Dr. Duarte says you're really good at that sort of thing."

Rizo felt a weird feeling in his chest that made him smile slightly. "Uh, thanks," he said. "I'm decent at it." They made their way to the living room.

"Dr. Duarte said you can hack a NETLINK," Nova said, her eyes wide.

"It took a while," Rizo said honestly.

"Don't be so modest. I could never do something like that," Nova said.

"I'm sure you could if you really tried. You're really smart," Rizo said encouragingly, painfully aware of the fact that they had reached the living room and were being watched by many people.

"Anyway," Krackers said, rolling his eyes. "Can you guys stop flirting? We have more important things to do."

Rizo felt his face grow hot. "I'm not flirting," he mumbled. He avoided Nova, quite sure that her face was the same shade as his.

Dr. Duarte ignored this interlude and said, "We need to discuss more important matters. We have a plan of action. Because Kyrie and Rizo are not fully recovered, they will be our backup and will be mission control. Nova, Anala, and Ryder will create a small diversion nearby involving some C-4 while Jared, Mikaela, Krackers, and I will go in for the gold. Got that? Kyrie, you need to hook up these earpieces to the GAMMALINK I brought with me. Now Rizo, we need you to hack into the security mainframe and disable some of the sensors, cameras, everything you can. Everyone else, come with me to discuss some finer points. We have less than 24 hours."

Concentration

Chapter 26

June 14, 2473

Rizo found it extremely hard to concentrate when he was surrounded by fever-pitch excitement. While he bent over the small GAMMALINK Dr. Duarte had brought and squinted at the chains of code, Ryder and Anala were setting off small amounts of C-4, claiming that they were "practicing". At the same time, Mikaela and Dr. Duarte were loudly discussing courses of action, Jared and Kyrie were arguing over who knows what, and Nova was pacing back and forth distractedly, occasionally shooting dirty looks at Krackers, who was preening his feathers condescendingly from his perch on the couch.

"Could you all quiet down?" Rizo tried weakly. Nobody heard him except Mikaela, who wrinkled her forehead. She whistled, and everyone froze in their tracks. A bit of C-4 detonated, shattering the silence.

"Rizo needs to concentrate," Mikaela said. "Let's keep it down. Anala and Ryder, you've used quite enough of that C-4. If you carry on like this, we won't have enough to explode anything. Honestly, is *anyone* practical around here? Rizo, go to you room and shut the door. That way it'll be a little less noisy."

"When did you become the boss?" Ryder asked.

Mikaela shot a steely glare at him, and he immediately shut his mouth and turned away.

Rizo took Mikaela up on her suggestion and moved to his room and sat on a chair and set the LINK on his desk, trying to fight the headache that was threatening to escalate into a full-blown migraine. Rubbing his temples, he turned his gaze to the LINK that was giving him so many problems. The GAMMALINK was projecting three holograms around him, and Rizo began manipulating them with his hands.

Needless to say, the security system of a covert Netrhaphalin factory was *insane*. There were so many layers that needed to be peeled off the whole thing, and Rizo was surprised that he actually had a talent for hacking and had improved on his skills after simply reading one book and practicing on Dr. Duarte's fake NETLINK.

After all, he had had some training in the past (courtesy of Dr. Duarte, who insisted that they learn the basics) and had displayed a knack for it, but hadn't thought he would have actually become good at it.

As nice as this thought was, Rizo knew it wouldn't mean anything if he didn't fully hack the system in time. He channeled all his concentration into the LINK and the lines of code before him.

A few hours later, Rizo had no idea if he was any closer to hacking the system than he was when he first started. He knew everyone was counting on him, yet he started to doubt his ability to hack at all. Darkness seemed to close around him. A sound from the door alerted him and he whipped around.

"Nova?" He asked.

"How are you doing?" Nova asked, looking over his shoulder. "Man, that looks confusing."

"It *is* confusing," Rizo admitted.

"You can do it," Nova said, bumping his shoulder good-naturedly.

"Thanks," Rizo said. "How long have I been here?"

"A few hours," Nova said, biting her lip. "Um, actually I came here to ask if you were almost done. We're moving out in T-minus 60 minutes, as Dr. Duarte says."

"Nova, I have no idea where I am. I could be done soon or later, I don't know," Rizo said, wrinkling his forehead.

"Well, I'm sure you'll get it soon," Nova said, with less confidence than Rizo would have liked.

"Hopefully," Rizo said uncertainly, tapping out another series of commands. "Can you keep me company?"

"Won't I distract you?" Nova asked.

"No, it's fine." Rizo said. Nova summoned a chair and sat down beside him. She watched silently as Rizo frowned and pressed a series of buttons. Lines of code flew in and out of the screen. Rizo sat back, just watching the code move in and out of his view.

"What are you doing now?" Nova asked.

"I'm scanning the code for irregularities," Rizo said.

"What?" Nova asked, confused.

"It's a bit complicated," Rizo shrugged. "Basically, I'm just looking for places to get in."

"Oh," Nova said, though she still looked puzzled.

"It could take a bit of time," Rizo said. "Like-" He abruptly stopped and leaned forward. "There!" He said, pointing at a chain of commands. He highlighted them in red. His fingers flew as he directed the code to do his will. A few long minutes passed. Rizo still kept typing and muttering to himself.

"Here goes nothing," he said. "I've been trying to crack this barrier for the last two hours."

Nova shuddered.

Rizo entered in the code and crossed his fingers and held his breath. He had stopped doing this a few hours ago, but having Nova there gave him renewed hope. A minute later, the screen flashed green, and he let out a whoop.

"You're a good luck charm!" he said to Nova ecstatically. "I did it!" He then turned back to the multiple holograms. "I think I have enough time to do what I call 'bouncing'."

"What?" Nova asked.

"It's probably not the right term," Rizo said. "But I'm pretty much leaving a fake trail behind that goes from one LINK to the next. Just when they think they've figured out where I hacked from, they'll discover a trail leading back to another LINK. I should probably be able to do one in forty-five minutes. I just have to be strategic about where I bounce to."

"Okay," Nova said, not looking quite as if she had just understood everything he had said. "I'll tell Dr. Duarte the good news."

She bounded off, and Rizo sat down to add some finishing touches to his masterpiece.

Half an hour later, Dr. Duarte called a team meeting.

"Kyrie and Rizo, are you all good?" He asked. Kyrie and Rizo were sharing the LINK now, which Rizo had set up in the living room.

"Yep," Kyrie said in an unusually calm voice for the situation at hand.

"Nova, Ryder, and Anala?" Dr. Duarte asked.

"All ready, Dr. Duarte," Anala said excitedly, bouncing up and down. "WE are going to ACE this!"

"I appreciate your enthusiasm," Mikaela said in only a half sarcastic voice.

"Do we really have to do this?" Nova asked. "I mean, it seems so... violent."

"Violent?" Mikaela rounded on Nova. "You think *this* is violent?"

"Mikaela," Dr. Duarte said weakly.

"The Netrhaphalin killed my family!" Mikaela exploded. "They killed them! Is that violent or not? Besides, it's not like we can poison the Netrhaphalin with arsenic."

"I just think-" Nova started.

"You don't understand and you never will," Mikaela snapped. "I *knew* you were a wimp. In your sheltered and peaceful little tunnels you probably think that everything is always sunshine and rainbows."

"Drop it Mikaela," Dr. Duarte said. "We need to work together."

Breathing heavily, Mikaela turned away. Nova looked down, tears gathering in her eyes. Rizo wanted to comfort her, but didn't know how. Anala put a hand on Nova's shoulder.

"Don't worry," Anala said. "Mikaela doesn't mean it."

"Yes, I do," Mikaela growled.

"You're holding us up," Dr. Duarte said, resorting to threats. "It you don't stop arguing, we're not going to be able to pull this off. And Mikaela, no more snide comments or you're off the mission."

Mikaela glowered at Dr. Duarte but didn't say anything.

"All right folks, let's go then," Dr. Duarte said wearily.

"Good luck Dad," Kyrie said.

"Yeah, good luck," Rizo said, looking at Nova. "I know you'll be fine."

"Don't worry," Nova said softly. "I'll be fine."

Kyrie wordlessly handed out earpieces to everyone.

"Move out, troops," Dr. Duarte said as everyone stuck the earpieces in their ear.

"Goodbye and good luck," Kyrie said.

Everyone left, reluctantly or eagerly. Kyrie closed the door and put her headset on. Rizo did the same. Thankfully, he wasn't as sore as he had been a few hours ago. He set to work disabling as many security systems as possible.

"We are teleporting in T-minus 5 seconds," Dr. Duarte's voice came over the headset. "The video will go dark for a bit." Dr. Duarte had mounted miniscule cameras on all of them so that Kyrie could monitor their progress.

"Got that, Dad," Kyrie said, tapping a few things on the hologram that was showing the videos from the party. In quick succession, all of the videos went dark.

Rizo turned and disabled a security camera that would have recorded their entry into a Telecube Station and watched as the videos on Kyrie's screen popped up again.

"Splitting up now," Ryder said, and the videos diverged, with Nova, Anala, and Ryder going one way and the others going in another direction. Rizo pulled his eyes away from the action and focused on his task. Disabling the security cameras of the overzealous Netrhaphalin was a hard task, as there was one every three meters.

"Are you in position?" Ryder asked. Anala could be heard in the background, begging Ryder to let her speak.

"I'm the group leader, Anala," Ryder said sternly. "Sorry about that. Are you in position?"

"Copy that," Mikaela's voice came over, tinted with barely suppressed glee.

"Diversion incoming," Ryder said. "Going radio silence now. This could get hectic. Keep an eye on us, Kyrie."

"We're ready," Dr. Duarte said.

Rizo watched as Ryder bent forward, set the C-4 up and stood back.

In a few seconds, an explosion rocked the screen. Ryder seemed to be running. Anala's screen was still. Rizo could see Nova helping Anala through the cloud of debris through Ryder's screen.

Rizo glanced at Dr. Duarte's screen. They were infiltrating the factory, slowly but surely.

"Rizo!" Dr. Duarte hissed. "Security!"

"Oh, sorry, I forgot!" Rizo said, turning to disable a few cameras and sensors that were ahead of them.

Rizo then turned his attention to Ryder's screen. Anala and Nova were making slow progress.

"Are they okay?" Rizo asked Kyrie. She shook her head.

"Ryder? What's up with Nova and Anala?" She asked.

"Don't worry," he said. "We've got it covered. There are three whole squads investigating the explosion."

"Just don't get caught," Kyrie said.

"Don't worry," Ryder repeated.

"All right," Kyrie said uncertainly.

"Stop fighting both of you," Nova gasped. "Ryder, help me."

"I can't!" Ryder said. His camera was moving erratically now. "I just... can't." A Netrhaphalin flew in and out of his video. Ryder was breathing heavily, trying to save his breath.

"We should go in for them," Rizo said, worried.

"No," Kyrie shook her head. "Give them a few more minutes to sort themselves out."

Rizo ground his teeth while he disabled a few cameras and sensors absentmindedly. He hated that he had to stay behind.

"Rizo!" Pay attention!" Dr. Duarte said. "We almost got caught with a sensor back there."

"Sorry, sorry!" Rizo apologized, frantically disabling a few more sensors.

"Just focus," Dr. Duarte snapped.

Rizo kept his eyes on his task- for a few seconds. He glanced at Ryder's video.

"We lost them," Ryder panted. "It was epic!"

Rizo could see Anala and Nova right in front of Ryder. Both were beaming. Anala gave Rizo a wave through Ryder's camera.

"That was AWESOME!" She told him.

"Glad you think so," Rizo said. He took a deep breath. His sister was fine. Maybe they were going to get through this unscathed after all.

"Rizo!" Dr. Duarte yelled. Rizo whipped around.

"What?" He asked frantically.

Rizo watched in horror as Netrhaphalin surrounded Dr. Duarte, Mikaela, and Jared while shoving Krackers into a cage. Rizo turned to Ryder's video and saw Nova and Anala clinging to each other while the Netrhaphalin closed in.

Kyrie shut down her earpiece and indicated that Rizo should do the same.

"They can't answer us. Who knows if the Netrhaphalin have their earpieces by now?" Kyrie asked, shutting down the videos. "You have to go in by yourself. I want to, but I'm afraid that I'm too heavily injured to do something like that. I did take the pill, but it's not a miracle cure."

"Me? Against all the Netrhaphalin?" Rizo asked.

"Yes," Kyrie said. "No doubt they've bugged the place, so I doubt I can get away with talking to you."

"I thought I disabled all the bugs," Rizo said.

"I think you missed some," Kyrie said bluntly. "Nevertheless, we can't risk it. You're their only hope."

"But I'm not good at that kind of stuff," Rizo protested. "Can't you come with me?"

"No, I'll only slow you down," Kyrie said. "Just go, Rizo! Take the telecube- go." Rizo looked at Kyrie and realized that she was scared. She wanted to help her family, but she couldn't.

"Can you give me anything that can help me?" Rizo begged. "Please."

"That, I can do," Kyrie said. She handed him some leftover C-4, a pen that could shoot a bullet, and an old taser that Dr. Duarte had modified to short-circuit a Netrhaphalin.

"Electricity is their biggest weakness," he had said. "That's why they banned any electric conducting weapons. Luckily, I managed to salvage a few from museums."

"Thank you," Rizo said.

"Good luck," Kyrie said, handing Rizo 5 bullets for the pen. "Don't mess things up. I really can't do much right now, which means I can't save you and everyone else. Oh, and Rizo? I'm sorry, but you're going to have to wing this whole operation."

Rizo glanced around and gulped. How could he do this? Then he thought of Anala and Nova, trapped and scared. He really couldn't delay any longer. Without hesitating, so that he wouldn't overthink it, Rizo primed the telecube, then stepped into it and let himself be whisked away.

Solo Infiltration

Chapter 27

June 14, 2473

Rizo was teleported to a blindingly bright white room. He held the taser, which doubled as a flashlight and an ALPHALINK, up so that he was ready to strike at any moment. He turned on the ALPHALINK part of the old taser, and a single hologram flickered to life. Rizo pulled up a map. It seemed like he was underground. Rizo sighed. Why did he always have to be like a mole, going from one tunnel to another?

Rizo went to the door and realized that it needed a code to open. Rizo took a step back. Would he already have to abort the mission? Turning the taser in his hand, he realized that there was only one way to do this. Yes, it would be messy, and yes, he would probably alert the Netrhaphalin to his presence. Also, it was the craziest and most foolish thing he had done in his entire life. But when he thought about Anala and Nova, he took a deep breath. No way he was going to pass up this opportunity to save them and live with that knowledge for the rest of his life. Rizo took the C-4 and split it apart carefully, then jammed some into the door. He loaded the pen and stepped back as far as he could. Then he took aim and fired. His shot was nowhere close to the wad of C-4. The bullet lodged itself in the wall a good foot from the explosive. Rizo took a deep breath and tried again. Still no luck. If possible, Rizo had been off by even more. Luckily, the pen was silent. If it hadn't been, every Netrhaphalin would be baring down on him right now.

Third time's a charm, Rizo said to himself. He lined himself up with the C-4, then shot. The bullet ricocheted off a titanium bar and hit a centimeter away from the explosive. A few sparks flew. That was all it took. There was a deafening bang, and the wall crumbled. Rizo jumped through the debris and ran for his life, hiding in a room marked COMMUNICATION. A lone Netrhaphalin was there, monitoring a NETLINK and talking to another

Netrhaphalin. Rizo flipped on the taser and jabbed it at the Netrhaphalin. It collapsed. Rizo flipped the Netrhaphalin over and realized that it had letters on it. It read CRUZ. Rizo also realized that all Netrhaphalin had a series of letters on them, he just hadn't noticed before. Rizo did not dwell on this revelation and instead exited the room through another unmarked door.

This led to a simple drop. Rizo groaned as he realized that Netrhaphalin could fly down this and therefore had no need for stairs or elevators. Rizo contemplated this before searching the room for anything that could help him get down. There was nothing. Rizo could hear Netrhaphalin searching for the cause of the commotion a little ways away. He glanced down the shaft again. On closer inspection, Rizo saw that there were small metal rods jutting out from the concrete. Rizo decided to climb down them.

It was a nerve-wracking journey, and Rizo's hands grew slick with sweat. The shaft was long, and Rizo's foot slipped. With great effort, he regained his footing. He knew he didn't have much time, as it wouldn't be long until the Netrhaphalin discovered Cruz on the floor. And yet, he still had about ten meters to go. Rizo wiped his hand on his shirt and kept descending slowly. Finally, he was only a meter and a half from the bottom. He let go and landed heavily, admiring how much he had risked on a whim. Not that he would do the same if he could actually stop and *think*.

He walked out of the shaft, breathing heavily. He realized that he actually had no idea where everyone was, so he decided to go to security first. Then, he could hopefully see them through a camera. Rizo relaxed. Finally, he had a plan. Well, somewhat of a plan. An outline of a plan.

A hologram directory was conveniently down the hallway. Rizo peered at it and deduced that the security room was behind a number of checkpoints but otherwise easy to get in. *Well*, Rizo thought grimly, *maybe I should say there are no other obstacles except those, which are pretty terrifying.*

Rizo crept along the halls, trying hard to be unnoticed. Thankfully, he didn't bump into any Netrhaphalin. Suddenly, a clanking noise that grew louder seemed to be coming from an unmarked door. He pushed it open, curious. It was the factory! Rizo watched as gears flipped and half-formed Netrhaphalin emerged into view for a second then vanished into another machine. Rizo crouched behind a massive machine that had four letters. One letter was constantly flipping, and Rizo watched as the letters formed Salh, then Salj, and then Sall. Those letters were then printed on to the disjoined bodies of Netrhaphalin to-be.

"Ohhhh," Rizo said out loud. The "names" of the Netrhaphalin indicated when they had been made. The earlier the letter, the older they were. No wonder Jami had called Rerl a 'rookie'. The first letter on this machine was 'S', and Rerl had been an 'R'. Rerl was fresh out of the factory. *No wonder they have funny names*, Rizo thought. All the names were computer-generated. Rizo frowned as he realized that the letter machine had skipped the letter 'K'. Rizo wondered if it skipped 'K' because of Kano. Maybe the letter K was not used out of respect for him.

Rizo watched, mesmerized, as partly-formed Netrhaphalin emerged and disappeared in an out of different machines. He watched as the letters on the naming machine clicked through the alphabet. He just sat on the cold stone floor. He didn't know how many minutes- or maybe hours- had passed when he remembered that he had a mission. He got up with a start and accidently bumped into a lose piece of equipment. It fell with a loud clatter. Rizo jumped. He looked around to see if any Netrhaphalin had noticed. It seemed as if none had, but he still stayed alert and more careful.

Rizo crept along to the first checkpoint and hid in a closet. A Netrhaphalin was there, floating from side to side restlessly, looking at a hologram.

"No, I haven't seen any humans around," the Netrhaphalin said. "Really? They blew up the Telecube portal? Do you need any help?"

There was a stiff pause. Then the Netrhaphalin said, "A Netrhaphalin needing re-naming?" Was it a factory error?"

Another pause.

"In the hands of humans? No way? Resistance groups? What's its name right now?"

Another pause. Then the Netrhaphalin gave a snort of disgust.

"Hope? What kind of name is that? It probably has nothing to do with its status, I bet."

Another pause. Rizo raised his eyebrows. Hope was going to be re-named? In this very factory? Did she even remember them now?

"I'll be there. No, the checkpoint is fine. A human can't even get down the shaft. You'll probably catch them soon."

Rizo grinned. Obviously, this Netrhaphalin had heavily underestimated him.

"Deva, I'll be fine. I'm Bope, if you haven't forgotten. That's a whole 2 letters above you," the Netrhaphalin said bossily.

Rizo swallowed his laughter. What kind of self-respecting Netrhaphalin would be called Bope?

"Stop dithering, Deva, I'm coming." Bope glided out of the room, failing to see Rizo watching him from the closet. As soon as he was gone, Rizo tried to open the door. Of course, Bope had left it unlocked. Rizo pushed it open and found himself facing an angry Netrhaphalin. Whipping out his taser, he jabbed it at the Netrhaphalin, which made a "Ahhhh" sound and crumpled. Rizo went to the hologram that was asking to enter a code. Rizo flipped the Netrhaphalin over and saw that the letters printed on it read EVVE. Rizo keyed this in. ACCESS DENIED flashed across the screen. This message was closely followed by the words LOCKDOWN IMMINENT. YOU HAVE A MINUTE TO DISABLE LOCKDOWN WITH TODAY'S CODE. In a panic, Rizo looked around desperately. On another hologram were Evve's messages. He scrolled through them. One caught his eye. It was headlined: PASSCODE FOR SECURITY CHECKPOINTS.

Rizo tapped the message. It read:

To all Netrhaphalin in Factory 4:
The code for the following checkpoints are:
Checkpoint 1: PRVS147
Checkpoint 2: JMO788
Checkpoint 3: KANO44
Checkpoint 4: 3E4R5T6

MYRAH898

-Arin
Director of Security
Factory 4
Letter: A

Rizo quickly typed in the passcode for checkpoint #2. The LOCKDOWN IMMINENT message vanished and was replaced by the words, ACCESS GRANTED. HAVE A GOOD DAY. The door slid open. Rizo jotted down the passcodes on the ALPHALINK and walked forward. He copied down the last sequence; even though he didn't know what it was for. The next checkpoint was around the corner, and Rizo held his taser at the ready. However, this checkpoint was deserted. Rizo quickly typed KANO44 into the hologram, and the door opened. He saw the security room ahead of him. He ran, tapped the passcode into the nearby LINK, and burst through the door. Two startled Netrhaphalin turned around. Rizo zapped both of them with his taser before they could react, then stepped over their limp forms. He then took a look at the camera feeds playing out on multiple holograms.

He realized that there must be two separate security systems, as there were two NETLINKS, one showing half of hallways and one showing the other half. Rizo realized that he had only hacked into one system, and that was why they had gotten caught. This knowledge gave him a sense of overwhelming relief. He wasn't responsible for his friends' capture after all. Well, he wasn't completely responsible for it. He could have paid a bit more attention, but it wouldn't have done any good. Rizo scanned the holograms, looking for his friends. After a few minutes, he found them on a monitor. They seemed to be talking to a Netrhaphalin or someone that was just out of view. Dr. Duarte looked extremely stressed and worried.

As Rizo watched, a Netrhaphalin carried Anala forward. She looked terrified. Rizo watched in horror as the Netrhaphalin talked to Dr. Duarte. It seemed as if the Netrhaphalin was angry. Rizo stood, rooted to the spot as the Netrhaphalin shot lasers directly at his sister. She writhed in pain. Rizo couldn't hear what was going on, but he was sure that Anala was screaming in agony.

"Anala!" Rizo cried. He turned to the map in the security room and found that his sister was being held in the interrogation amphitheater. He plotted out a quick route to the amphitheater. Holding a taser in one hand, he ran out of the security room and into the hall. He ran as fast as he could, hoping that the Netrhaphalin hadn't stunned her- or worse. Whatever they were doing, they were certainly using her as a hostage. Rizo made a left, then right. He paused to catch his breath, clutching at the stitch in his side. Dr. Duarte had always told him that he was out of shape, but he had never really known that until he had gone out into the real world.

Gulping down air, he sprinted forward. He had to help his sister. He had typed the directions down on the ALPHALINK, so he consulted the hologram.

He rounded a corner and promptly slammed into three Netrhaphalin.

"Oof," Rizo winced, falling down.

"Ah, little human," one Netrhaphalin said, smiling menacingly. "We've found you at last."

Rizo looked up and jabbed the Netrhaphalin with his taser. Its look of pleasure turned into one of shock, then disappeared altogether. Rizo jabbed the other startled Netrhaphalin with the taser. One crumbled, but the other dodged his blow. The Netrhaphalin grabbed Rizo from behind. Rizo twisted around and hit it with the taser, but not before it called for reinforcements. Rizo made a run for it. Unfortunately, he made a wrong turn in his haste.

A Netrhaphalin was there, manning a NETLINK. Rizo stunned it easily, then turned around. He was faced by five Netrhaphalin, all who were forming a wall around him. Rizo jabbed at one, but to his surprise, the taser did nothing. Pocketing the device, he ran for it. The Netrhaphalin blocked off his escape, gliding soundlessly.

"Give up," one of them called. "and we will spare you."

Rizo doubted the validity of this statement and crouched, scanning his surroundings.

"How come this doesn't work on you?" Rizo asked, holding up the taser.

"We are a special force," A Netrhaphalin named Pewe said. "We do not run on electricity. We run on gears and cogs only. Rudimentary materials, but the way we are made is extraordinary."

Rizo gazed at the letters PEWE on the Netrhaphalin and again experienced the sensation of trying hard not to laugh at such an absurd name.

"How does your AI run?" Rizo asked, stalling for time. "I mean, you do not have any electricity in you."

"Ah, such things will not make sense to inferior beings like you," Pewe said. Rizo noticed that it spoke with a lisp, as if it was choking out the sentence. Every word was strained.

"Why am I in trouble?" Rizo asked, feigning innocence. He slowly slid towards a glass window that looked into the factory. His mind was slowly forming something that he could do to escape, but he needed as much time as possible.

"You know why you are in trouble," Pewe scoffed. "Or are you too stupid to think like us?" Another Netrhaphalin laughed behind Pewe. Its laugh sounded like metal grinding metal. Rizo cringed.

"I don't know, really, I don't," Rizo said, widening his eyes. He slid closer and closer to the large window.

"Ha, you are not fooling me, Pewe!" The Netrhaphalin sneered. Rizo had to pinch himself to keep a straight face.

"Is something the matter? What smells?" Rizo asked pleasantly.

"What? Oh, I am saying my name, you idiot. Pewe. Pewe!" The Netrhaphalin flung out his arm in a dramatic pose, and Rizo took this opportunity to whip the bullet-firing pen out of his pocket. Taking aim, he shot the window.

There was a tinkling of glass, and a layer of the glass shattered. Reizo picked up a shard with a sharp, pointed edge and slashed it across Pewe's eyes. He had watched Mikaela and Kyrie execute this move many times, so it wasn't difficult. While Pewe roared, Rizo took advantage of the situation and slashed the other Netrhaphalins' eyes. He ran away as fast as he could towards the place where Anala and Nova were. At the end of a long corridor there was a nondescript double door. To his relief, it was unlocked. He pushed it open and took in the scene before him.

Anala lay sprawled on the floor, breathing heavily. A trickle of blood was coming from a cut on her arm. A Netrhaphalin stood over her, knife in hand. The others were being restrained by Netrhaphalin, struggling against their captors even though they were bound and gagged.

"Anala!" Rizo yelled, rushing towards his sister.

"Ah, Rizo, how nice of you to join us," a cool voice with a British accent purred. "This makes things *very* easy."

Rizo looked into the eyes of someone he had hoped he would never see again. Dr. Nikita was standing on a raised dais, her hands calmly folded behind her back.

"Now you tell us exactly what is going on..." Dr. Nikita paused benevolently. "or your little sister dies."

Confrontation

Chapter 28
June 15, 2473

Rizo stopped.

"I-I don't know anything," he stuttered.

"Yes, you do," Dr. Nikita said. She paced up and down the dais, shaking her head. "And if you knew better, you would tell me what you know." Even though Dr. Nikita was threatening Rizo, her accent made her voice sound pleasant.

"What are you doing here anyway?" Rizo asked.

"I'm asking the questions, not you," Dr. Nikita raised an eyebrow.

"I just want to know," Rizo shrugged.

"Don't give me sass," Dr. Nikita said threateningly. She flicked her wrist at the Netrhaphalin tormenting Anala and he moved the knife closer to her throat.

"Okay!" Rizo said. "I'll tell you everything!"

"Very good," Dr. Nikita said triumphantly. "Now, where will we begin? Oh, yes, why are you here, in a secret Netrhaphalin factory?"

"We were-" Rizo paused, searching for a believable lie he could tell Dr. Nikita.

"Spit it out," Dr. Nikita ordered. She snapped her fingers, and the Netrhaphalin holding the knife over Anala held it even closer to her neck.

"We were going to try to bug it!" Rizo said quickly. "We wanted to see what you all were up too. We didn't know it was a factory."

Dr. Nikita's eyes narrowed, as if she was trying to sense a lie beneath Rizo's words.

"You did not know it was a factory," Dr. Nikita paced some more.

"No," Rizo said, trying to sell the lie as best he could. He glanced at Mikaela and Nova, hoping that they would have something that would help them get out of this mess. Rizo copied Dr. Nikita's pacing, waiting for her to say something.

"Stand still," Dr. Nikita said sharply. "If you don't, I can have some Netrhaphalin *encourage* you to stop moving." Dr. Nikita's lips turned up into a menacing smile.

"Yes, ma'am," Rizo said quietly, standing as still as he could. He did not want any Netrhaphalin to 'encourage' him to stand still. That form of persuasion was most likely torture.

"Now, about your story. You know what I think?" Dr. Nikita said, leaning forward. "I think that you are a liar." She hissed the last word so quietly so that Rizo was the only one who could hear her. "Well," she said in a normal voice. "I gave you a chance." Dr. Nikita clapped her hands. "Irmo, bring in the truth-telling device."

Rizo shuddered. He watched as a Netrhaphalin entered with a metal chair that was so heavy that it was swaying with the weight.

"You know you have no choice. Either you tell the truth- or your sister dies *and* you get shot painfully with electricity," Dr. Nikita said clinically. "It's definitely poetic, don't you think? You brought down so many with that taser of yours, and now you are at the mercy of my electricity. I've been meaning to test how much shock a human can withstand until they die, but I've been too busy studying $LD_{50}s$ on other human test subjects." Dr. Nikita sighed dramatically.

Rizo glanced at Dr. Duarte, who looked both furious and appalled at the same time.

"What are $LD_{50}s$?" Rizo asked cautiously.

"You don't know? Tsk, tsk," Dr. Nikita clicked her tongue disapprovingly. "Doesn't my ex-colleague teach you anything? I suppose he thought such a topic was too sensitive for your ears. Well, a LD_{50} is the amount of chemical that will kill half, or 50%, of all test subjects."

Rizo was pushed into the chair by a Irmo and put up no protest, he was too stunned at what Dr. Nikita had just said.

"You're testing poisons on *humans*?" He asked, horrified. "That's just sick."

Rizo glanced at Nova. She looked as nauseous as he felt. Mikaela's face was a stony mask of hatred, while Dr. Duarte mirrored Jared's face, which was etched with disapproval and disgust. Ryder looked shocked.

"One thing I admire about the Netrhaphalin is that they do not let *ethics*," Dr. Nikita spat this word out like it was a rotten tomato. "get in the way of science. That's one of the reasons I joined them. I was on the brink of discovering something revolutionary when Dr. Duarte here destroyed all my years of hard work. In exchange for my services, Kano sends me some Netrhaphalin to aid me in my experiments." She pulled up a hover chair more forcibly than she needed to and sat down huffily. This was a fancy one that had a desk built-in. A hologram appeared in front of her, and she tapped it thoughtfully.

"Let's get back to business," Dr. Nikita said calmly. Rizo barely heard her, he was too disturbed by this revelation. What a wicked, nasty thing human experimentation was. Dr. Nikita was a human herself. Didn't she have compassion for any of her victims?

"Tut, tut," Dr. Nikita looked up. "Rizo, I suggest you not think such brutal things."

Rizo sat up, shocked for the millionth time that day. A hologram was spelling out the words in his head at that very moment.

"You're reading my mind?" Rizo gasped, struggling to stop anything from appearing on that hologram.

"You could say that," Dr. Nikita said, taking notes on her hologram. "You know, it's the first time I've used this. How interesting. It is only reading your most prominent thoughts. Disappointing."

Rizo let his mind go blank, and tried to keep it that way. He imagined covering his mind with a dark cloth, and, to his surprise, the hologram dimmed. His thoughts, for he could not stop them, were dark and flickering. Rizo concentrated on making the cloth a wall, and the hologram blacked out completely.

Dr. Nikita frowned, though Rizo did not see the corners of her mouth dip down. He was focusing so hard on that wall that he thought his head might explode.

"Rizo, why did you come here?" Dr. Nikita's cool voice asked.

"To bug this place," Rizo said as convincingly as he could. "I told you!" Answering had lifted the wall for a second, and Dr. Nikita had caught a glimpse of something else. However, she did not know what she had seen. Rizo glanced at Mikaela, whose hands were flying. With a flash of understanding, Rizo realized she was using sign language.

Dr. Duarte had forced them to learn it, even though it had been dead for hundreds of years since the surgery that could cure one's deafness.

"It's useful," he had said.

Mikaela was signing frantically. Rizo caught the words 'taser' and 'me'. He squinted at her. He finally realized that she wanted the taser. His face screwed up in concentration to keep his mental wall up, he slowly moved his hand toward his pants pocket. The Netrhaphalin were not as smart as they thought they were. They had forgotten about his weapons. And truth to be told, Rizo had, too.

"I asked you a question, Rizo," Dr. Nikita said crisply.

"Oh, sorry?" Rizo said, concentrating hard.

"Who is that?" Dr. Nikita pointed at Mikaela. "I do not recognize her."

"Uh, Sharon," Rizo said, going with Mikaela's alias that she had used with the Rockets.

"So she was telling the truth," Dr. Nikita muttered, making a note on her hologram.

"Excuse me?" Rizo asked.

"I was just making sure that Sharon was who she said she was. She was a bit quick to answer my question," Dr. Nikita said, drumming her fingers rhythmically on her desk.

"You mean that question was a trick?" Rizo asked.

"No, it was simply cursory. I had to make sure that nobody was lying." Dr. Nikita looked down at her desk, and Rizo moved his hand into his pocket. His face was contorted in concentration as he kept up the wall guarding his thoughts.

"What's that?" Rizo asked loudly, pretending to be alarmed. While everyone was distracted, he pulled out the pen and fired it at a window that looked into the factory. Heads swiveled in the direction of the shattering glass. Dr. Nikita jumped up and made her way to the window, the rest of the Netrhaphalin on her trail. Rizo quickly drew out the taser, placed it on the floor, and kicked it over to Mikaela while slipping the pen back into his pocket. Mikaela bent down hastily and scooped up the taser. She whisked it out of sight and zapped the Netrhaphalin holding her while it was distracted. It slumped slightly. Luckily, she had backed up against the wall so that the Netrhaphalin didn't fall to the floor. While Mikaela was straining to hold her Netrhaphalin in place, Dr. Nikita marched over to Rizo.

"Did you do that?" She asked, pointing her finger into his face.

"N-no," Rizo stammered, leaning away from her. "I didn't do anything!"

Dr. Nikita slapped him across his face. "Tell me the truth," she hissed. "I am not a cruel person, contrary to what you might think. I do everything in the name of science. I simply believe that we should not let our conscience get in the way of discovery."

"Then you're evil," Rizo said, glaring at her defiantly. Dr. Nikita looked taken aback.

"I am *not*!" She exclaimed. She looked quite offended. "I'm actually finding things out about this world that will benefit all of us."

"That doesn't matter one bit if you are hurting other people in the process!" Rizo argued. "Do you really have to know everything? I mean, if it's dangerous to find out, just make a guess, or wing it, or- I don't know; just do something less destructive!"

Rizo had reached a tipping point, and he now realized that he was okay with just going along with the flow. If you tried to find out everything about your situation, people could get hurt.

"I mean, science is cool and all, but do you really have to know everything, even the stuff that can hurt you? I mean, knowing less is sometimes knowing more. If you don't know something, you can be more creative."

"Fool!" Dr. Nikita said. "Those half-cocked impulses will just get you killed."

"Well, I've done quite a few spur-of-the-moment things, and I'm not dead yet," Rizo countered. "Besides, you *are* having people killed. It's not like knowing things will help their situation."

"Sacrifices must be made in the name of progress," Dr. Nikita said through gritted teeth.

"Not sacrifices this big, Dr. Nikita. You're killing people just to know the precise amount of arsenic that will kill them? Come on. Just say, arsenic is lethal and leave it at that. Testing chemicals on vermin are one thing. Testing this stuff on humans is an entirely different matter," Rizo said earnestly.

"You don't understand," Dr. Nikita spat.

"I don't," Rizo said. "I don't understand why you would kill people for science. That's just horrible. Don't you have any heart?"

"It's for science!" Dr. Nikita seemed to explode. She walked over to Rizo as if she was going to hit him. At the last moment, she stopped and composed herself.

"This is not the point of this interrogation," she muttered, taking deep breaths. "I am questioning you, not the other way around."

Rizo glanced at Mikaela. She signed for him to keep stalling Dr. Nikita. Rizo was very glad that Mikaela had a plan, and that the taser was in competent hands. Even though he was okay with winging a mission, he still was slightly partial to plans.

"But-" Rizo started, looking directly at Dr. Nikita.

"Hold your tongue," she snapped. "I am trying to calm down. If you have enough nerve, speak and feel my wrath."

Rizo shut his mouth. Even though he knew he had to stall Dr. Nikita, he didn't want to deal with her rage. The moment of silence gave him time to marvel about the fact that it was easier to keep the wall on. It was becoming sort of a second thought, rather than a first one.

Rizo sucked in a slow breath, relaxing slightly. He glanced at Mikaela again. She discreetly signed that he get everyone's attention quickly. Rizo jerked his head up to show her that he had understood and looked at Dr. Nikita once more.

She was muttering to herself. "I am perfectly calm and not evil. That boy is lying! I am calm. Very calm."

Rizo considered Dr. Nikita with interest. Perhaps she did have a heart after all, if she hated the thought of being evil.

Of course, she could also just be convincing herself that Rizo was horrible and deserved to die. Rizo had to shut down this rather morbid and discouraging train of thought. He had to stay calm, no matter what.

"Dr. Nikita?" Rizo asked.

"Shut your mouth," Dr. Nikita snapped. "I did warn you." She pressed a button on a controller that Rizo hadn't seen before. Pain coursed up and down him. He was writhing in pain, every nerve in his body was on fire.

And then it stopped. Rizo slumped in his chair, breathing heavily.

376

"I hope you've learned your lesson," Dr. Nikita said. "Hmm, I thought that would completely take away your mental barrier. Interesting."

Rizo sat up in surprise. He craned his neck to see that his wall was flickering, like a black veil fluttering in the wind. He concentrated, and his wall solidified.

Dr. Nikita looked at Rizo up and down. Her gaze traveled to the pen, which had half-fallen out of Rizo's pocket while he had been thrashing around.

"What is that?" She asked, her voice sharp.

"Nothing, just a pen," Rizo said, struggling to keep his voice calm. He pushed it back into his pocket.

"Likely story," Dr. Nikita said. She lunged at him, grabbing at the pen. All the Netrhaphalin turned to look at her.

Mikaela threw herself into action. She zapped every Netrhaphalin holding the others, including the one standing over Anala, then ran over to where two shocked robots were cleaning up the glass. She stunned them and grabbed a shard of glass off the floor. She slashed the nearest Netrhaphalin's eyes, then made her way to Rizo, immobilizing robots as she went. Dr. Nikita's eyes widened, and she whipped around.

"Stop her!" She screamed.

"Get the explosives!" Mikaela yelled to Rizo, pointing to a huge lump of C-4 in the corner of the room. Rizo ran towards them and scooped them up.

He ran towards the factory and plunked the C-4 down smack dab in the center of the machines. Dr. Duarte ran into the factory, holding a long-range detonator.

"I'll blow it up when we're ready!" He yelled. "Go help the others! I need to hook this up and amplify it!"

Rizo dashed off. Jared had scooped up Anala, who was unconscious, so Rizo darted towards Nova.

"We have to evacuate! Now!" He cried. He pulled Nova away from the throng of Netrhaphalin who were chasing her and located Jared, Anala, Krackers, Ryder, and Mikaela with his eyes. They ran towards him, and he ran down the hall. When he found the security checkpoints, he typed the passcode in with ease.

"What?" Mikaela asked, dumbstruck.

"I'll tell you later," Rizo panted.

Mikaela took the lead, taking Rizo to a part of the factory he had never been to before. It had a huge glass floor looking down into the factory.

"We need to make a way for Dr. Duarte to escape," she said.

"How will we break the glass?" Nova gasped, clutching her side.

Rizo felt in his pocket for the extra C-4 that he had saved from when he had blasted the telecube station door off.

"Here," he handed it to Mikaela.

"Excellent." She put it on the glass. She had retrieved her pen from the Netrhaphalin, and now she aimed it at the C-4 from the concrete platform.

"Stand on something solid," she instructed them. As they moved to a safer spot, she took aim and fired. The glass shattered, layer by layer, until there was a hole. Mikaela pulled out some wire and lowered it down from the hole.

Rizo glanced around. He paled as he saw a horde of Netrhaphalin advancing towards them.

"Mikaela!" He said, pointing. Her eyes grew wide.

"Shoot," she said. Looking down the hole, she yelled. "Dr. Duarte! Catch!"

Dr. Duarte held on to the wire, and everyone strained to pull him out of the hole. He scrambled up, and Mikaela let go of the wire and slammed her taser into the arm of the closest Netrhaphalin. Because all of the robots were so densely packed together, she took out half of them with one electric current.

While she struck out again, Rizo and the others ran past the Netrhaphalin. Unfortunately, one of the Netrhaphalin whisked the detonator out of Dr. Duarte's hand.

No one realized what had happened except Rizo. Without waiting to tell the others, he pounced on the Netrhaphalin. Picking up some lose glass as he tumbled around the floor, he slashed the robot's eyes so that he could not shoot him with lasers.

Rizo wrestled the detonator out of the metal hand and ran for his life. He ran to the Telecube station and joined the others, who were looking worried.

"I've lost the detonator!" Dr. Duarte said to Rizo.

"No, I've got it," Rizo said, gulping air down. "Let's go."

Dr. Duarte fiddled with the controller; Mikaela right next to him.

"They've shut it down!" Mikaela said, her face filled with panic.

"We have to get out another way!" Rizo said. "Come on!" He ran out of the station and took random turns, the others following him. He skidded to a halt as he saw around ten Netrhaphalin coming towards him. He could tell that they were all electricity-immune, as their movements were jerky and because Pewe was in the lead.

However, he also saw the emergency exit behind Pewe.

"They're immune to the taser!" He called to his friends. They stopped, gazing at the Netrhaphalin coming their way. Mikaela hesitated for a second before she sprang at the robots with a glass shard in her hand. Rizo looked down and realized that he still had some glass, too. He let himself marvel that such a simple weapon could take down such a formidable enemy only for a second before throwing himself into the fray. Slashing a path towards the door, he threw himself at the emergency exit.

He knew just by a glance that it needed a password to open. With a sudden flashback, he remembered the code that had been on the message with no explanation and entered it in. The door swung open. Rizo beckoned everyone to come through, then slammed the door behind him, locking it. Outside, it was nighttime, though you could barely tell because of the light pollution. He could see that the sun seemed to be peaking over the horizon, so it was very early in the morning.

"Let's go!" He said, beckoning to the rest of them.

"Wait," Mikaela said. She was in exceptionally good shape, as she wasn't breathing as hard as the rest of them. "I want to see this factory blown to smithereens."

"Here," Rizo handed her the detonator.

"You should do it," Nova said. "You saved us."

"Oh, okay," Rizo said, flushing slightly at Nova's compliment.

With a sense of thrill and the knowledge that he was doing the right thing, Rizo slammed his fist into the detonator.

It was finally time that the Netrhaphalin got what they deserved.

KANO

Explosions

Chapter 29
June 15, 2473

Rizo waited. Nothing happened. Just as he was turning to the others to ask if Dr. Duarte had hooked things up correctly, a rumbling shook the pavement under his feet. Rizo fell down.

"Run!" He yelled. "This is about to blow!"
Everyone scattered.

Rizo watched from a safe distance as the road shuddered. Then, with a deafening bang, it caved in on itself. The screech of metal assaulted his ears, and rancid smoke made him cough.

"Let's get out of here," he said, blindly trying to find his friends. He bumped into Nova.

"Let's go!" He yelled to her over the cacophony of sound. People were yelling, sirens were wailing, and metal groaned ominously.

Nova nodded, and they both ran like the wind.

Rizo didn't stop until he could no longer hear or see the explosion.

"Where are the others?" He asked Nova, looking around.

She was doubled up next to him, gasping for air. "I- don't- know," she croaked.

"How are we going to get back?" Rizo asked. Nova simply shook her head. Rizo decided to sit down on the soft grass to catch his breath a wait for someone to tell him what was going on. Nova followed his lead.

"I'm so tired," Rizo said, lying down.

"Same," Nova groaned.

"I just want things to go back to the way they were," Rizo admitted. "I mean, all the stuff we did was for a good cause, but I feel like now I'll never be able to look at somethings the same way again."

"I know what you mean," Nova said. "Do you think Dr. Nikita survived the blast?"

"I have no idea," Rizo said. "She *was* pretty evil, so although I won't say that she deserved it, she didn't not deserve it, either."

"I know," Nova said. "I can't believe she tested chemicals on humans. That's diabolical."

"I don't even want to think about it," Rizo shuddered.

Suddenly, Nova giggled. "I think she's the definition of a mad scientist," she said. "Not the just plain weird kind, more of the I'll-do-anything-for science kind of crazy mad, if that makes sense."

"It does," Rizo said. He gazed around the area to see if he could spot any of their friends. "Hey! There's Mikaela!" He exclaimed, pointing.

"Over here!" Nova yelled, waving her arms.

Mikaela ran over to them.

"There you are!" She said. "We've been looking for you everywhere! We're all a kilometer down the street. Honestly, you two running away from the scene sparked a lot of questions. People thought you two had blown half the street up."

"We sort of did," Rizo said.

"I know," Mikaela said impatiently. "But what I mean is, it put you in a bad position. Dr. Duarte had to say that you were taking Nova away because she had breathing problems and you didn't want her to choke on the dust."

"Thanks a ton," Nova said, sitting up.

"Well, it was either that or something else dramatic," Mikaela said.

"Still, why didn't you say that *Rizo* had the breathing problems?" Nova groaned.

"Enough about that," Mikaela said. "You know, there was something weird, when Dr. Duarte said that, Ryder got really quiet and looked really strange."

"There's probably no reason," Nova said quickly.

"Is there something wrong?" Rizo asked.

"No, there's nothing," Nova said. "Could you just stop asking questions?"

"Okay," Rizo said slowly. "Are you sure?"

"I can't talk about it now, just drop it," Nova said sharply.

"Okay," Rizo said again, exchanging a puzzled glance with Mikaela. "Take us to the others. Is Anala fine?"

Mikaela winced. "She's not the greatest, but she'll come around. The damage is mostly superficial."

"I don't know if I'm supposed to be concerned or comforted," Rizo said wryly.

"Just be mad at the Netrhaphalin," Mikaela said.

"No, then I'll just be like you, hating everyone," Rizo said.

"I don't hate *everyone*," Mikaela said.

"Pretty close," Nova said ruefully.

"Come on, I don't hate either of you," Mikaela said, smiling slightly.

"That's a relief," Nova said, smiling back.

"Yeah, I've seen you in action. It's better to be on your side when we're in a fight," Rizo said.

They all walked in silence, side by side, for a bit.

"Hey, I hope Kyrie knows that we've completed the mission and that we're all alive," Rizo said, breaking the silence.

"I hope so, we'll probably be able to get in contact with her soon," Mikaela said.

"Hey," Rizo said. "Did you know that Hope was going to be renamed at that factory. I really hope we didn't blow her up."

"Hope? Good riddance. And what do you mean by 'renamed'?" Mikaela asked.

"It's a long story, I'll tell you later," Rizo said. "When we're all together and I don't have to tell everyone multiple times. I mean, the whole sneaking in by myself part will probably take about an hour."

"Yeah, I forgot that you did that," Mikaela said. "Thanks."

"You're welcome," Rizo said.

"Hey, they're just down that block," Mikaela said. "Race you!"

"No thanks," Nova said.

"Oh, fine," Mikaela sighed. "I've *got* to get you guys in shape."

A minute later, they were reunited with the others.

"Let's go home," Rizo said wearily.

"We can do that," Dr. Duarte said.

"Awesome," Anala said groggily. "Rizo, you slowpoke. I just want to go to sleep."

"I'm just glad you're awake," Rizo said. "I can't believe that the Netrhaphalin used you as leverage."

"Neither can I," Anala said. "That is so RUDE. Luckily, you blew them up, so no hard feelings."

Rizo smiled. Anala was back to being herself. He envied how cheerful she was.

"How are you all?" Rizo asked the group.

"Fine," Dr. Duarte said. "I think that was successful."

"The only thing that went right," Rizo nodded.

"Well, there were some bumps in the road," Jared said.

"Definitely," Ryder agreed. "Too bad Kyrie isn't here. She's probably still worrying about us."

"She's worried about you?" Jared looked at Ryder in disbelief. "I thought she said you were a pain in the neck."

"She didn't mean it," Ryder said.

"Um, I know my sister, and when she says something, she means it," Jared said.

"Whatever you say," Ryder said, shrugging.

"You know, I just want to go home," Rizo sighed.

"That's a good idea," Dr. Duarte said. "There's a telecube just down the street."

All of them walked down the street, finally united after long days of fighting. Rizo smiled as Dr. Duarte quickly punched MYRAH898 into the keypad as Rizo had suggested. He wasn't exactly a fan of explosions.

To his surprise and delight, the code Rizo had indicated worked.

"It must be like a master passcode," Nova said.

Rizo just nodded. He was all relief, but he was really tired. He hadn't gotten much sleep in the last few days, and all he wanted was a nice shower and maybe even a cup of hot chocolate.

As he watched all of his friends disappear into the telecube, he smiled.

The mission had been a success.

Rizo stepped onto the telecube and let it whisk him away.

>>> 10 hours later...

Rizo was awakened by Anala bouncing on his bed.

"GUESS WHAT!" She yelled.

"What?" Rizo asked groggily.

"I'm completely healed!" Anala announced.

"That's great!" Rizo said. "Now can I go back to sleep?"

After they had gone home, Kyrie had fussed over them a bit, but then they had taken a shower and gone to bed. Rizo had slept soundly the whole night, never getting up once.

"NO!" Anala rolled him over. "Get up, sleepyhead! I'm so BORED. The only other person awake is Kyrie. She's great and everything, but she doesn't know how to have fun! I mean, I even asked if we could play *Crush that Robot*, and she said no! Why wouldn't she want to? I guess she's stressed about her dad, is all."

Rizo had not been listening to Anala's monologue, but at the mention of Dr. Duarte, he perked up slightly.

"What?" He asked.

"Oh, did I mention? Dr. Duarte said he wasn't hurt, but he really WAS. He has some bad cuts and a bruised rib. He also has a twisted ankle. Kyrie says he has high pain tolerance."

"Oh," Rizo said. "Well, I hope he gets better."

"I hope so, too." Anala kept bouncing up and down.

"Anala- could you get out so I could, er, change?" Rizo asked.

"Sure thing!" Anala bounded out of the room, as chipper as ever.

Rizo got dressed quickly and found Kyrie in the kitchen, weary after listening to Anala for so long.

"Rizo!" She said, starting a few things in the kitchen. "Thank goodness! How can you stand your sister? She's a doll and everything, but Lord have mercy she is loud."

"I know," Rizo whispered. "It takes a lot of patience."

"That's one thing I don't really have," Kyrie grumbled.

"I'm really hungry," Rizo said, changing the subject. "Is there anything to eat?"

"Oh, yes," Kyrie said. "While you were away and I was going stir crazy, I baked an apple pie. I'm heating it up now."

"That sounds great," Rizo said. "I'm starving."

"I'm not surprised. I also baked cherry and blueberry pies; I was so bored and worried. Ah, it's done now!"

Kyrie pulled a scrumptious pie out of the instant oven. She laid in on the stove and cut her, Anala, and

Rizo generous slices. As Kyrie passed out plates, they all took their pie eagerly and dug in.

It was the best thing Rizo had ever tasted.

"Wow, Kyrie, this is amazing," he said between mouthfuls.

"It's my mom's recipe. The secret ingredient is a dash of apple cider." Kyrie smiled. "I'm glad you like it."

"LIKE it? LOVE IT!" Anala yelped.

"Shh," Kyrie said. "You'll wake the others."

"But they need to try some of this," Anala reasoned.

"I made other pies that they can eat," Kyrie shrugged.

"More for us," Rizo grinned.

"That's right," Kyrie nodded. She looked over Rizo's shoulder.

"Hi, Ryder!" She greeted him. "We're having apple pie. Too bad there's not enough for you."

"I think there's plenty," Ryder said, helping himself to a slice. Sitting down, he took a big bite. "This is delicious!" He exclaimed.

"What do you say?" Kyrie said, raising an eyebrow.

"Thank you," Ryder said.

"Oh, yeah, thanks," Rizo said.

"THANKS!" Anala yelled. "Kyrie, you are AWESOME!"

Kyrie winced slightly, as Anala had just yelled in her ear. "I'm going to go check on my dad," she said, clearing her place and exiting the room.

"Is Dr. Duarte that bad?" Rizo asked.

"I just woke up," Ryder shrugged. Both of them looked at Anala.

"Well," she hesitated. "Kyrie did say that she thought something else was wrong that she couldn't find."

"Oh," Ryder said, looking down at his pie. "Should we try to help her?"

"You know how Kyrie is," Rizo said. "She'll probably just get upset. Let's just do stuff that she would've done, so that she doesn't have to do it later."

"Good idea." Ryder cleared all of their dishes, as they no longer felt like eating. Rizo helped clean up, and Anala pitched in as well. Soon, the kitchen and dining room were sparkling clean.

Just as they were finishing, Nova came in, rubbing her eyes.

"What's up?" She asked. Then she noticed how spotless the place was. "Wow, you've been busy."

"We're trying to help Kyrie without actually helping her," Ryder said.

"That makes no sense at all," Nova said.

"Don't worry about it," Rizo said. "Anyway, we think that Dr. Duarte's really hurt and we want to help Kyrie help him. Except Kyrie probably would get frustrated with us, so we decided to just do the stuff she was going to do so she doesn't have to do it."

"Could you repeat that?" Nova asked.

"Never mind," Rizo sighed.

"What NOW?" Anala asked.

"I think-" Rizo started before Kyrie burst into the room. She looked from one person to another.

"He's not here?" She asked, fear in her rising voice. "I thought he would be here, where is he?"

"Calm down, you'll wake the others," Ryder said, concerned. Kyrie sank into a chair that Ryder pulled up for her, and started crying. Rizo had only seen Kyrie lose it like this once before, and that was in pretty dire circumstances.

"What's wrong?" Anala asked, her cheerful attitude diminished.

"I've looked everywhere," Kyrie sobbed. "He's not in the living room, in his room, anywhere! I even checked the secret compartment. I don't know where he is!"

"Kyrie, who are you talking about?" Ryder asked.

"Everyone else is here," Kyrie babbled. "They're all safe. He isn't. He has injuries!"

With a flash of insight, Rizo realized who Kyrie was talking about.

"Oh, no," he breathed.

"What's WRONG?" Anala demanded.

"Dad," Kyrie gasped. "Dr. Duarte. He's missing."

Acknowledgements

Thank you to my family for all your support- I couldn't have done it without you. Nina- thanks for being the first human (other than me) to read my book. Jeremy- thanks for putting up with all the time I spent editing. Dad- thanks for helping me with the plot. Mom- thank you a million for helping me format, edit, and actually get all my stuff done. You're the best! And thank you Mocha, for being the best dog ever. I'm so glad that I have so much love and support. For now, I'm on to book 2!

Made in the USA
Coppell, TX
02 March 2021

51119239R10236